MW01130973

DON'T WAKE THE DEAD

The Wraith Files, Case #53

by
C.C. Wood

Cover by
Jena Brignola, Bibliophile Productions

Editing by
Tania Marinaro, Libros Evolution

Table of Contents

Chapter One 1

Chapter Two.. 7

Chapter Three... 17

Chapter Four 23

Chapter Five 31

Chapter Six... 37

Chapter Seven.. 45

Chapter Eight 51

Chapter Nine 61

Chapter Ten 69

Chapter Eleven... 75

Chapter Twelve 83

Chapter Thirteen 89

Chapter Fourteen.. 95

Chapter Fifteen... 99

Chapter Sixteen 105

Chapter Seventeen 111

Chapter Eighteen 119

Chapter Nineteen.. 123

Chapter Twenty.. 129

Chapter Twenty-One... 137

Chapter Twenty-Two 145

Chapter Twenty-Three 153

Chapter Twenty-Four.. 159

Chapter Twenty-Five 163

Chapter Twenty-Six 169

Chapter Twenty-Seven 173

Chapter Twenty-Eight 181

Chapter Twenty-Nine 185

Chapter Thirty 191

Chapter Thirty-One 197

Chapter Thirty-Two 205

Chapter Thirty-Three 209

Chapter Thirty-Four 215

Chapter Thirty-Five 221

Chapter Thirty-Six 229

Chapter Thirty-Seven 233

Chapter Thirty-Eight 237

Chapter Thirty-Nine 243

Chapter Forty 249

Chapter Forty-One 255

Chapter Forty-Two 261

Chapter Forty-Three 267

Chapter Forty-Four 273

Epilogue 279

Contact C.C. 280

About C.C. 281

Titles by C.C. Wood 282

Dedication

To T.A. Thank you for being my real-life Teri and making me laugh all the time. When we die in 40 or 50 years, I hope we can be ghost friends and scare the shit out of people together.

CHAPTER 1

IF I'D REALIZED he was in the elevator, I wouldn't have stepped inside. I always tried to avoid him, but I wasn't paying attention that morning.

"It's you."

I looked up from my phone and fought not to cringe. Immediately, I returned my attention back to the screen of my phone.

He leaned into me. "Why won't you talk to me?"

Ducking my head, I focused on responding to Jonelle's text as I pretended that he didn't exist.

Suddenly, I felt an icy cold tingle on the side of my face. I jerked away from him, banging my shoulder into the wall. He stood next to me, his tongue hanging out of his mouth like some sort of overgrown puppy.

The other two people in the elevator, a man and a woman, turned and gave me concerned looks. Then they looked at each other as if to say, "You'll help hold her down if she loses her shit, right?"

I smiled wanly. "Sorry, I tripped."

The woman glared at me, but the man eyed me speculatively. I shrugged, trying to look as harmless as possible.

They turned their backs toward me but I could tell that they were on guard. Irritated, I glared at the man to my right. Quickly, I pulled up the note app on my phone and typed him a message.

Leave me alone. And don't ever lick my face again, asshole.

"I just wanted your attention. Why won't you talk to me?" he complained, his voice quieter this time. "You're the only one who seems to see or hear me."

Bcuz I am.

"But why? Why do they all pretend they can't see me?" Now his tone was verging on whiny.

They can't. You know they can't.

"I don't understand. Why can't they see me?"
Usually I tried to be considerate when talking to someone in his position, but we'd had this conversation before. In fact, we'd had this conversation at least once a week since I'd been hired at the insurance firm. If I was alone in the elevator, I would express my annoyance out loud but this time I was hampered by the two other occupants. He knew it too, which was why he was still bothering me. If anything, he was tenacious and willfully ignorant.

I've told u a million times, Jerry. Ur dead. Uve been dead for a long time.

"I can't be dead," he argued.
Sick of arguing with him, I typed him a final message.

U R a ghost. Don't bother me again or I'll come back with holy water and banish ur ass.

Though I wasn't even sure if holy water would work, it seemed like a viable threat. Maybe my words were cruel, but Jerry had been haunting this building daily for the last four years that I worked here. At first, I managed to ignore him, but I made the mistake of responding to his questions once when I was alone. Since then, he tried to talk to me every time he saw me. I was pretty sure he looked for me.

"Bitch," he muttered.

I realized then that not only did Jerry understand that he was dead, he enjoyed being undetectable. He liked moving among the living mostly unseen. The harassment he dished out to me was his way of relieving boredom.

Still, he had no intention of moving on. He wanted to remain here, even if no one else could see or talk to him. Probably so he could look up women's skirts or lick their toes in the elevator, the pervy fucker.

When the elevator reached my floor, I rushed off, accidentally bumping into the woman near the doors.

She huffed in annoyance.

Glancing back, I apologized, "Sorry."

I didn't wait to hear a response from her or Jerry, already hurrying down the hallway toward the offices that held the insurance company that employed me.

The receptionist, Claire, smiled and waved at me as I entered. I nodded to her and headed straight toward the break room where the employee lockers were located. I put my purse inside my locker and took a quick trip to the ladies room. Once I was done, I headed back into the break room for a cup of coffee. It was the same routine I went through every workday morning.

As I added sugar and creamer, my boss, Mike, stuck his head into the break room.

"I need to see you in my office before you start your shift," he stated.

"Okay," I replied.

Before I could ask him if everything was okay, he disappeared.

That was a bad sign. Mike might not be the friendliest man I'd ever met, but he never ended conversations so abruptly.

My stomach twisted as I stirred my coffee. I might not be clairvoyant, but I had an idea what was coming. I'd been hearing rumors about company restructuring for a couple of months.

I made my way to Mike's office. I noticed halfway down the hall that I'd left my coffee on the counter in the break room. It didn't matter. I wouldn't have been able to drink a drop right now anyway.

I knocked on his open door and stuck my head in when he called out.

"Hey, Mike."

His face was serious as he gestured for me to come inside. "Please close the door behind you."

That's when I knew my worries were well founded. Mike had a stringent open-door policy in the office. Meetings, unless they were reprimands or terminations, were always held with the door open. Mike wanted his employees to trust him and refused to hide in his office.

I shut the door and took a seat in the chair across from his. Lacing my fingers together, I rested my hands in my lap and waited.

Mike sighed and mimicked my pose, his expression unhappy. "You're an intelligent person, Zoe, I'm sure you already have an idea of why I called you in here."

"If this has something to do with the rumors of company restructuring, then yes," I answered.

"I'm afraid it does."

"Go ahead and spit it out, Mike," I invited.

"General Insurance is eliminating over a thousand positions this year. All claims centers will pare down from five hundred to four hundred claim reps. As much as I hate this, I have to terminate people based on seniority and you're one of my newer reps."

My eyebrows lifted. "After four years, I'm a newer rep?"

He shrugged. "It's twenty percent of my staff, Zoe. A few of these terminations are for people who've been here longer than you." His face fell. "For what it's worth, I hate doing this and I'm sorry."

"It's okay, Mike," I replied.

Even though it wasn't okay as I claimed, I couldn't be angry with him. He had a job to do, even if he didn't necessarily like it.

I hauled myself out of my chair. "So I take it I have the day off?"

He sighed and I felt a twinge of remorse for my quip. "I've enjoyed working with you. Please put me down as a reference. I'll give any prospective employers a glowing recommendation."

My smile was half-hearted but I appreciated his effort. "Thanks, Mike."

I trudged out of his office, unsure of what to do next. Retracing my steps, I returned to the break room. My full coffee cup was still sitting on the counter. I poured it down the sink and washed the mug.

I didn't bother to go to my cubicle. I stopped bringing personal items to work when I realized that Norma, the woman in the workspace directly behind me, was a kleptomaniac and stole everything on my desk that wasn't nailed down. Except for my work files. Those she was happy to leave.

Removing my bag from my locker, I left the break room and took one last look around the place I'd worked for the last four years. The bland grey carpet and white walls weren't much and the generic landscape paintings hanging throughout the offices were actually damn ugly, but I'd enjoyed my time here.

Now, I was leaving for good.

I said good-bye to Claire as I left. She seemed to know exactly what was going on because she looked sad.

The elevator doors opened up and I was face-to-face with Jerry the Annoying Ghost again. He sneered at me as I stepped on.

"Back so soon?" he asked.

After I pressed the button for the first floor, I faced him. "For the last time. I gotta tell you, Jerry, I won't miss you."

"Miss me?" he asked.

I was actually kind of glad I was alone in the elevator with him so I could speak freely without people thinking I was a fruitcake.

"It's my last day. I won't be back."

He actually looked surprised. "But who'll I talk to?"

I laughed. "No one, Jer. No one. You should really think about moving on."

The elevator steadily descended toward the bottom floor with no stops.

"You can't leave me," he demanded. "I won't let you."

The elevator dinged as it halted on the lobby level.

"Good-bye, Jerry," I replied.

"I'll find you. I won't let you leave me here alone," he spat out. His words were venomous and full of menace, but they were empty. He'd never be able to leave the elevator unless he went to the next plane.

"Fuck you, Jerry," I answered levelly, marching off the elevator car as the doors slid open.

I could hear him screaming at me as I walked through the lobby and out the front doors, but I didn't look back.

Like all ghosts, he was stuck in the past and that's where I intended to leave him.

CHAPTER

2

As soon as I walked through the front door, Teri materialized in the living room.

"What are you doing back so early?" she asked. "You get fired or something?"

I dropped my purse on the floor and tried to hang my keys on the hook by the front door. I missed the hook and they hit the floor with a clatter. I left them there.

"Zoe?"

"Got it in one," I answered. "I was fired."

"Shit. Does this mean you're gonna move out? It's been kinda nice having someone to talk to after all these years."

Sighing, I kicked off my shoes and stripped off my jacket. "No, I have some money saved and the mortgage is low enough that it'll last me a while. Thanks to you."

Teri grinned at me. "Hey, I can't help it if everyone in town believes the rumors about this place."

She didn't know the half of it. The Kenna gossip mill insisted that six people had died in this house over the years and that it was haunted by a demon.

In reality, there had been two deaths here, but nothing like they thought. The first owner had died in her sleep at the ripe old age of ninety-five. Teri had been found hanging in the garage in an apparent suicide. She was adamant that wasn't case, that she'd been murdered. In fact, she mentioned it a lot.

Whether it was true or not, it had happened thirty years ago, so there wasn't much I could do about it.

"We should get drunk," Teri stated.

"*We* can't get drunk, Teri. You're a ghost. Ghosts don't drink."

"I know. I fucking miss it too. That and smoking." She paused. "And sex. God, do I miss sex. Do you know how difficult it is to have an orgasm when you don't have a physical form?"

I clapped my hands over my ears. "TMI! Do not tell me things like that!"

She sneered at me. "Well who am I supposed to tell? My pickings are slim for friends. You're my best friend by default."

"Oh great, so even the ghosts in this town would rather be friends with someone other than me," I quipped.

"Hey, that slutty girl likes you."

I glared at her. "Jonelle isn't slutty. She just isn't ready to settle down."

"She goes through men faster than a teenage boy goes through hand lotion."

I grimaced at her analogy. "Ick."

Teri nodded. "Yes. It's also accurate."

I shook my head and walked past her toward the kitchen. I didn't intend to get drunk but a bottle of hard cider, or two, wouldn't be unwelcome right now.

As usual, Teri was exaggerating. Jonelle did date a lot, but only because she didn't want to settle down. She wanted to enjoy her youth while she still had it...at least that's what she claimed. I had a feeling it had more to do with the fact that she didn't trust any man to stick around when the going got tough.

"Speaking of the cock hopper, you should call her."

I glared at Teri over my shoulder. "First of all, don't call her a cock hopper. Ever. Or I'll be forced to revoke your daytime TV privileges."

Teri gasped. "You wouldn't."

"I would. Secondly, why would I call Jonelle right now? It's the middle of the day, she's probably at work."

Jonelle worked at a salon in Weatherford. Fridays and Saturdays were her busiest.

My resident ghost rolled her eyes. "Because she's your best friend and she might want to know you just got canned so she can be supportive or some shit."

"I'll call her later." My phone slid across the counter toward me and I jumped, whirling to face her. "Dammit, Teri, I told you not to do stuff like that."

She smirked at me. "I'm getting better at moving things. I've been practicing."

I regretted encouraging her to interact with objects. Once Teri figured out how to move things, she liked to freak out my friends and family when they came to visit. After a couple of years, my mother refused to set foot in my house anymore.

"Call her," Teri insisted.

"Fine," I snapped, snatching up the cordless phone. I sighed, realizing I would probably have to cancel my landline soon in order to save money.

Jonelle picked up on the third ring. "Hey, girl. Are you sick?"

I hesitated. "Uh, no. Why do you ask?"

"You're calling me from your home phone at ten in the morning on a weekday," she explained.

"Oh. Um, no, I'm not sick."

"Is something else wrong?" she asked.

I sighed when I felt Teri's cold finger prod my shoulder. "Yeah. I got fired this morning."

"Damn. Did you finally lose your shit on that sneaky, thieving bitch in the cubicle next to yours?"

I huffed out a laugh. "No. They're downsizing. My office alone is cutting one hundred reps."

"And you're one of them?" Jonelle prompted.

"Yeah."

"That blows, sweetie. Are you going to be okay? Do you need some cash or anything?"

I smiled at her offer. Jonelle was such a generous friend. "I should be good. I have some money saved."

"Okay, well let me know if that changes," she stated. "I can float you a loan.

"Thanks, Jonelle."

We chatted a few more minutes, then her client arrived and Jonelle had to hang up.

I put the phone back on the charging stand and found Teri staring at me, her arms crossed over her chest.

"Feel better?"

I scowled at her. "Yes."

"Then stop frowning at me. It'll give you wrinkles."

Rolling my eyes, I grabbed my hard cider and carried it into the living room.

Teri followed me. "Well, it's ten-fifteen."

"Okaaay," I drawled in response, unsure why she was announcing the time to me.

"The firefighter next door likes to workout in his backyard this time of day."

I stared at her blankly.

"Shirtless."

I shrugged. "So?"

She shook her head in disgust. "There's no hope for you." Then she moved through the wall, her faded outline dissipating against the cool blue background.

My resident ghost was slightly obsessed with my neighbor, Preston. She'd been telling me since I'd moved in that I should ask him over for coffee or dinner. Or sex. I hadn't done either. Mostly because I thought Teri was pushing me toward my neighbor in an effort to live vicariously through me.

Also, I resisted because Preston just wasn't my type. He was a nice man in his early thirties, good-looking, and employed. All the things most women would want in a potential mate.

But he wasn't for me.

Like so many other people in the small town of Kenna, Texas, Preston Rogers thought I was…peculiar.

And for good reason.

When I was five, I died. No one could ever figure out what happened. My heart just—stopped. I was dead for nearly two minutes. The only reason I recovered was because the woman who lived across the street from us was a nurse. She saw me collapse on the front lawn and ran over to help. To this day, twenty-two years later, my mother refers to it as *the incident.*

When I regained consciousness in the hospital, I saw a man standing by the door to my room. I asked my mother who he was, but she insisted that there was no one else there.

It took me a while to realize what I was seeing. For the first few months, I told everyone I knew about the people I saw that no one else did.

As I grew older I began to understand that they were ghosts. By then it was too late, everyone in my small town thought I was more than a little off since *the incident.*

Then, in high school, I'd gone to the local cemetery with a group of kids. They dared me to go in alone. When I did, two of the fresh graves nearby opened up and out climbed a couple of corpses. Needless to say, the kids who I'd desperately wanted to befriend had left me stranded in that graveyard.

Discovering what was happening to me became vitally important. After that night, I drove to Fort Worth and spent hours poring through books about the supernatural. I assumed that the bodies I'd raised in the cemetery were zombies, but I hadn't intended for them to rise from the grave, so I doubted that I was a necromancer.

Then there were the ghouls. Once I turned eighteen, men noticed me. However, it was only certain men and their interest was borderline creepy. Okay, forget creepy, it was borderline frightening.

I didn't understand what they were until I finally confronted a young ghoul with my can of pepper spray and a whole lot of attitude. He'd stammered out an explanation of what he was, which was unsettling in itself, and then I'd asked him not to continue when he'd begun talking about how he couldn't resist me. Eating dead flesh was a massive turn off. Add in stalker tendencies, and I was ready to give him a blast of pepper spray just on principle.

Over the years, I'd stopped acknowledging my abilities. When I was a child, I constantly talked about the people only I could see and it alienated me from other kids.

I quit talking about it with my parents because my mother would freak out or loudly demand that I stop lying.

The only person who seemed to understand and accept what was happening to me was my paternal grandmother. She listened to me when I told her the stories and described what I saw.

Not long before she passed away, she said to me, "Sweetie, when you died and they revived you, I think a piece of the other side came back with your soul."

I still found those words comforting though my grandmother had been dead for seven years now.

"Oh, hell yeah! Take it off, baby!"

Teri's voice cut through my maudlin mood as she whooped and hollered. Clearly, Preston had begun his workout in his backyard.

Taking a sip of my hard cider, I picked up the TV remote and settled in to watch true crime shows.

There was a knock on my door a couple hours later. Teri had gone quiet, which was typical for her. Sometimes I wondered if she took a nap in the afternoon like a whiny toddler. Or a bitchy she-ghost.

I hauled myself off the couch, feeling more than a little tipsy. Peeking out the small windows that ran up each side of the doorjamb, I saw Jonelle standing on my front porch.

Throwing open the door, I asked, "What are you doing here?"

She grinned at me and held up a bottle of sparkling wine. "Celebrating."

Though I was half drunk, her answer still made no sense to me. "Huh?"

She brushed by me as she entered the house. "I'm helping you celebrate moving on from that job. You've mentioned changing careers several times in the past few months. Maybe this is an opportunity."

I ignored her statement, even though it was true. "Don't you have clients?"

Jonelle shrugged, brushing her blonde hair off her shoulders. "I only had a couple. I rescheduled them for tomorrow."

"Jonelle…"

She shoved the bottle of wine at me. "Take the wine. Pour me a glass. No complaining. You've had a shitty morning and we're going to take a day to goof off."

I couldn't help but grin at her. "Yes, boss."

Nodding, she replied, "Damn skippy."

Rolling my eyes at her goofiness, I carried the wine into the kitchen. I laughed when I realized that the wine was screw top. Clearly we were going to be classy bitches and drink cheap wine.

"I see the cock hopper showed up," Teri said behind me.

I twisted around and pointed at her. "That's it. I'm leaving tomorrow for the entire day and I'm going to put Tori Amos on repeat. Do not call her that!"

"Call her what?" Jonelle asked as she walked into the room, passing right through Teri's opaque body.

Teri wailed, "Goddammit, I hate it when she does that!"

Though Jonelle swore she couldn't see Teri, I think she could at least sense her because she did that a lot.

"Teri was calling you a not-so-nice name. I was planning to punish her with *Happy Phantom* on repeat, but you just walked right through her so that may be punishment enough."

"So what did she call me?" Jonelle took the glass of wine I held out to her. When I hesitated, she sighed. "As if anything that demon poltergeist could call me would hurt my feelings."

"Cock hopper," I stated.

Jonelle choked on her wine as she guffawed. "Oh my God, that's a good one. I've got to remember that."

I turned my gaze to Teri, making sure my displeasure was clear. "Go see if Preston is still working out and we'll talk later."

Jonelle's eyebrows rose at my statement. "Preston is working out right now? Is he shirtless?"

I sighed. Though Teri seemed to despise Jonelle, they did share a common interest in my neighbor. Probably because he wouldn't have sex with either of them. He seemed skittish around Jonelle, as if she was a bomb he expected to go off at any second.

"I'll be right back," Jonelle commented, disappearing through the door. I heard her footsteps fade as she walked to the formal dining room across the hall. It had an unobstructed view into Preston's back yard.

Though their bickering required my participation and annoyed me to no end, it had accomplished the one thing I hadn't thought possible.

It took my mind off the fact that I was now unemployed.

CHAPTER

3

Two Months Later

"SO HOW'S THE job hunt going?" my mother asked, her voice high and chipper as though she expected me to have great news for her.

"It's going," I replied.

I felt her annoyance from across the room but didn't look up from my phone.

"Zoe Rose Thorne, don't you take that tone with me."

I took a sip of iced tea before lifting my gaze to hers. "Sorry, Mama."

She put a hand on her hip and studied me closely. Though she was fifty, my mother didn't look it. Sarah Thorne always made an effort to look her best. Her brown hair was the same shade as my own, but now due to the grace of her hairdresser rather than God. Her skin was smooth, pale, and carried few lines.

Though she abhorred exercise, my mother walked for half an hour every morning and ate healthfully. She also avoided alcohol, coffee, and sweets.

If she could see all the junk food in my kitchen at the moment, she would lose her mind.

"Have you heard anything from the jobs you applied for?" she persisted.

I shook my head. "Nope. I've put in for several other positions this week, but things are moving slowly." I didn't mention to her that the job market was flooded with desperate people, many who were better qualified than I could ever hope to be.

She shook her head, as though my continued unemployment was intentional in my effort to make her life more stressful. "You'll just have to try harder," she stated. "Start calling some of those companies. Call them every day."

I bit back a sigh. Persistence paid off, but if I called some of these businesses one more time I was liable to be charged with harassment.

"I am working regularly with the temp agency," I replied.

"Three days a week," she snapped, turning back to the pots and pans on the stove.

Every week, I ate dinner with my parents on Thursday night. My mother insisted I come over early to "help" yet never let me do anything but wash dishes after we ate. When it came to cooking, my mother wanted things done in a particular fashion and it was best just to stay out of her way.

"I'm doing okay, Mom," I insisted. And I was. I might not have as much spending money as I used to, but my bills were getting paid and I'd barely touched my savings. Of course, I'd cancelled my cable subscription and started buying the manager's specials at the grocery store, but I wasn't broke.

Yet.

My mother shook her head and scoffed, keeping her back to me as she began to mash the hell out of the potatoes she'd just drained.

I was saved from further lectures when my father appeared at the back door, carrying his lunchbox from work.

His weathered face broke into a wide, sincere smile as he greeted me. "Hey, Zoe."

Though he spoke to me first, he went straight to my mother and kissed her hello. My relationship with my mother might be contentious, but it was sweet to see how devoted my father was to her. For as long as I could remember, the first thing my father did when he came home from work every night was kiss my mother.

A shaft of longing pierced my heart. I rarely thought about dating or marriage, but those memories suddenly made me yearn for someone to come home to me at night. Someone who would walk through the door and straight to me to kiss me hello.

I shook off the thoughts. At twenty-seven, I'd given up on the fairy tale ending years ago. Right now I'd be happy to find a man who didn't think I was a freak or expect me to be so grateful for his attention that I'd let him treat me like shit.

As she had for the last thirty years, my mother immediately brought dinner to the table as my father washed his hands.

While we ate, my father and mother carried most of the conversation. After everyone was finished, I cleared the table, loaded the dishwasher, and washed the pots and pans.

I was just finishing up when the phone rang and my mother carried the cordless handset out of the room to continue her conversation.

"Let's go out on the back porch and talk," my dad suggested.

I hung the dishtowel on the rack and nodded.

"Want a beer?" he asked.

"Sure."

He pulled two bottles from the fridge and popped the tops. I followed him out to the back porch and settled into one of the deck chairs.

May typically brought warmer temperatures during the day, but the evenings were comfortably cool. When I was younger, we would sit outside after dinner almost every night. Sometimes we would talk, but most of the time we sat in silence.

Before he sat down, Dad pulled his wallet out of his pocket and took out a slip of paper, holding it out to me.

I took it from him and blinked at the check for five hundred dollars, made out to me. "What's this?"

"It's for you. I know you said you're doing okay, but this way I'll be sure."

"Dad…"

He shook his head and sat down next to me. "Don't argue with me. If you really don't need it, save it for when you do. I know your mom is giving you a hard time about not having a job yet, but it's just because she's worried about you."

I didn't respond verbally, just shrugged. Dad always seemed to think the best of my mother's intentions. It was difficult for me to do the same since I was the one on the receiving end of her directives.

"Who do you think wrote out that check?" he asked.

I stared at the check in surprise. It was clearly her handwriting now that I took the time to look at it.

"Thank you," I murmured.

"Tell your mother that before you leave."

I nodded. "I will."

We sat there for a long while, sipping beer and talking occasionally about things we'd heard around town.

"Well, I'd better get going," I commented after I finished my beer. "I have a temp job in Fort Worth tomorrow morning and I can't be late."

I gave my dad a hug and kiss on the cheek and went in search of my mother. When I thanked her for the check, she looked as uncomfortable as I felt.

As I drove home, I thought about my dad's words. Maybe my mother's bossy demeanor was her way of showing she cared. If so, she must love me a lot. I chuckled to myself on that epiphany. My mother could spit out commands faster than an auctioneer at an estate auction.

I hadn't been lying when I told my parents I was doing okay. I'd cut back as much as I could, so my temp job was covering my bills, just without much room for extras.

Though I had a mortgage on my house, it was very low. Because of the rumors that surrounded the Craftsman home, no one would buy it. After sitting vacant for years, the city was going to tear it down in an effort to entice someone to purchase the lot.

I'd approached someone in City Hall about it and within a few weeks, I was a proud first time homeowner.

Because I'd bought the house for so little, my mortgage was cheaper than rent on an apartment.

I loved my little Craftsman style home. It needed renovating when I moved in, but with some elbow grease and a lot of help from my dad, it was almost as good as new.

I even liked having Teri around. Though she could be a pain in the ass, she was a lot of fun. She was also the reason my mother refused to come to my house anymore. Teri had played one too many pranks on her in the last few years and she'd given me an ultimatum; either move somewhere else or she wouldn't come over any longer.

Clearly, I'd chosen to keep my house and my mother's unexpected visits stopped.

As a thank you gift for Teri, I purchased a calendar that featured naked French firefighters. It was hanging in the guest room so she could enjoy it privately.

As I pulled up in front of my home I was even more determined to keep it. I'd worked long and hard for a place to call my own, even if it included a smartass ghost and a long list of home improvements.

I *had* to find a steady job. And soon.

CHAPTER

4

TWO DAYS LATER, I was lazing on my front porch swing in the warm afternoon sun. I had a historical romance novel in one hand and a spoon in the other. An open jar of peanut butter was between my hip and the back of the swing and a huge glass of milk sat on a table beside the swing. In other words, I was in Heaven.

Engrossed in the novel, I dipped the spoon in the jar and stuck it in my mouth. I refused to listen to the subconscious echo of my mother's voice scolding me about all the germs and bacteria I was introducing into the jar. What woman hasn't resorted to eating peanut butter directly from the jar when she's depressed?

"Excuse me."

I nearly choked on the sticky wad in my mouth and looked up. For a split second I wasn't sure if he was a living, breathing human being or an apparition. Then the sun came out from behind the clouds and reflected on his glasses and I knew he was real.

As I studied him, he came up the steps. "Hi, my name is Mal Flemming. I'd like to talk to you about your house."

He held out a business card and I glanced at it, annoyed that my quiet time was being interrupted.

Malachi Flemming,

Paranormal Investigator and Host/Creator of The Wraith Files

My eyes jumped back up to him, narrowing in suspicion. I reached out and grabbed the milk, washing the last bit of peanut butter from my mouth.

Apparently, the guy could sense I was about to tell him to get lost because he squatted down so that we were almost eye level and ran a hand through his short black hair, leaving it spiky and messy.

"Please just let me explain before you say no," he pleaded.

Since my tongue felt as though it were glued to the roof of my mouth I couldn't answer, which he took as acquiescence.

"I'm in the area for the next few weeks, filming my YouTube show, *The Wraith Files*, at the Baker Hotel and some other sites in the vicinity. Someone in Mineral Wells suggested this house, but they thought it was still vacant. I just want to ask you if you've seen or experienced anything out of the ordinary here."

As he spoke, he took off his black framed glasses and his eyes immediately made me forget what I intended to say. They were dark brown, flecked with gold, and something about them made me hesitate.

I took another gulp of milk, finally washing down the last of the peanut butter. "Listen, Malachi-"

He flinched. "Please, call me Mal. Malachi makes me think of Children of the Corn."

I caught myself chuckling. "Sorry," I apologized.

Mal shook his head. "Don't worry about it. It is funny. I'm pretty sure my mom was still high on painkillers after my birth when she picked my name."

My mouth quirked into a half-grin. It was beyond my control. Though I didn't want to like this guy, his sense of humor was similar to my own. Still, that didn't mean I was going to let him film at my house.

"Okay, Mal. I have to tell you, I haven't experienced anything weird. I think that the small town gossip mill sent you on a fool's errand."

No sooner had the words come out of my mouth when Teri appeared behind Mal.

"Oh, he's cute." She tilted her head sideways and bent down at the waist. "And he has a *very* nice ass. You should let him do whatever he wants here."

I glanced over his shoulder and gave my head one small shake.

"God, you act like you're an old biddy. You're young and gorgeous. You should be dating. Or at least getting your freak on with hot geeks like him," she insisted. "The nerd glasses are a nice touch."

I bit my bottom lip to keep from telling her to shut the hell up. If I spoke to her, Mal would think I was a complete nutcase.

"You okay?" he asked.

I looked back toward him and saw the curiosity in his gaze. "Uh, yeah. Sorry. I thought I saw the neighbor's cat. He's a bit of an escape artist."

Out of the corner of my eye I saw Teri slowly open the screen door. Before I realized what she was doing, she released it and it slammed with a loud bang.

Mal jumped to his feet and whirled around. "What in the hell was that?"

Suddenly, the porch light overhead started flashing off and on, over and over again. I knew it was Teri and cursed beneath my breath.

"Does this sort of thing happen often?" Mal asked me, his eyes wide.

I shook my head. "This is the first time."

And it was. Teri pulled this shit when she was trying to freak out Jonelle or my mom and only when I wasn't around because she knew it pissed me off. If she was going to play poltergeist she could have at least been original.

"This is amazing," he breathed, staring up at the light as it flickered a few more times.

"Whatever you say," I replied, shifting so I could see through the small windows that ran down each side of the doorjamb. When my eyes met Teri's, I glared at her. She grinned, completely unfazed, but she did let go of the light switch.

"These sorts of phenomena are extremely common in hauntings of residences. I would love to record here and see what we can find," Mal stated.

"Look, I don't know-"

"I'll pay you. One thousand dollars."

I blinked at him. "Uh, just to film at my house?" I asked incredulously.

Mal nodded. "Absolutely."

Staring at him in consternation, I queried, "Do you, um, pay people often?"

"No, not usually. Typically, people contact us and ask us to investigate or try to cleanse the areas. I've never seen this kind of activity as soon as I enter the premises."

I heard Teri's giggle behind me and knew she'd returned to the front porch. "He said *enter the premises.*" Then she snorted and dissolved into gales of laughter. "Please say yes. I want to know if he can see me on video or hear me on one of those....what are they called?" She paused for a moment. "I remember! EVP's!"

I ignored her, even though her giggling made me fight a smile of my own.

"Mal, seriously, this kind of stuff just doesn't happen here. I'm sure it was just the wind or something."

My excuse sounded lame, even to my own ears. The door, yes, it could have been the wind, but the overhead porch light wouldn't have flickered for several seconds because of it.

He studied me closely for a moment. "Just think about it for a couple days and call me when you decide. I'll pay you fifteen hundred dollars."

I squinted up at him. "I thought you said a thousand."

"Something tells me you need a little more incentive before you'll consider agreeing."

He turned and bounded down the steps of my front porch. I watched him walk away and I had to admit that Teri was right.

He had a fantastic ass.

LATER THAT EVENING, I was going over my bills and bank statements for the month. I was drinking my second bottle of hard cider for the night because looking at my finances was stressful enough when I was gainfully employed. Now that I was relying on my temp work, it was downright terrifying.

Looking at my bank balance and calculating how much income I would need to get by, I realized that I was going to have to start dipping into my savings soon. I usually worked at least two or three days a week at my temp jobs, but there were weeks they didn't need me at all.

My eyes strayed down to the card that Malachi Flemming had left earlier that day.

Leaning back on my couch, I lifted the card up and studied it. The glossy black surface looked sleek and minimal until you tilted the card. Then thin tendrils of smoke or mist seemed to appear around the edges. The only information on the card was his name, job title, phone number, website, and email address. They were all in bold white typeface.

I tapped the card against my fingertips several time before tossing it onto the keyboard of my laptop. With a sigh, I snatched up my cell phone. I'd canceled my landline a few weeks after I'd been fired in an effort to save money.

"Hey, girl. What's up?" Jonelle greeted after one ring.

"I'm having trouble making a decision," I responded.

"About what?"

I told her about Malachi and his offer of fifteen hundred dollars to film a paranormal investigation show at my house.

"Hang on," she said. "I want to look this up."

I rolled my eyes. "Why? It's all bullshit anyway."

"Says the woman who has a ghost in her house that she sees and talks to on a daily basis. And let's not forget the zombies that rise out of their graves to greet you or the ghouls that follow you around like little lost puppy dogs, desperate to hump your leg."

I grumbled beneath my breath at her last comment. "Fine, so those things happen to me, but you can't see or hear everything I can. Neither can most people. I don't think five thousand dollar infrared cameras and digital recorders will change that."

"Maybe, but I am curious what the show is like. That should have some bearing on your decision."

She was silent for a few more moments. "Holy fucking shit, you didn't tell me that he was a sexy geek type."

I shrugged, even though she couldn't see me. "I didn't notice."

"There has got to be something wrong with you. That man is hot. Not only hot. Hot and nerdy."

I sighed. "If you say so."

I could hear the murmuring of her computer in the background, but not the dialogue. After a few moments, I heard the click of her shutting her laptop.

"You should do it," she stated.

"Why?"

"Well, he seems to take it seriously and he has a very scientific approach."

"How would you know?" I argued. "You watched all of two minutes of one episode."

"Okay, forget if he's scientific or not. It's fifteen hundred bucks and he's fucking hot. Take the money then take him. You need both the cash and to get laid. It's a win-win situation for all parties involved."

I choked on my hard cider. "Oh my God, I'm not going to sleep with him."

"Why not?" she asked.

"I barely know him," I sputtered.

"So?"

"So, I don't have sex with strange men. It's one of my personal standards."

"Why not?" she repeated.

"God, Jonelle. I realize not every woman feels the way I do, but I'd like to at least know a guy well enough to decide if he's an asshole before I get naked with him."

She sighed. "You should give it a try. Sometimes the assholes are the best lay."

I shook my head. "Whatever you say."

"Fine, forget the sex. I still say you should take the money and let them film. Fifteen hundred dollars will help you a lot, right?"

"Yeah," I answered quietly.

"So do it. It's not like he asked you to be on the show, did he?"

I thought for a moment. "No, he didn't. Even if he did want me to appear, I'd say no."

"I figured," she replied dryly.

"Hey, I'm just not comfortable on camera."

"Sometimes you need to push yourself outside your comfort zone, Zoe Thorne. You might be surprised."

I huffed out a breath. "Maybe. Maybe not."

"Just try something new. It's a YouTube show, not a marriage proposal. Who knows, there are probably only five or six people who watch it anyway."

"Fine," I grumbled. "But only this one time."

She laughed. "Good girl. Now, I need my beauty sleep. I'll talk to you tomorrow."

After she disconnected, I picked up Mal's card and ran my fingers along the edges.

Then I deliberately set it to the side and settled my computer on my lap. It was time to do some research. If I was going to let Mal film his show in my house, I wanted to know more about it.

I pulled up the YouTube site and started searching.

CHAPTER 5

I WOKE UP well after ten the next morning.

It was the strangest thing. The night before, when I started watching the episodes of Mal Flemming's YouTube show, *The Wraith Files*, I was hooked. I watched all fifty episodes, back-to-back. I didn't fall asleep until after two a.m.

Mal was charismatic and articulate, and I never got the sense that he was acting.

There were several episodes in which he debunked all the claims that the areas were haunted. That was what finally convinced me to allow Mal and his crew to film in my house. I felt that he would treat me, and my home, with respect rather than a circus sideshow.

After I rolled out of bed, I took the time to shower and drink a cup of coffee before I picked up my cell phone to call Mal.

Our conversation was brief, but I could hear the undercurrent of excitement in his voice. He explained that he would want to come over and walk through the house before he filmed. Then he asked if he could come by today.

Since the temp agency didn't need me the rest of this week, I was definitely free.

After we settled on a time that afternoon, I hung up and stared out my kitchen window, fighting the urge to call him back and tell him I'd changed my mind.

"Is that gorgeous hunk of manmeat coming over again today?" Teri asked from behind me.

I sighed. "Yes, he is. Would it be too much to ask for you to be on your best behavior?"

A wicked chuckle was her only reply and I felt her leave the room.

Later that afternoon, my doorbell rang. Teri didn't appear by the front door, but I knew her well enough to know that she was loitering nearby.

I opened the door to reveal Mal standing on the other side. Today, I wasn't distracted by his sudden appearance and I took the time to study him. His dark hair stood up in spikes all over his head. I realized that his face wasn't conventionally handsome when I watched his television show, but there was something about him. I couldn't have explained it out loud, but his features were strong, striking, and they drew the eye.

I also hadn't realized how tall he was yesterday, or how broad, but standing a few feet from him I felt as though he dwarfed me. He looked as though he worked out. A lot. For a split second, I worried about how easily he could overpower me and how Preston wasn't next door, but pulling a forty-eight hour shift at the firehouse.

My fears dissipated quickly as Mal stepped inside and looked around.

"Wow. This place is gorgeous," he stated. "I'd heard it was abandoned for a while, but it looks as though it was just built."

I felt a surge of pride. "It needed quite a bit of work when I bought it, but it has come together nicely in the last couple of years."

My house was neater than it ever had been when I worked full time. One benefit of unemployment was plenty of time to clean. I had picked up some of the clutter that was scattered in the living room and my bedroom, but there wasn't much else to tidy before he arrived.

He walked through the living room. "Did you do this work yourself?"

"Most of the cosmetic stuff like the floors and the walls. My dad helped with the bigger things and I hired a plumber to handle the bathrooms and kitchen."

He turned back toward me, his gaze speculative. "You seem young to own a house like this."

I shrugged. "I got a great deal."

Somewhere upstairs, Teri slammed a door. He jumped, his eyes moving quickly to the ceiling.

Then he looked at me again and chuckled. "I'll bet."

I heard heavy footsteps upstairs. Teri was sure as hell playing it up for Mal. She walked through the hall and started down the steps, stomping on each tread like a damn elephant.

He whirled as though he expected to be able to see her, which of course he couldn't.

Teri grinned cheekily at me as she hopped with both feet down the last two steps, making the table at the base of the staircase shudder.

"Do you hear that?" he asked me, his voice rising. "Tell me you heard that."

Teri moved forward and grabbed a handful of Mal's muscular ass.

"Holy fucking shit!" he yelped, leaping at least two feet into the air. "It just touched my ass!"

Teri dissolved into a fit of uncontrollable laughter. "God, I wish I could have really felt that," she gasped. "They're such pretty buns, I couldn't resist."

It was difficult for me to keep my mouth shut, listening to Teri guffaw wildly and seeing Mal's wide, wheeling eyes. Somehow I managed it.

Chest heaving, Mal stared at me. "What in the hell was that?"

"I don't know," I answered, desperately trying to keep a straight face.

His eyes narrowed. "You're lying to me."

"Why would I lie?" I shot back, squaring my shoulders.

Silent, he continued to watch me for several long moments, his breathing still accelerated. "Okay, okay. You're right. Why would you lie? I'm overreacting."

It was clear he was making an effort to take slow, deep breaths and I felt a stab of guilt.

I shouldn't be laughing, even if it was internally, at the poor guy. He had no idea what was going on. He couldn't see or hear Teri to know that she was just playing with him and didn't mean any harm.

My conscience pricked and I exhaled hard. "Okay, so I've seen and heard some weird things since I moved in, but not much. I don't think that she means any harm."

"She?" He perked up.

Shit, I'd slipped up.

"Yeah, I think the spirit or whatever is a she. And she seems more like a goofy practical joker than anything else."

"Okay, good to know. Have you seen her or heard her? Maybe tried to call in a medium?"

If he only knew.

I shook my head. "Just a glimpse of her. I just got the impression the ghost is a female. She seems harmless, even if she can be annoying, so I didn't call anyone."

"Hey!" Teri exclaimed. "I'm not annoying."

I forgot myself for a moment and glanced at her, giving her a hard stare.

"Okay, so maybe I only annoy you," she grumbled.

"Do you see something?" Mal asked me.

"Uh, no. Sorry."

Once again, he studied me and my scalp tingled. For an insane moment, I thought perhaps he was reading my mind.

"I'm going to talk to her for just a moment, then I'd like to continue to look around your house."

"Knock yourself out," I replied with a shrug.

Teri moved across the room and stood shoulder to shoulder with me. I rubbed my left arm, which was covered in goose bumps from where her transparent flesh touched mine.

"What do you think he's gonna say?" she asked.

I shot her a sidelong glance but didn't answer.

"I think he knows you can see and hear me," Teri continued. "He looked awfully suspicious earlier."

I shifted slightly away from her, annoyed by her comments.

"If you're still here," Mal began, "I just want to learn more about you and talk to you if you're willing."

Suddenly, I didn't feel like laughing at him. He seemed so earnest in his desire to talk to Teri. I felt like a heel for enjoying his earlier freak out.

Then I felt Teri lean closer to me, her mouth near my ear. I shivered from the cool sensation, but didn't swat at her as I usually would have.

"Should I grab his ass again?" she whispered.

I dropped my head and stared at the floor to keep from laughing out loud. Teri might do her best to irritate the hell out of me, but she also made almost everything funny. She rivaled Jonelle in her ability to crack me up.

"Would you mind if I brought a medium in to try and communicate with the spirit when we film?" Mal asked me.

At his question, I brought my head up. "I guess not."

He nodded. "This is going to be a great place to film," he stated, rubbing his hands together as he looked around my living room.

"He's right, this is going to be fun!" Teri cried out in my ear.

Wincing, I muttered beneath my breath, "If you say so."

CHAPTER

6

LATER THAT EVENING, after Mal left to do whatever ghost hunters did at night, I read through the paperwork he left for me. Legal jargon wasn't my forte, but I understood the gist of one particular section and I did not like it at all.

Frowning, I snatched up my cell phone and called Mal. He didn't answer, so I left him a message.

"Hey, Mal. It's Zoe. I'm reading the contract you left me and I have a problem with one of the sections. We need to discuss it. Please call me back."

I disconnected and re-read the entire contract again. I was fine with everything else.

Within five minutes, my phone rang and it was Mal.

"Hey," he greeted me, sounding slightly breathless. "Sorry I missed your call. I was at the gym. What's wrong with the contract?"

Well, that reaffirmed my belief that he must work out regularly.

"Not a lot, except for the fact that you expect me to appear on camera."

After a brief silence, he prompted, "You have a problem with appearing on camera?"

"Yes."

"May I ask why?" he queried, his tone even.

I got the sense I was beginning to try his patience. The thought made me grin. Malachi Flemming seemed like a laid-back guy and some perverse part of me liked the idea that I might ruffle that calm exterior. Damn, Teri was rubbing off on me.

I didn't want to answer honestly, but if he'd been asking around town about my house then he'd probably gotten an earful of the rumors about me as well. Still, I wasn't going to bring it up unless he did.

"I'm just not comfortable with it."

"The homeowners are usually on camera," he stated.

"Not this one," I shot back, my tone firm.

"It's part of the show, Zoe. People like hearing about the experiences of the people living in these houses. It'll just be a few minutes of conversation."

"Then maybe this was a bad idea. If appearing on camera is a requirement, then I can't allow you to film in the house."

"Seriously?" he asked. He sounded absolutely shocked that I would turn down fifteen hundred dollars over a short interview.

"Yes."

I needed the money but people in my hometown would find out about the show. They would watch it and think I was even kookier than they already did. After witnessing my childhood propensity for talking to ghosts, and my vehement insistence that they were real, the townspeople of Kenna, Texas labeled me as peculiar. That tag stuck for twenty years after I finally stopped trying to convince them that there were spirits walking among them unseen and unheard.

To this day, people my age and their parents avoided me and children stared at me, probably remembering all the things they'd overheard adults whispering about me.

Leaving Kenna wasn't an option, though. While anonymity would be nice, living in the city meant more people in less space and that included ghosts. Cities tended to be more haunted than anyone realized. The short time I'd lived away from home for college had been hard as hell because everywhere I went, I ran into an apparition. They were usually just lonely. Some were lost and confused. Then there were ghosts like Jerry at the insurance firm, the dead who seemed to enjoy bedeviling the living.

And they all wanted my attention when they realized that I could see and hear them.

"Fine," Mal conceded, interrupting my thoughts. "You don't have to appear on camera. I'll go back to my hotel room and remove that clause. If you have a printer, I can email it to you."

"That would be great."

"I'd like to film tomorrow. Will that work for you?"

"That's fine," I responded. It was more than fine. The quicker this was over, the better.

"We'll be over around three to set up our equipment. We'll be going to dinner after that, if you'd like to join us."

His invitation surprised me. "Uh, okay. That sounds nice." I hesitated. "We can order pizza and have it delivered if that's more convenient for you and your crew."

I had no idea why I issued the invitation. Just a few seconds ago, I'd been looking forward to this being over.

"That would be great," Mal answered. "And it will make things a lot easier for the crew."

"Then I'll see you all tomorrow at three."

THE NEXT DAY, my house was invaded. There was no other way to describe it.

At three o'clock sharp, my doorbell rang. Teri, who'd been waiting impatiently all day, came sailing down through the ceiling, something she rarely did. She claimed that moving through objects and people felt, in her words, "weird as hell".

"They're here!" she cried. "I wonder if Hunkypants' friends are as hot as he is."

I rolled my eyes at her words. If Teri was this obsessed with sex thirty years after she died, I didn't think I wanted to know what she was like when she was alive.

When I walked to the door, she pressed right up against my back and I couldn't suppress the shiver that ran down my spine.

"Back off, Teri," I mumbled. "You know I hate it when you do that."

"Do what?" she asked absently.

"Brush up against me. I have goose bumps all over my body now."

"Oh, sorry," she apologized.

I felt the intense cold move away from my body and relaxed. "Thanks."

"No problem. It's not like touching you gives me the warm fuzzies either."

I glanced over my shoulder. "I bet these guys cleanse haunted homes. Maybe I should ask them."

"You wouldn't," she gasped.

"Don't tempt me."

I felt her move away as I answered the door. I wasn't serious about having the crew cleanse the house, but the threat might keep her in line tonight. We'd had a long discussion this morning about what constituted sexual harassment and why it was wrong to go around grabbing a person's ass even if you weren't human any longer. I still didn't believe for a second that Teri would keep her hands to herself, but I had to try.

"Hi," I greeted Mal. "Come on in."

When I stepped back to allow Mal and his crew into the house,

I heard Teri sigh.

"*Damn*, his friends are as hot as he is," she muttered. "I don't know where to start."

I managed to clamp down on the urge to tell her to back off. I could only hope that Mal and his two friends wouldn't be offended by a little groping from a horny ghost.

Mal gestured to his friends. "Zoe, this is Blaine and Sean."

I held out my hand to Blaine. He was tall with shoulder length blonde hair and blue eyes. He looked like the quintessential surfer stereotype. His body was lean, but his shoulders were broad.

"Nice to meet you, Zoe," he said with a big grin. Dimples appeared in both cheeks. After he released my hand, he elbowed Mal. "Dude, you didn't tell me what a knockout she is."

My cheeks heated up just a little at his flirtation. I didn't take it seriously because I got the impression that Blaine flirted with every woman he met, both young and old.

"Quit flirting with her," the other man stated, stepping in front of Mal and Blaine. He looked down at me and I found myself staring into a pair of gorgeous hazel eyes with lashes long enough to make most women envious. "I'm Sean, but everyone calls me Stony." His shaggy brown hair wasn't as long as Blaine's but it was definitely overdue for a cut.

I took his hand, but he didn't shake it. He merely held it as he looked down at me.

Feeling a little uncomfortable, I asked, "Why do they call you Stony?"

Mal appeared beside us. "Because he was stoned for most of his college career," he answered shortly. "Stony, let Zoe go. You're making her uncomfortable."

Stony smiled at me. "I'm not doing that, am I?"

"Uh…"

Still grinning, he released my hand. "My bad. Your eyes distracted me. They're really pretty."

Damn, these guys were laying it on thick. I almost rolled my eyes, even as the blush in my cheeks intensified.

"Girl, I've never seen you blush!" Teri cackled. "This is awesome."

Her words broke the spell. I was acting like a swoony teenage girl and I didn't like it.

"From now on, no flirting," I stated firmly, looking from Blaine to Stony.

"It's not flirting if we're just stating the truth," Blaine quipped.

"Okay, how about this. Flirting with me will get you absolutely nowhere," I expounded.

"Why?" Stony asked.

"Why what?"

"Why won't it get us anywhere? You got a boyfriend?"

I groaned. "No, but that's not the point."

"Oh, I get it. You like girls," Blaine said. "That's cool. My sister does too. She's single and almost as good-looking as me. Want me to introduce you?"

"Thanks for the offer, but I'm straight." I replied. I eyed Blaine. "And you might want to ask your sister if she's okay with you setting her up on blind dates before you offer them," I chastised him. "Someone could get their feelings hurt."

His smile widened into a shit-eating grin. "So you like men?"

I nodded. "Yes, I like men, but I'm not sure you and Stony qualify. You seem boyish to me."

Stony groaned, clutching his chest in mock pain. "Oh, man, that's cold."

Blaine elbowed him. "You're proving her point, dude. Stop."

"Okay, that's enough screwing around," Mal snapped. "We're here to work, not for your two to hit on Zoe. Help me unload the van."

Mal marched outside, the screen door slapping shut behind him.

"Can men have PMS?" Blaine asked Stony.

"I don't know, B. Maybe we should get Mal some Midol just in case."

They continued their conversation as they followed Mal.

"I like them," Teri said, her voice close to my ear.

I jerked, startled by her sudden appearance. "You like anything with a nice ass and a penis."

"True, but I like more than their manly attributes. They're funny and they were hitting on with you. You should jump one of them. Or all of them. Oh, *ménage a quatre*. It's like a smutty book or something."

"Go away, Teri," I retorted.

"Just sayin'," she muttered. "You'd be in a much better mood if you got laid."

"Teri." My voice was little more than an angry growl. She was beginning to sound like Jonelle.

"Fine, fine. I'll shut up."

I felt her presence retreat, but not before she said one last thing.

"Besides, having regular sex makes you prettier."

Before I could reply, she disappeared. That was just like Teri. She always had to have the final word.

CHAPTER

FOR ALL THEIR silly behavior earlier, as soon as Blaine and Sean began unpacking equipment, they were all business. Teri vanished, claiming she was bored and wanted to take a nap before her "special appearance" tonight.

I tried to stay out of their way as they began setting up cameras and various other electronic devices. I found myself fascinated by what they were doing.

"What's that?" I asked Stony as he removed a black box from one of the cases.

"It's an EMF meter."

A couple of days ago, his explanation would have meant nothing to me. After watching all the episodes of *The Wraith Files*, I knew it was an electromagnetic field meter. The device looked different in person than it did on video. It was widely believed that ghosts used electromagnetic energy to manifest physically or to make themselves heard aurally. The meter would gauge the strength of the electromagnetic field.

"Won't the electricity in the house affect it?" I questioned, my curiosity getting the better of me again.

"Mal's already been through the house and checked everything, right?"

I nodded.

"Then he knows where the electrical stuff is and he's already made notes," Stony explained.

I backed away then and continued to watch them. When they were done, I found the revised contract Mal emailed me and handed it to him.

"I really wish you'd reconsider being on camera," Mal commented as he looked over the signed papers.

"Wait, you're not going to let us film you?" Blaine asked in surprise. "Why not? You'd look great on camera."

"Well, I have my reputation to worry about," I answered lightly.

"I call bullshit," quipped Stony. "If you actually give a damn what other people think about you, I'll strip down naked and run around the block."

"As pleasant as that sounds, I'll pass," I responded. "I'm just not interested in being a YouTube celebrity."

"Please?" Blaine wheedled.

I shook my head.

Before they could continue pleading, my cell phone rang. I excused myself and carried the phone onto the front porch. It was Jonelle.

Instead of a traditional greeting, she asked, "Hey, how's it going so far?"

"Wow, hello to you, too. I'm fine. How are you?"

"C'mon, Zoe. Tell me what's happening."

I sighed. "Nothing much. They're setting up their equipment."

"Are Blaine and Stony the only ones there?"

"How did you know their names?"

"Because I watched the show last night. I gotta tell you, I'm tempted to invite myself over just so I can watch them in action."

I laughed. "I think you'd be too much of a distraction."

"Yeah. I am pretty sexy. Wouldn't want them to forget about

Teri. She'd get jealous and do something really vindictive, like flush my lipstick down the toilet again."

I bit back another chuckle. Though she talked trash about my resident ghost, I think Jonelle actually liked her. In an I'd-have-to-kill-you-if-Zoe-wasn't-your-friend kind of way.

"Well, call me when it's over. I want to hear all the dirty details."

I scoffed. "Uh, no way. I'm going to sleep as soon as they leave. Mal said they'll probably be here until sunrise."

"Damn. Yeah, don't call me at sunrise. I need my beauty sleep."

We disconnected a few moments later and I went back inside the house. I could hear the men walking around, talking to each other as they finished setting up their cameras and other equipment.

I decided to get a cold drink and settle down in the kitchen until they were done and ready to order the food. When I walked through the door, I paused. There was a huge cooler sitting in the middle of the room.

I hadn't noticed them bring it in.

"Hey, we're just about done," Mal said as he entered the kitchen behind me. "What do you like on your pizza? I'm just about to order."

"Anything but anchovies, olives, and jalapenos. Why is there a gigantic cooler in my kitchen?"

"Oh, we brought snacks and drinks and stuff. We don't want to eat all your food."

I nodded. "That's nice."

"I'm going to order the pizza then."

"Wait, let me get you some cash," I offered. "I need to pay for mine."

"Our treat. We're invading your house for a night. It's the least we can do."

I didn't mention that he had already given me a check for fifteen hundred dollars, which was tucked away in my wallet.

"There's soda and stuff in the cooler, so help yourself. I'm going to call this in before Blaine and Stony stampede downstairs and start bitching about how hungry they are and how they're going to starve to death before we even get started."

I grinned at him as he left the room.

"You know he likes you right?"

I jerked and whirled to face Teri. I opened my mouth to yell at her then remembered I wasn't alone in the house. I couldn't believe I hadn't sensed her enter the room. Usually it was something I couldn't ignore.

After a quick check to make sure Mal was out of earshot, I whispered, "No, he doesn't."

"Oh, yes he does."

"I doubt that, but so what if he does?"

Teri shook her head. "I give up. You're never going to get laid."

"Yeah, because I don't want your perverted ass watching me have sex with somebody!"

I heard footsteps approach and put a finger to my lips.

"Hey, Zoe. Is someone here?" Stony asked as he came into the kitchen and made a beeline for the cooler. He removed a can of soda, cracked it open, and chugged.

"No."

He lowered the can from his mouth. "Weird. I thought I heard you talking to someone." Then he covered his mouth with a hand, suppressing a burp. "Well, we're all set to go. Mal said the pizza'll be here in a half hour and then the medium will show up at seven. We'll start filming at full dark."

As he spoke, Teri walked around him, looking him up and

down. Then she fixed her eyes on me. "He's got a nice ass, too."

I closed my eyes, knowing what was about to happen and hoping that Stony wouldn't spill his drink all over my freshly mopped kitchen floor.

"There! Did you hear that?" Stony asked. "I couldn't make out what they were saying, but I heard a woman speaking."

Teri froze, staring at me in shock. "Holy shit, he heard me!" She leaned closer to Stony, her mouth almost touching his ear. "Can you hear me, sexy?"

Stony shivered. "Damn. Mal was right. This place is definitely haunted. I just heard it again and got a cold chill." Then he grinned at me. "I can't *wait* to get started."

He sauntered out of the room, drinking his soda. Teri and I merely gaped at each other. It seemed at least one of the men on Mal's team was sensitive to the presence of ghosts. Well, more sensitive than the average person.

"I'm going to go whisper dirty things in his ear and see how much he hears," Teri marveled, moving to follow him.

"Fine, just keep your hands to yourself."

She flipped me the bird as she floated by me. "I make no promises and tell no lies."

When I didn't hear screams or cursing a few moments later, I assumed she took my advice despite her mischievous attitude. I doubted it would last the night.

CHAPTER

8

A COUPLE OF hours later, we were done eating and I was cleaning up the shocking amount of garbage that three grown men generated. Blaine and Stony were bickering about some place they'd filmed earlier that week as they huddled around my dining room table. Mal helped me wash plates and wipe up crumbs, which made me think of what Teri had said earlier. About how he liked me.

When the doorbell rang, Mal quickly rinsed and dried his hands. "That must be Marcy, the medium."

Marcy the Medium? Now that was an alliteration.

I followed him to the front door, pasting a civil smile on my face. It had been my experience that most mediums or people who claimed to talk to the dead were con artists out to make a quick buck.

"Hey, Marcy. Glad you could make it."

He stepped back to allow her inside. I was surprised by her appearance. I expected her to be a middle-aged woman wearing lots of rings and amulets. Instead, she was young, only a few years older than me, and very attractive. Her long blonde hair was pulled back into a ponytail and her full, pouty lips were slicked with red gloss. She wore a purple button-down shirt and tight black pants. From the tips of her stilettos to the top of her head, she looked professional and successful. With the exception of the glaring display of cleavage she was currently aiming at Mal, and the sultry smile that curved her mouth.

"Of course, Mal. *Anything* you need."

I felt Teri's presence a split second before I heard her make a gagging sound behind me. "I changed my mind. Jonelle isn't a cock hopper. *That* is a cock hopper."

I snorted, quickly covering the sound with a quiet cough. "Excuse me."

This brought Marcy's heavily made-up eyes to me. She narrowed them, staring holes into me without speaking.

"Marcy, this is Zoe. She owns this house, and I gotta tell you this is one of the hottest places I've ever been to," Mal stated.

I held out a hand to Marcy. I could tell by her body language that she didn't want to shake my hand, which was part of the reason I'd done it. "Pleasure to meet you," I lied, hiding a grimace when she laid her hand in mine. I hated dead fish handshakes, where the other person's muscles were limp, making their hand seem boneless. It felt creepy.

"I'm sure," she murmured.

When Stony and Blaine came out of the kitchen, still arguing over whatever had happened two days ago, Marcy perked up.

"Well hello, boys," she greeted them.

"Is this bitch for real?" Teri grumbled behind me. "If she's supposed to be a medium, why can't she see me? Or at least hear me?"

I jerked my left shoulder up in a miniscule shrug, telling her without words that I didn't know.

"Ugh. I'll be back when they start filming." I heard a wicked chuckle come from behind me. "Maybe I can scare the shit out of Prissy Pants there."

"Maybe," I whispered.

"What was that?" Mal asked.

I glanced up at him. "Nothing. Just thinking about something else."

Mal disengaged Stony and Blaine from Marcy and asked everyone to gather in the kitchen to discuss the game plan for the night.

By the time the meeting ended, the sun had sunk below the horizon. I watched as Mal filmed the introduction to the show. It took him several takes, but it was interesting to see how his demeanor changed as soon as he was in front of the camera.

Once that was complete, their investigation began. Mal introduced Marcy and they began walking from room to room downstairs. I followed them, Teri right behind me.

"I feel a spirit here," Marcy stated, tilting her head back and closing her eyes. "A female spirit. She's in great pain and so sad."

"Hell yeah, I'm in pain," Teri mumbled. "It hurts to watch this bullshit."

I bit back a laugh.

"Seriously, now I don't want to appear at all," she continued. "At least not in front of this hack."

I shrugged. Teri could do what she wanted. Though I almost felt sorry for Mal since his fifteen hundred bucks would be for nothing.

"Do you know what her name is?" Mal asked Marcy.

Marcy's brow furrowed slightly. "I'm getting something with a T. Tessa? Trina? No, no, Teresa. Her name is Teresa."

"Always hated that name," Teri stated behind me.

I barely refrained from rolling my eyes because all it would take to learn that information was a quick Internet search of the address. The archived articles were one of the first things to pop up.

"How did she die?" Mal asked.

Marcy paused, obviously for dramatic effect. "She killed herself."

Mal glanced back at me. "Did you know this?"

I nodded.

"That's it. I'm going upstairs," Teri snapped. "I'm not dignify-ing this farce with my presence."

Though I agreed with her, I didn't have much choice but to stick around. This was my house after all.

I felt Teri leave as I continued to follow the group around downstairs. Marcy "made contact" with the spirit in my house a couple more times.

A few minutes later, I distinctly heard a door upstairs slam shut. Everyone around me jumped.

"What was that?" Blaine asked, his voice loud and excited.

"A door upstairs," I replied.

Everyone dashed up the steps, but I followed at a slower pace. Marcy was just in front of me, probably because running in stilettos was nearly impossible.

When we crested the stairs, we saw Mal standing in front of the closed bathroom door, talking into the camera.

"Earlier this evening, when we were setting up, we left all of the doors upstairs open," he explained. "Now, this bathroom door is shut."

Before he could continue, we could clearly hear the shower come on. All the guys got excited, speaking all at once.

Marcy stepped in front of all of them. "Let me talk to the spirit here," she insisted.

There was some back-and-forth as they decided the best way to film the moment, and all the while my shower ran. If Teri kept this shit up, that check from Mal would be required to pay my water bill.

I leaned forward as Marcy reached down and slowly turned the doorknob. The door swung open on silent hinges because there was no way in hell my dad would let me live in a house where the doors squeaked.

She stepped into the steamy room and began speaking. "Teresa, I'm here. You can speak to me."

Blaine followed her into the small space, moving around to film her face as she spoke.

Suddenly, the shower curtain slid back, the loud sound of the metal rings against the bar making everyone jump. I could see Teri standing in the tub, grinning maniacally.

Marcy crept closer to the shower, clearly unaware of Teri's presence. "Teresa? Please talk to me."

The shower shut off. Marcy gasped, inching even closer to the bathtub.

I smiled then because I realized what Teri was up to when her hand lifted the removable showerhead from the stand.

"Oh my God, tell me your getting this," Blaine whispered.

"I am," Mal replied, his voice equally quiet.

The tension in the bathroom grew as Marcy stopped right beside the bathtub, peering into it. Teri looked at me and winked. The spray head rotated until it faced Marcy, then with a flick of her thumb, Teri gave the medium a face full of water.

Marcy shrieked, arms pinwheeling as she scrambled back from the tub.

Teri followed her mercilessly, spraying her head and soaking her clothes.

The men backed up quickly, never looking up from their cameras as they filmed the incident.

"Help me!" Marcy yelled, diving out of the bathroom to escape the cascade of water.

As soon as she could no longer reach her, Teri shut off the showerhead again and let it fall into the bottom of the tub with a clatter.

Everyone jumped again except for me.

Marcy stumbled downstairs, yelling and cursing as her wet stilettos slid on the treads. The men followed quickly behind her, asking if she was okay.

I stepped into the bathroom and grabbed a hand towel. "Good girl," I murmured to Teri, who was hovering in the corner.

She winked at me again and disappeared, probably to go downstairs to witness the upheaval she'd caused.

I looked around the bathroom and sighed. It was a mess. I tossed a couple of bath towels on the worst puddles, snagged another towel for Marcy, and left the room. Clinging to the handrail, I slipped and slid my way down the stairs to the living room.

I nearly fell off the bottom step when I got a load of Marcy's face. Her dark eye make-up had run down her cheeks, leaving black and grey streaks against her skin.

Then there were her eyebrows. Well, what was left of them as they dripped down her temples to her jawline.

As soon as she saw the towel in my hand, she snatched it and began wiping at the mess on her face. I winced at the dark stains that appeared on the white cloth. There was no way they were coming out.

"Shut the camera off," she snapped at Blaine, who was hovering nearby.

"I need to document-"

"SHUT IT OFF!" she screamed.

He lowered the device immediately, his wide eyes shooting toward Mal.

"I think you need to calm down, Marcy," Mal began. "This is an amazing phenomena that we've caught on tape."

I sucked in a breath at his first words. Clearly he hadn't had many girlfriends because telling a pissed off woman to calm down was like taking a stick of dynamite out of the freezer—which meant an explosion was imminent.

"Calm down?" she asked, her chest heaving. "Calm down? I was just attacked by a ghost! An evil entity that obviously intended to harm me!"

"It's just a little water," Stony stated. "It didn't truly hurt you."

I shook my head and bit my bottom lip. These guys were fast digging themselves into a hole they'd never be able to climb out of.

"Excuse me?" Marcy hissed to him.

"Uh, never mind."

Then she turned toward me, pointing a finger in my direction. "And you! You knew this would happen."

I felt my eyebrows lift. "Pardon?"

"You had to have known that this ghost would attack me. Why didn't you warn us that it was dangerous?"

I drew my shoulders back and straightened from my slouch at the stair railing. "I've never experienced harm at the hands of any spirits here. Not even a scratch or a spook. This is the first time that I've seen anything like this happen."

Marcy shook her head wildly. "Well, it'll damn well be the last! I'm going to cleanse this place if it's the last thing I do."

I frowned as she darted over to her purse and began rummaging around inside of it. Now that most of her make-up was gone, I could see that she was much younger than she looked. Maybe in her early twenties.

She yanked out a bottle that contained a clear liquid.

"What's that?" I asked.

"Holy water," she snapped, moving toward the front door.

"Now, wait a minute-" I began.

"I cleanse this house," she murmured, wetting her thumb with holy water and making the sign of the cross on the top of the doorjamb.

58   C.C. WOOD

"Stop that, right now!" I cried, moving forward.

My foot hit a small puddle and shot out from under me. I hit the floor with a crash. Immediately, Mal was at my side.

"Are you okay?" he asked.

I blinked up at him, taking stock of my body. "I think so."

I tried to sit up and winced as I felt a twinge in my lower back.

"No, you're not okay. Let me help you to the sofa," he offered.

Before I could respond, he lifted me into his arms and carried me across the living room. I clutched his shoulders and felt my eyes widen as I felt the steely muscles beneath my fingers. I had to suppress the urge to move my hands over his chest to see if the muscles there were just as firm.

Gently, he sat me on the sofa, tucking a couple of throw pillows behind me.

"Seriously, I'm fine," I insisted. "More startled than hurt."

"Sit here for a minute," he commanded.

With a sigh, I crossed my arms over my chest and looked around to find Stony and Blaine eyeing me speculatively and Marcy at the end of the couch, her holy water clutched loosely in her hand.

"Why don't you want me to cleanse this place?" she asked, her eyes narrowed.

"Because I know for a fact that the spirit here is harmless."

"Weren't you upstairs just now?" she queried scathingly. "Didn't you see what that ghost did to me?"

"Yes, I did. I saw everything. Especially the fact that you're a liar and a fake. You can't see or feel ghosts."

She gasped just before her hand flew out, dousing me with the holy water. "Bitch!"

Before I realized what I was doing, I was on my feet, shoving Mal out of my way. "Get out of my house, you scheming con artist! You couldn't see Teri when she was right in front of you!

And if you had been able to *connect* with her as you claim, you would have known that she swears she didn't kill herself. She was murdered!"

Everyone in the room gaped at me.

"Fuck," I muttered quietly. I took a deep breath. "I want you to leave, Marcy. Right. Now."

She huffed, but moved quickly to gather her things. Just as she got to the front door, Teri appeared and flung it open. The so-called medium squealed in surprise, then scurried outside as fast as her spike heels could carry her.

No one seemed surprised when the door slammed behind her.

"Good riddance," Teri stated, brushing her hands together as if she was dusting off dirt.

"I'm going upstairs to clean up the mess in the bathroom," I said, avoiding the eyes of the men around me. I didn't want to see the skeptical expressions on their faces or the pity in their eyes. "Feel free to keep doing what you're doing."

I started up the stairs, then paused. Leaning down over the railing, I looked at them. "Don't even think about cleansing the house or I'll chase you out of here with the shotgun my daddy bought me as a housewarming present."

They were all still silently gaping at me as I straightened and stomped up the steps.

CHAPTER

9

ON MY HANDS and knees, I cleaned up the puddles of water all over my bathroom. There was even water on the walls and the toilet.

The place was a mess.

"Next time you decide to scare the shit out of a fake medium, please find a less messy way to do it, okay?" I mumbled to Teri. "This is a pain in the ass. Literally."

My butt and lower back ached continuously from where they'd come into contact with the hardwood floor downstairs.

"I'm sorry, Zoe," she replied. "But did you see her face?"

I snickered. "Yeah. It was kind of worth it, wasn't it?"

"Totally!"

We both chuckled as I wiped up the last of the water and threw away the roll of toilet paper that had somehow managed to get soggy.

"Oh, Hunkypants at six o'clock," she warned me.

I straightened from my crouch and turned to face Mal. He stood in the doorway, his arms raised as his hands hooked on to the top of the doorjamb. I tried to ignore the little flutter in my belly at how sexy he looked lounging there.

Dammit, Teri's horniness was rubbing off on me.

"Hey," I greeted him, dumping the towels in the plastic hamper by the bathtub.

"Why did you lie to me?"

It seemed Mal intended to get right to the point.

I sat on the edge of the tub, wincing as my butt came into contact with the unforgiving porcelain.

"Because I learned a long time ago that people don't want to hear the truth. At least not about me and what I can see," I answered bluntly.

He tilted his head to the side. "Why not?"

I shot him a disbelieving look. "Seriously?"

He shrugged, bringing my attention back to the bulk of his arms and chest.

"Well, golly gee, Mal, most people would think I was crazy if I started telling them that I can see ghosts. Oh, and talk to them," I replied sarcastically. "It's not as if most people are open-minded. I'd end up in a straightjacket and doped up on anti-psychotics faster than you could say 'hallucination'."

He released the doorframe and crossed his arms over his chest. "No need to get snarky," he commented.

He was right. I wasn't truly angry with him anyway. I was mad at a world that couldn't, or wouldn't, accept me for who I was. A world full of people that would avoid me like the plague if I told them the truth they didn't want to hear.

Then again, there was always the occasional desperate person from Kenna that had heard the rumors about me. They would show up on my doorstep, asking me to contact their Grandpa Jack or their twin sister because they could no longer bear their grief or loneliness.

"You're right. I'm sorry," I sighed. "I've just been living with this…secret for a long time now. When I was younger, I tried to tell people what I saw, but they always thought I was making it up. As I grew older, I learned to keep my mouth shut before I got into trouble."

He studied me, as if weighing my words. I couldn't say I blamed him, considering I'd already lied to him once.

"Have you always had this ability?" he queried.

I shook my head. "Not always."

"What happened?"

I stood up, rubbing my back. "Let's talk about this downstairs. I need a comfortable chair and something alcoholic to drink."

A few minutes later, I was settled on the couch with a bottle of hard cider in my hand. Mal sat on the opposite end and Stony and Blaine were slouched on the chairs that faced the sofa.

"I died when I was five," I began. "No one could ever figure out why. My parents took me to doctor after doctor, convinced that it could happen again. My heart just…stopped."

"Damn, that sucks," Stony commiserated.

I shrugged. It did.

"The woman who lived across the street was a nurse. When she saw me hit the ground, she rushed over and administered CPR until my heart and breathing started back up again. I don't remember the trip to the hospital but as soon as I regained consciousness, I could see people. People that no one else could see."

Mal leaned forward, resting his elbows on his knees. "Do they look different from regular people?" he asked.

"Yeah. It's hard to describe. They're almost flat. There's no sheen to their skin or hair. Sometimes it's hard to tell the difference until they turn their head or someone walks through them."

"Did you tell anyone?" Blaine questioned.

I took a huge drink of my cider. "Well, yeah. I was five. I didn't understand what I was seeing. The first time I saw one, it was a man in a cowboy hat in my hospital room. I asked my mother who he was and she insisted that no one was there. At first I think that she believed I was just disoriented, but when I kept asking her about other people that she couldn't see…" I paused.

Mal frowned, but didn't say anything.

"Let's just say that she got upset with me. Then I told the kids at school and, well, the rumors flew fast and furious after that. I think that's what truly pissed my mother off—the fact that the entire town thought I was the *peculiar Thorne girl*."

"That's why you didn't want to be on camera, isn't it?" Mal asked.

I nodded. I didn't want to fuel the flames of the gossip that burned swift and viciously in Kenna. In a town this small, there wasn't much else to do but talk about what was going on with your neighbors.

"Yeah, but without your weird shit, I wouldn't have you," Teri stated, appearing between Mal and I on the couch. "I'd still be lonely and bored out of my skull."

I grinned at her. "That's true."

"What?" Mal questioned.

"Sorry, I was talking to Teri."

"Teri? The ghost?"

"Yeah."

"She's here?" His voice rising in pitch, as though he were excited.

I laughed. "She's sitting right between us."

"*Really*?" He sounded equal parts excited and freaked out. As if he wasn't sure whether he wanted to reach out and try to touch her or jump up from sofa and run across the room.

Teri turned and put a hand on Mal's thigh, patting gently. "Sure thing, Hunkypants."

Mal jumped to his feet. "Oh my God, did she just touch my leg?" he cried out.

I couldn't help myself. I laughed. "Yeah. She calls you

Hunkypants.''

Stony and Blaine burst out laughing as well.

"Hunkypants!'' Blaine guffawed, pointing at Mal.

Mal grimaced at me. "You're making that up,'' he accused.

I shook my head. "Nope.''

"We don't get nicknames?'' Stony asked, sounding almost disappointed.

Shrugging, I looked at Teri. "Do you have nicknames for Stony and Blaine?''

"Not yet,'' she answered.

I shook my head at the guys, amused at the crestfallen expressions on their faces. "I'm sure she'll come up with something sooner or later,'' I offered.

"Dammit!''

I jumped and stared at Mal, who was staring at me in dismay. "What?''

"You can actually talk to Teri and tell me what she's saying and doing, but you refuse to be on camera. The show would be so much better if you appeared!''

"Yeah.'' Stony and Blaine chimed in, their voices in unison.

Lifting my hands, I shook my head vehemently. "The show will be just fine without me, guys. Teri promised to give you lots of juicy stuff. Knocking, cold spots, electronic voice phenomenon, and maybe even a misty apparition on video.''

"Yeah, but she ran off our medium,'' Blaine complained.

I scoffed. "That woman wasn't a medium. She was a con artist. She couldn't see or hear Teri.''

"Then how did she know all that stuff?'' Stony asked.

"Because she researched this house at the library or online. The articles about Teri's death aren't difficult to find on the Internet.''

"Maybe. But still—'' Stony argued.

I interrupted him. "Teri was with us nearly the entire time she was talking about her, I could see her and hear her. If the medium had even a little ability, she would have picked up on that. She also would have known that Teri hates being called Teresa. And I wouldn't say that she committed suicide while you're here either. She'll end up giving you an earful about how she was murdered."

"She was murdered?" Blaine asked incredulously.

"Yeah. It sucked," Teri answered shortly, even though she knew he couldn't hear him.

"Did you hear that?" Stony asked.

I nodded. "Yeah, Teri just answered Blaine's question."

"You mean I can hear her?"

"Did you hear exactly what she said?" I inquired.

Stony shook his head. "But I could hear a murmur of a woman's voice, as though she were speaking in the next room but I couldn't make out what she said."

"You heard her earlier in the kitchen, too," I explained.

"She was in there?" His eyes widened. "Wow. I can't wait to review my digital recorder and see if it picked up an EVP."

I glanced at Teri and bit my lip. There was no telling what all she said to him. If I didn't know any better, I would have sworn she was blushing.

"Well, if Teri's ready to get started, so are we," Mal stated.

She nodded and floated to her feet.

"She's ready," I told him. As the other guys got to their feet, I realized something. "Uh, I forgot to ask earlier, but what's your stance on cursing. Teri swears like a sailor. You're EVP's might be useless."

"Shit, I didn't think about that," Teri mumbled. "Wait, what's an EVP?"

"Electronic voice phenomenon," I whispered, rolling my eyes. Teri had brought up EVP's a few days ago when Mal was here. I swear her memory had more holes than Swiss cheese.

"Ah, gotcha," she replied.

"We'll work it out," Mal assured me.

"I hope so, because all my dirty talk will sound stupid if I can't use words like *ass* and *cock*," Teri complained.

I almost felt sorry for the guys concerning what they would find when they went back over their digital recordings. I only hoped that the devices didn't pick up everything.

CHAPTER

10

"Zoe."

A hand cupped my shoulder, rubbing gently.

"Zoe, wake up."

My eyes opened slightly and I saw someone hovering over me. I jerked back, startled.

Mal lifted his hands. "Sorry, I didn't mean to scare you."

I blinked rapidly. "It's okay." I sat up and winced as the movement pulled the bruised muscles in my lower back. I must have fallen asleep on the couch while the guys did the rest of their investigation. Pale, pearly light leaked around the curtains, an indication that the sun was beginning to rise.

"Something wrong?"

"Just a twinge in my back," I explained with a chuckle. "I'm still a little sore from falling on the floor."

"You didn't tell me you were hurt that badly," he stated. "Let me take a look."

I lifted a hand. "No, no. I'm fine. You don't need to."

"Zoe, let me take a look. You might need to go see a doctor."

Since the pain wasn't letting up and Mal looked as if he was prepared to sit there all day until I let him examine my injury, I turned slightly away from him.

"It's just my lower back," I explained. "I'm pretty sure it's only bruised."

I felt Mal lift the back of my shirt a few inches and tried not to tense.

"Jesus, Zoe," Mal hissed. "You're black and blue. We should have put some ice on this."

"I'm sure it'll be fine," I argued. Anything else I might have said was forgotten as I felt the light pressure of his fingers as they trailed across my lower back, just above the waistband of my jeans.

"Does this hurt?" he asked.

"Not really," I replied hoarsely.

His fingers skimmed over my spine once more. "Are you sure?"

"It's fine, Mal," I insisted, leaning forward and pulling my shirt free from his grip so that it fell across the waist of my jeans. "Some rest and ibuprofen and I'll be as good as new in a few days."

He frowned at me. "Okay. Well, the guys and I are all packed up and ready to leave. I didn't want to wake you, but I thought I should let you know that we were going."

"Did you get anything good?"

Mal's face broke into a huge grin. "Oh yeah. Teri grabbed Blaine's ass the way she did mine the other day. It was hilarious." He paused. "How in the hell did you keep a straight face when she did it to me?"

I shrugged. "I'm used to hiding my reactions and not responding to ghosts when people are around."

His smile vanished at my words. "Yeah, I guess you are." He got to his feet. "Well, thanks for letting us film here. It's been a lot of fun. Between what happened with Marcy and Teri copping a feel on Blaine, this episode will probably get a lot of views."

I rose as well. "You're welcome. I'm glad I let you talk me into it. I wasn't sure at first, but this was a lot of fun."

I followed him out onto the front porch, waving at Stony and

Blaine as they loaded the last of their equipment back into their van.

They both jogged over.

"It was great meeting you, Zoe," Stony said, shaking my hand briefly before yanking me into a quick hug. "I hope we see you again."

When Stony released me, Blaine grabbed me and hugged me as well. "Yeah. I liked hanging out with you, even if the ghost in your house is a pervert who likes to grab an unsuspecting man's ass. It made me feel dirty."

"Oh, shut up," Stony insisted. "You loved it."

Blaine shrugged. "Dude, any time a woman recognizes all this sexiness and wants a piece, it's cool with me. Even if she is dead."

I laughed and shook my head at their antics as they walked back out to the van, ribbing each other good-naturedly.

Mal smiled and held out his hand. "This was probably the most fun we've had while filming, Zoe. Thanks again for changing your mind."

I took his hand, suddenly conscious of the warmth and roughness of his palm. While touching the others hadn't affected me in the least, something about Mal made me hyper aware of the feel of his flesh against my fingers and how his hand engulfed mine.

"You're welcome."

He held my hand for a moment longer and stared down at me in silence.

"Good-bye, Zoe Thorne. I truly enjoyed meeting you."

Just like that, he released me and walked away.

As I stood on the porch and watched them drive away, I realized that I probably wouldn't see them again in person and felt a wave of sadness. It had been nice to meet people who hadn't judged me for the things I saw and heard, but embraced my abilities.

"I think we'll be seeing them again," Teri said as she appeared next to me on the porch.

"Why do you say that?" I asked as their van disappeared around the corner.

"Just a hunch. Now, we both need our beauty sleep. Being on camera is hard work."

I chuckled weakly. "If you say so."

I followed her into the house, shutting the door behind me.

MINDLESSLY, I SCROLLED through the Netflix listings. Nothing piqued my interest but I didn't feel like reading or cleaning so I intended to watch something mind-numbing on TV.

Since Mal and his team filmed at the house, I'd gotten a call from the temp agency. They wouldn't have any work for me for at least two weeks.

"Moping again, I see?" Teri asked as she plopped down on the couch next to me.

"I'm not moping," I grumbled as I browsed the horror movie listings.

"Coulda fooled me. Ever since Hunkypants left, you've been downright surly."

I glanced at her out of the corner of my eye. "Surly?"

She shrugged. "Best word for your attitude lately."

Without responding, I chose a movie to watch.

"Admit it, you enjoyed being around those three."

I ignored her and wrapped myself up in a throw from the couch.

"You were able to tell them the truth and they didn't judge you," Teri stated. "You can't tell me that you didn't like that."

"I told Jonelle the truth and she doesn't judge me," I shot back, refusing to look at Teri.

"Yeah, but this is different. Jonelle accepts the truth. These guys work in your truth."

That got my attention. I turned to study her. "What do you mean?"

"Jonelle is your friend because she likes you, but she doesn't always understand you. Mal, Stony, and Blaine do. They believe in the paranormal, they seek it out. Their world revolves around it, sorta like yours does."

I stared at her silently.

"What?" she asked, her tone defensive.

"That was just...unexpectedly insightful," I replied.

She scowled at me. "I can be profound."

"Yeah, like a fortune cookie."

"Whatever. All I'm saying is that I think you should consider that you might be happier if you acknowledged your abilities instead of living as though they don't exist."

Before I could think of a response, my cell phone rang. I picked it up and stared at the screen with wide eyes.

"Who is it?" Teri asked. Instead of waiting for an answer, she moved around me to stare at the screen. "Holy shit, speak of the devil."

I lifted the phone to my ear. "Hello?"

"Hey, Zoe. It's Mal. How are you?"

"Uh, I'm fine."

"Listen, if you're free tomorrow, the guys and I would love it if you came by our hotel to look at our footage and digital recordings so far."

"Uh-"

Teri motioned to me. *Go*, she mouthed.

"That sounds like fun," I answered.

"Great. We're in Weatherford. That's not too far for you, is it?"

"Um, no. It's a short drive. What time should I be there?"

After we settled on a time in the afternoon, he said, "Oh, and there's something else I want to discuss with you. See you tomorrow."

Before I could ask him what he wanted to talk about, he disconnected.

"I wonder what he wants to talk to me about," I mused to myself.

"Hopefully, mutual nudity."

I shot a dirty look at Teri. "What is it with you and your obsession with my sex life?"

She shrugged one shoulder. "One of us should have one and you're the only one with a pulse."

With a sigh, I started the movie and went back to ignoring the oversexed ghost that lived in my house.

CHAPTER 11

THE FOOTAGE OF Marcy the Medium getting hosed down in my bathroom was my favorite.

"Play it again, Blaine," I insisted.

"This is the third time," he groaned.

"Yeah, but I'm really enjoying it."

Stony laughed. "You've got a mean streak. It's sexy."

"You think everything is sexy," I quipped, rolling my eyes at him.

"True," he answered, sipping his beer. "But I still have standards."

"Low ones," Blaine muttered beneath his breath.

"I heard that."

"How about you two jackasses quit fighting long enough for me to talk to Zoe?" Mal interrupted. "Better yet, how about you go to your own room?"

Complaining and groaning, they got to their feet and exited through the door that connected their room to Mal's. Mal shut the door behind them with a sigh.

"Some days it's like we still live in the damn frat house," he complained.

I laughed, because he had an excellent point. Still, I liked hanging out with Blaine and Stony. They were funny.

"Maybe, but I like them. I think they're sweet."

Mal scoffed. "Don't let them hear you say that. Their heads will swell." He sat down next to me in front of the makeshift desk they'd set up using the dining table in the corner of the room. "So, what did you think of the footage?"

"It's great," I stated enthusiastically. "I didn't realize how many EVP's you caught. Teri will be happy to know that her voice will be forever immortalized on the Internet."

Mal chuckled. "Teri sounds like an interesting person." He paused. "I'd like to ask you a question, but I'm not sure if you'd be insulted or not."

"The only way to know is to ask me," I answered.

"Okay, but no pressure if you feel like this is too intrusive," he stated, holding his hands out in a gesture of peace.

I nodded.

"What's it like living with a ghost? I mean, does she randomly go through the house slamming doors and flushing the toilet, or does she talk to you? How does that work?"

I laughed because there was no way his question was insulting. Maybe a bit personal, but not bad at all.

"Well, it's kind of like living with a slightly annoying roommate. She shows up at the most inopportune times, she talks a lot, and she's constantly trying to get me to hook up with my neighbor because she has the hots for him and she wants to live vicariously through me."

Mal's eyes widened at my words. "Whoa."

"Yeah. Usually she doesn't leave a mess. The other night was an anomaly brought on by the fact that she didn't like Marcy at all."

"That's…interesting," Mal stated.

He had no clue, but I didn't reply, merely lifted a shoulder in agreement.

"Uh, do you see other ghosts?" he asked.

"Not always. It really depends on where I am and how crowded it is. The greater the concentration of population, the more spirits I see. That's why I like Kenna so much. Teri is one of the few ghosts I see regularly."

"Really?"

"Oh, yeah. I lived in Dallas for a while when I went to college. It was hell. Sometimes I would respond to a ghost on autopilot before I fully recognized that no one else could see or hear them. Most of the girls in my dorm thought I was a little odd."

Mal smiled. "I'll bet. Surely some of them weren't freaked out."

I gave him an arch look. "These are college girls we're talking about. Most of them wanted nothing to do with me."

"Have you ever thought about, I don't know, using your talents to earn money?" Mal asked casually.

I sensed that we were getting to the real reason he wanted me to come to the hotel today.

"Not really."

"Would you consider it in the future?"

"Why don't you just ask the question you really want to ask?" I prompted him.

Mal smiled. He was wearing his glasses today and he looked every bit the sexy nerd that Jonelle had called him. "I was trying for subtlety."

"Subtlety isn't my strong suit," I replied. "I prefer honesty."

"I'm beginning to see that," he said with a nod. He took a deep breath. "Look, the guys and I really enjoyed working with you the other night. We were wondering if you'd be interested in working with us again."

"As in, be on camera? Tell you what the ghosts are saying?"

"Something like that," Mal responded. "I think you'd be an excellent addition to the show."

I studied him for a moment. Teri was right earlier when she said that Mal, Stony, and Blaine lived in the same world I did, that they would understand me in ways no one else would. "Are you offering me a job?"

He nodded.

Still unsure, I leaned back in my chair. "I'm not sure, Mal. I've never done anything like this before. I could ruin your show."

"I don't think that's possible," Mal answered with a chuckle.

"How long will you be in this area?" I had an idea.

Mal seemed surprised by my question. "Uh, probably until the end of the month. We're filming at some of the more well-known sites in the area like The Baker Hotel."

That had possibilities. The end of the month was a little under two weeks away.

"What if we did a temporary thing?" I asked. "I would film with y'all for the remainder of your stay, but that would be it."

"What if we want you to stay on longer than that?" he shot back.

I shrugged. "Mal, I'm not sure I'd be comfortable with doing this long term. I also don't feel right about asking people to pay me to *investigate* their haunted homes."

Mal shook his head vehemently. "No, we don't charge people money to come into their homes. Everything we do is in the name of discovery and to help people understand what's happening around them."

"Then who would pay me?" I asked, frowning at him.

Mal fidgeted in his chair, a sheepish expression on his face. "Uh, me."

I felt my frown deepen and made an effort to stop. I didn't want Mal to get defensive. "Okay, maybe it's wrong of me to ask this, but where in the heck are you going to get the money to pay me?"

He ran a hand through his hair, leaving it standing in spikes all over his scalp. "Well, we have advertisers."

"Yeah, but I'm sure that barely pays your travel costs and a small salary for y'all."

Mal sighed. "I'm going to tell you something, but I need you to promise that you won't get mad."

Those words almost guaranteed that whatever he had to say would probably stir my ire.

"Promise I won't get mad?" I queried, lifting my eyebrows.

"Okay, just promise you won't yell."

"Just tell me, Mal. Unless it's illegal. In that case, don't tell me because I'd feel obligated to turn you in."

He laughed. "No, it's not illegal. You see…" he sighed. "You know my last name is Flemming, right?"

I nodded.

"As in *Flemming Telecom*."

My eyes widened. Holy shit, the Flemmings were well known and among the wealthiest families in the state of Texas. They owned several large companies, one of which was Flemming Telecommunications.

"So, they fund your show?" I asked incredulously.

Mal huffed out a laugh. "Uh, no." Then he considered. "Well, in a way, I guess they do." He noticed my confusion. "I use my trust fund to finance the show. At least for now," he stated.

"Trust fund?"

"It won't be forever," he continued as if he hadn't heard me speak. "I'm shopping the show around to networks. Paranormal investigations are doing well right now in television. It may take a little time, but we'll get there eventually."

"So, you would be paying me out of your personal trust fund?" I asked again, this time a little louder.

"I think our chances of being noticed by a network would improve greatly with you on the show."

"Seriously, Mal? Just answer my damn question!" I yelled.

He winced. "I thought you promised not to yell."

"I only yelled because you weren't listening," I replied. "Now, are you saying that you would be paying my salary with your trust fund?"

He nodded.

"Do you pay Stony and Blaine a salary the same way?" I asked.

"They won't let me pay them," he stated.

"*Won't let you?*" My voice was rising again.

"Well, they have trust funds of their own, you see."

I got to my feet. "So what? You see that I don't have a job and you decide to offer me one because, hey, money is no object with you?"

Mal mirrored my movements, the sheepish expression disappearing from his face. It was replaced with annoyance. "Of course not."

"What am I? The token poor chick?" I sneered.

"What? Why would you even think that?" Mal asked, looking both angry and bewildered.

"Why in the hell else would you ask me to be on the show?"

"Maybe because you can see ghosts!" he yelled back. "We wouldn't have to worry about dealing with mediums who are full of shit and charge enormous fees anymore. We'd have our own. Oh, and let's not forget you're pretty damn hot. Having you on the show would guarantee more views, not just from women, but from men as well."

I heard the connecting door between the two rooms fly open.

"Dude, why are you yelling at her?" Blaine asked. "We want her to work with us, not take out a restraining order."

I was too distracted to say anything. Mal thought I was hot? I wasn't sure how to even process that information.

Stony walked over to stand beside me. "Mal, man, she's in shock. What the hell is wrong with you, yelling at her like that?"

Mal groaned and tore his hands through his hair. "Dammit." He turned and stomped away from us.

"You okay, Zoe?" Stony asked me, putting his hands on my shoulders.

That knocked me out of my trance. "I'm fine, Stony." I moved from beneath his hands, not wanting him to get the wrong impression.

Mal was pacing by the window, messing his hair up even more than it had already been.

I stood in front of him, forcing him to stop. "What kind of salary are we talking here?"

He blinked down at me, clearly confused. "Huh? I thought you didn't want to do it."

"I didn't say that," I stated. "I was upset at first because I thought…well, forget what I thought. What's the starting salary?"

"Seven-fifty a week," Mal answered.

"Make it eight hundred a week, and we've got a deal. I'll work with y'all until the end of the month."

Mal came out of his daze. "And you'll consider filming with us more if it goes well?"

"I'll consider it, but there will be other terms we need to discuss before I commit to a full-time job."

He held out his hand. "Deal."

"Deal."

As we shook hands, Stony and Blaine whooped.

CHAPTER

12

MAL AND I had a slight issue concerning the first night I was supposed to film with them. They were going to a cemetery in Springtown to investigate a glowing tombstone.

As soon as Mal told me, I stated, "I can't go to a cemetery after dark."

Stony and Blaine gave me odd looks but went back to discussing their equipment needs.

"What?" Mal asked, not looking up from his notes on the location.

"I can't go to a cemetery after dark, Mal," I repeated.

I finally got his attention.

"What?" he asked again, his head coming up this time. "Why not?"

I bit my bottom lip. "It's difficult to explain."

"Try." He tossed his papers on the table in front of him.

With a sigh, I sat down opposite of him. "It's just that, well, I don't just see ghosts. There are…other beings out there that are drawn to me."

"Beings?"

"Like zombies and ghouls," I explained.

He frowned at me. "Zombies and ghouls? You expect me to believe that."

"Seriously? You believe in ghosts, Mal. Why would you find this any harder to believe?"

He scowled at me and picked up his paperwork again. "It'll be fine, Zoe."

"Mal, you don't understand—"

He lowered the packet and stared at me over it. "The city gave us special permission to film in the cemetery after it closes. We can't cancel at the last minute or we'll never get the opportunity again."

"Maybe I should skip this one, though," I hedged.

"We need you, Zoe," he insisted. "We've already run promo that you'll be in this episode. I can't take you out now. If we run into any zombies or ghouls or whatever, we'll be fine. I promise."

"Don't say I didn't warn you," I muttered beneath my breath, giving up the fight. I knew that the probable outcome at the cemetery wouldn't be dangerous, but it would certainly freak them all out.

Then I grinned. It might be fun to witness Mal seeing his first ever zombie.

"Uh oh," Stony said. "I don't like the looks of that smile. What are you planning?"

"Nothing. Just thinking about tonight."

IT WAS NEARLY nine when we arrived at the cemetery in Springtown, but it wasn't quite fully dark yet. The night was warm, which was typical of early summer in Texas, and a slight breeze moved through the trees, creating a hushed whisper in the air around us.

As I helped them unload the van, we were all quiet. Though we were the only people around, we spoke in hushed tones.

By the time we were ready, the night was completely dark. As we rounded the van together, the faint glow of the headstone was visible from outside the graveyard.

Stony and Blaine shouldered their cameras. I held a digital voice recorder since I would be the one to speak to the spirits that might be lingering and Mal held an EMF meter and a flashlight.

We took a few moments to film a short introduction by the cemetery gate and I felt surprisingly comfortable talking to the camera, maybe because it was Stony behind it. He and Blaine were both being very supportive and helpful.

"Just pretend you're talking to one of us without the camera between us," Blaine had suggested earlier. "It will seem less awkward that way."

After a few takes for the introduction, we made our way through the gates that had been left open for us. The caretaker would be back at midnight to escort us out and lock them again.

I could clearly see the faint glow of the headstone as we picked our way around the other markers.

"Do you see any ghosts yet?" Mal asked.

I shook my head. Strangely, ghosts didn't really hang around graveyards. They tended to be tethered to places that they'd frequented while they were alive. I'd only met one untethered ghost in my life and it was an experience I didn't want to repeat.

The glow of the headstone grew brighter as we approached. Mal had us all stop as he filmed a short segment on the history of the grave and the man who was buried there.

After that was done, we moved even closer. Then a few feet from the marker, the glow began to fade. By the time we were within arm's reach, it appeared to be an ordinary headstone.

Mal crouched down in front of it, looking over his shoulder at Blaine and Stony as they filmed.

As he talked, I heard a sound that was hauntingly familiar despite the fact that I hadn't experienced it since high school. The ground to my left trembled slightly and the sound of dirt shifting and separating filled the air.

"What was that?" Mal asked, still squatting in front of the marker.

"Oh my God," Blaine gasped. "Holy fucking shit! Are you seeing this, Stony?"

"Hell yeah, man. I'm recording it."

I turned slowly, knowing what I would see. I watched as a hand appeared at the edge of the open grave that hadn't been there a few minutes ago. The zombie dragged itself out of the grave, the dark suit it wore covered in dirt and other things I didn't want to consider.

"Fuck me," Mal muttered behind me.

The corpse righted itself and took a couple of tottering steps. The grave must have been fairly new and about one hundred feet away from where we stood.

The zombie staggered forward, his feet dragging as he tried to make his legs work. I could hear the men behind me breathing heavily as they watched.

"Zoe, what's happening?" Mal whispered behind me.

I twisted to give him a dirty look over my shoulder. "Exactly what I told you would happen."

"Zombies?" he asked, his voice weak.

I nodded and faced the dead man that now stood about five feet from me. His arms rested at his side with his head held high, as though he were a soldier at attention and awaiting my orders. Although he couldn't have been dead for that long, I was grateful to be upwind of him.

"Did he say zombies?" Stony murmured.

"Dude." That seemed to be Blaine's usual response when he wasn't sure what to say.

"What in the hell is going on?" Mal hissed.

I didn't look at him when I answered. "I tried to warn you. I can't come to cemeteries after dark without this happening."

"I thought you were exaggerating!"

The zombie took a step toward Mal when he raised his voice.

"Stop," I called out.

At my command, the dead man halted.

"Lie down and be at peace," I stated, keeping my voice calm and steady. I hoped the command worked. Since that night ten years ago, I'd done some research about zombies and necromancy in case I was ever in this position again.

The zombie walked unsteadily back to his grave, sliding down through the crack in the earth. Before our eyes, the dirt that had been displaced shifted back into place, covering the coffin.

"Whoa," Blaine muttered. "Did that just happen or did Stony sneak some magic mushrooms into our spaghetti dinner tonight?"

"Hey, those aren't cheap. No way would I waste them on the likes of you," Stony argued.

"Shut up," Mal bit out. His glasses glinted in the moonlight as he turned to look at me. "Zoe, I think we need to have a talk."

Typical. I tried to warn him what might happen and he hadn't listened, yet somehow I got the distinct impression he believed this was all my fault.

CHAPTER

13

WHILE STONY AND Blaine loaded the equipment in the van, Mal wrapped his hand around my elbow and pulled me a few feet away.

I didn't appreciate being treated like a recalcitrant child and yanked my arm free. When I tilted my head back to tell Mal as much, I was surprised by the excited expression on his face. Considering the grip he'd had on my arm, I thought he was upset.

"What was that?" he asked. "I've never in the two years we've been doing this seen anything like it."

I felt embarrassed because I didn't know how to explain it. I didn't even know how I did it. It just happened.

"I don't know," I finally answered. "That's just what happens when I go into a cemetery after dark."

"So during the day, nothing happens."

I shrugged. "Nothing like that."

He immediately caught on to my omission. "But something does?" he pressed.

"Just…a feeling I get," I answered on a sigh. Throwing up my hands, I stated, "I'm not sure I can put it into words."

"Please try. I'm trying to wrap my head around what I just saw."

"I feel a—" I hesitated, searching my brain for the most appropriate term, "Connection with the dead. I don't know how else to put it. I can just *feel* them."

What I didn't mention was that they could sense me as well. They recognized me as being similar to them, even though my heart still beat.

"So you don't mean to call the zombies?" Mal asked.

I shook my head. "Not at all."

"Have you ever tried to do it? Intentionally raise the dead, I mean."

"No," I answered shortly. "And I won't. It's not right to call the dead from their resting place. They deserve their peace."

He studied me in silence for a moment. "I suppose you're right."

He scrubbed a hand through his already messy hair. I was beginning to find the habit adorable when it should have been annoying. That wasn't a good sign. He was essentially my boss now.

"Well, I don't think we're going to get anymore work done tonight. Why don't we all go have a drink? Know any good places?"

I nodded. "Several. You want loud and rowdy or dark and seedy?"

Grinning back at me in the bright moonlight, he replied, "You choose."

As we walked back to the van, he reached down and squeezed my hand, holding it gently for a few moments. It was a brief touch, but it made my heart beat a little faster and a blush rise in my cheeks. For a split second, I was thrown back to junior high when the boy I liked held my hand at the movies. I found out later, he'd asked me out on a dare. A dare.

The memory doused any warm feelings I had and Mal had already released my hand.

OUT OF HABIT, I took Mal and the guys to Birdie's. Honkytonks weren't places I enjoyed, and Birdie's was the antithesis of that. The bar was dark and the only source of music was a jukebox full of albums recorded at least twenty years before I was born. You could order food, but that was limited to five items; wings, pizza, nachos, burgers, and fries.

I loved the place. Mostly because Birdie MacBride treated me the same way she treated everyone else; like shit. She was at least fifty years old and crotchety as hell. It was difficult to tell her exact age because she tanned every summer, smoked like a chimney, and dyed her hair a brilliant auburn. Her skin was leathery and wrinkled, but she dressed as though she were still twenty-two. I also couldn't remember ever seeing her smile.

Even with her grumpy attitude, I liked her a lot. Birdie laid it out for you and didn't hold back, even when it might hurt your feelings. She didn't pretend to be anything other than who she was and she expected the same from everyone else around her. Which meant she didn't give anyone special treatment. People were people as far as she was concerned.

After we were settled at a table, Mal looked around. "I see you went with dark and seedy," he joked.

"Well, the only honkytonk in town tends to get wild around midnight. I thought this would be better if you guys wanted to talk."

Stony smacked the table. "That's definitely what I want to do. I want to know what happened at the graveyard tonight. That was some freaky shit."

"Yeah, dude. I didn't think zombies existed until I saw one with my own eyes," Blaine stated.

We all looked up as Janice, our waitress approached. I was

grateful for the interruption. It was always unnerving to talk to other people about my abilities. There was always the risk that they would reject me. I didn't understand why I felt that way about Stony and Blaine, since they'd readily accepted the fact that I could see and talk to spirits.

"What can I get ya?" she asked.

Janice had worked as a waitress at Birdie's since the place opened up twenty-five years ago. I doubted that she would ever retire.

"Hey, Janice. I'll have a Woodchuck and a cheese pizza please," I answered.

The guys ordered beer and an assortment of wings, nachos, and pizza. My eyes widened at the amount of food they requested, wondering how they were going to eat it all.

"We get really hungry after filming a show," Stony explained.

"I'll say," I murmured.

After Janice walked away, Stony and Blaine looked at me expectantly.

I blew out a deep breath. "Okay, so I can raise the dead," I stated.

They looked at me blankly.

"Seriously?" Blaine asked.

I nodded.

Their silence made me nervous and I fidgeted in my seat.

Finally, Stony smiled widely. "That is so cool! Do you, I dunno, call for them or something? Or do they just show up?"

"Uh, they just show up," I answered, relieved that they didn't seem upset at the knowledge.

"Damn, I bet you're a lot of fun on Halloween," Blaine said.

I shook my head. "Definitely not. I usually stay home and pass out candy."

"You don't go around scaring the kiddies and such?" Blaine

asked sounding disappointed.

"Nope."

"Why not?"

I laughed. "Because I don't like scaring children or giving people heart attacks."

"But it could be fun," Blaine insisted. "We could all go together.

"Not doing it," I stated firmly.

"Fine," he huffed, sulking for all of two minutes until our drinks arrived. "Janice, you are an angel."

She gave him a cold stare in return. "Your food'll be here in a few." Then she turned and marched away.

"Ah, I think I'm in love," Blaine said as he placed his hand over his heart. "It turns me on when a woman scorns me."

Blaine and Stony seemed content with my broad explanation of what happened at the graveyard and the conversation moved on to other topics.

As we ate and drank, I realized that this was the first time I'd felt at home with people I worked with. At the insurance company, I'd always felt like an outsider, even when people tried to include me. It was so difficult to maintain the facade of normalcy whenever I was around other people. I had to pretend I didn't see or hear the things I did.

With Mal, Blaine, and Stony, I could just be myself. It was liberating. I didn't feel as though I had to constantly keep my guard up and watch what I said.

For the first time in my life, I could be Zoe Thorne…whoever she was.

CHAPTER

14

THE NEXT DAY Mal, Stony, and Blaine were all crowded around my kitchen table as we planned our trip to The Baker Hotel in Mineral Wells. I was also making dinner for them. I enjoyed cooking, but rarely entertained anyone but Jonelle. Tonight, I'd made a big pot roast with potatoes and carrots. I also had fresh green beans from the local farm stand and homemade garlic cheddar biscuits. I thought Stony's eyes were going to pop out of his head when I told them what we were eating.

As I finished cooking the meal, Mal laid out the game plan for filming the next night. When he asked if I'd ever been to the abandoned hotel, I laughed.

"Oh, yeah. Jonelle got it in her head that a group of us should go our senior year in high school."

Mal leaned forward. "Is it really haunted?"

I had to laugh again. "Definitely. You won't be disappointed. There's a very mischievous child named Nancy. She roams the place and gets up to all kinds of trouble. She loves it when people come to visit and does whatever she can to get their attention."

"So you think we'll get some good footage?" he queried.

"I'm certain of it."

As I served the meal, Blaine eyed it greedily. "I don't think I've had a home cooked meal in years," he commented.

I stared at him. "What have you been eating then?"

"Mostly take out and frozen dinners."

"Uh, you could have learned to cook for yourself, you know," I pointed out.

He and Stony looked at each other and laughed uproariously.

"What's so funny?"

Mal answered my question. "Blaine hasn't been allowed anywhere near a kitchen since the time he nearly burned down our apartment during senior year. Every time he's tried, it's been a disaster."

"Hey, I resent that. I made scrambled eggs one time," Blaine said defensively.

"You mean yellow rubber, don't you?" Stony teased.

Blaine had no response for that, so I assumed that they'd been inedible.

"Why don't we focus on the delicious meal that Zoe made for us?" Mal suggested.

As we ate, I was once again struck at how comfortable I was with these three men. After years of alienation and loneliness, I'd fallen into an easy camaraderie with a group of fellow misfits.

Teri had been correct when she said that they lived in my world. Most people walked around every day, completely blind to the things happening around them. Mal, Stony, and Blaine might not see the same things I did, but they were open to the possibilities.

After we ate, I scooped bowls of ice cream for everyone as Mal went over the scripts and shots he wanted to get. He'd been inside the hotel earlier in the week, planning which floors he wanted to focus on and looking for areas where activity would be concentrated.

As I read through the introduction and closing scenes in the script, I found myself tapping my fingers on the table. It wasn't necessarily bad, but it was a bit boring.

"Something wrong?"

I looked up to find Mal frowning at my drumming fingers. "Huh?"

"You've been doing that for the last ten minutes," he replied, nodding toward my hand. "Is something wrong with the script?"

I hesitated. I was so new to this that I wasn't sure I should even say anything. What did I know about filming a paranormal investigation show?

"Be honest," Mal encouraged. "I'd like to know what you think."

"It's just a little…bland, I guess." He didn't speak, just nodded, so I continued. "I mean, you three are so funny and entertaining in real life and, to me, the script doesn't show that like it should."

He seemed to consider my words. "What changes would you suggest?"

I picked up a pen. "May I?"

"Sure."

I went through the first sheet and made a few changes to the dialogue he intended to use for the introduction. When I finished, I slid the page over to him. Now that he was looking at it, I felt nervous. I didn't know anything about television or scriptwriting.

Before I could tell him to forget about the entire thing, he looked up at me. "I like this."

"Really?"

"Yeah. You're right. This sounds more like us when we're to-gether. I think the audience would enjoy this," Mal admitted, his eyes going back to the page. "Would you take a look at the other parts of the script I've completed so far and tell me what you think?"

"I'm sure they're fine, Mal. You don't need me to—"

"Just look at them, Zoe. Please?"

We all went back to our respective activities. Mal and I working on the screenplay while Stony and Blaine argued about who was going to carry certain pieces of equipment. Apparently, one of the cameras was "heavier" than the other even though they were both the same size. When their discussion became heated, I glanced at Mal to see if he was going to intervene.

He shook his head at me. "I don't bother anymore. They argue more than an old married couple."

"Who's married?" Stony asked.

When Mal and I burst into laughter, he looked bewildered. "What's so funny?"

"Nothing," answered Mal. "Let's get back to work."

He winked at me before he huddled behind his laptop once again.

I felt Teri before she leaned in behind me and I stifled a sigh. She'd agreed to stay out of the kitchen tonight and let us work. It was typical that she would decide to eavesdrop.

"I'm telling you. He likes you."

I discreetly flipped her off and heard her laugh before her presence faded from the kitchen.

Still, I couldn't stop thinking about her words. Surely she was wrong. Mal was my boss now. Getting involved would be a monumentally bad idea.

Right?

CHAPTER

15

I STOOD AT the base of the towering Baker Hotel, staring up at the building as the light of day faded away. The brilliant pink and orange hues from the sunset glinted off the windows, almost hiding the face of a little girl in a white dress. Her light brown hair curled in fat ringlets, a style from nearly a century ago.

Without thinking, I lifted my hand to wave at her, smiling as her eyes lit up and she waved back. Of all the spirits I'd met over the years, Nancy was one of the sweetest. I didn't understand why she was still tethered to The Baker Hotel. As far as I could tell she hadn't died a horrific or violent death, but somehow she hadn't moved on.

"Is someone up there?" Stony asked as he came up next to me.

"Yes and no," I answered softly.

"Huh?"

I turned and smiled at him. "It's Nancy, the little girl I told you all about last night. She's watching us from one of the windows."

Stony tilted his head back. His eyes narrowed as if he expected he would be able to see her if he squinted hard enough. Then, in an oddly sweet gesture, he lifted his own hand and waved too.

"Did she see me?" he asked.

I glanced back up to the window where Nancy had been. She was gone.

"I think so," I lied.

Stony seemed to sympathize with the spirits that were still around us. Considering how attuned he was with the spectral plane, I shouldn't have been surprised at his ability to empathize.

"Are we ready?" Mal asked.

I picked up the gear I'd brought from the van and followed the guys inside. As soon as the door shut behind us, the last rays of sunlight vanished, leaving the lobby of the hotel in murky twilight.

As I walked to the center of the room, I could already feel the spirits milling throughout the hotel. Some were merely echoes of the past, like recordings of random moments that were imprinted on the very walls. Mal and the guys called them residuals. Some had been drawn to this place in life, thus they were drawn here in death. You could talk to them, but they were muted and vague. The parts of them that made them human had already passed on, leaving behind a half empty, ethereal shell.

Others had suffered and died here. Those were usually the most coherent apparitions. Their thoughts and emotions were as sharp and clear as they had been while they were alive.

Those types of ghosts were the most difficult to talk to because they understood that they were dead. Even if they had long ago accepted it, there was sadness in them, as if the weight that tied them to a place had crushed their personality as well. They could communicate, but hearing their stories was heartbreaking.

They were all here, lonely and waiting. It made me sad to think of so many of them passing their days unseen and unheard, utterly alone.

A glimpse of white flashed in my peripheral vision and I turned my head. Nancy peeked out from behind a pillar, watching as Mal, Stony, and Blaine unpacked equipment. I smiled at her as I squatted down to open the bags I'd carried in as well.

She grinned back before scampering away, disappearing into

the gloom of an open doorway.

I doubted it would be the last time I saw her tonight.

Once all the cameras, meters, digital recorders, and flashlights were all looked over, the backup batteries were checked for a charge. Mal explained after the first time I witnessed the ritual that spirits often used the batteries in the devices as energy to manifest.

It also explained why I had to replace the batteries in my remotes and other appliances so often. And maybe even why my electric bill always seemed to be high.

We began on the ground level, working our way up to the floors that Mal had earmarked until we reached the top. Though I could see and hear most of the ghosts we encountered, Mal and the guys wanted to see if there was any sort of physical evidence, so I wasn't on camera much.

Until we reached the ballroom on the top floor.

I sensed Nancy's presence, but didn't see her. When nothing seemed to be happening, we took a short break and stood out on the narrow terrace. The full moon had risen and bathed everything around us in the pale light. It was beautiful and still, only a sporadic breeze broke up the heat left over from the warm late spring day.

After spending a half hour eating snacks and drinking water on the small balcony, we gathered the cameras and other equipment and headed back inside.

As soon as we re-entered the ballroom, the air changed. The temperature around us dropped dramatically.

"Do you feel that?" Stony asked.

Blaine lifted the digital thermometer they used to measure ambient air temperature. Before our eyes, it registered forty degrees Fahrenheit. I shivered and exhaled hard, my breath pluming in front of me.

"It's cold," I muttered.

I didn't recognize the presence I felt in the ballroom. Nancy was gone. This was something bigger. Darker. It scared the crap out of me because I'd never experienced anything like it before.

"Zoe, can you see or hear anything?" Mal asked softly.

My voice was nearly a whisper when I answered. "No."

We circled the perimeter of the room, taking measurements. Mal would occasionally ask me if I saw or felt anything. Other than the oppressive weight of the invisible phantom that hovered over the room, there was nothing.

"Well, I'd say this is a bust," Blaine stated.

Suddenly, all the hair on my arms stood on end and the nape of my neck prickled. Before I could warn the others that something was happening, the deep, deafening peal of a bell shook the room. The bell tower was empty, the bell long ago falling from its mounting.

Yet we all heard it.

I cringed and covered my ears with my hands as the bell clanged again, the reverberations shaking the entire floor.

As the vibrations began to fade, I turned to Mal. "We need to get out of here. Now."

In unison, we gathered up our things and made a mad dash for the old-fashioned elevator. The car began to descend just as another, final clash of the bell rang out.

The elevator shuddered and I fell over. Mal's hands closed around my waist, pulling me back and anchoring me to his body as he braced his back against the wall. I held my breath until the car stopped on the lobby level.

We spilled out of the elevator, all of us breathing hard.

"What the fuck just happened?" Stony yelled.

It was the first time I'd ever seen him ruffled. Not even after the zombie incident in the cemetery had he been unsettled.

Mal shrugged. "I have no clue."

They all turned and looked at me.

"Any idea, Zoe? You said you'd been here before." Mal's expression was expectant.

I shook my head. "I've never felt anything like that before. When we were here before, all the spirits I met were…harmless."

"Well, I sure as hell don't want to wait around and see if whatever that was intends to just scare the shit out of us or use our guts for garters. Let's get the fuck outta here," Stony exploded.

I guess everyone agreed because we had all the cases packed and outside the hotel in less than five minutes.

Within fifteen minutes, we were back on the road, heading toward Kenna. The interior of the van was utterly silent as Mal drove us along the rural roads I'd mapped out for him the previous evening.

"Anybody bring an extra pair of pants?" Blaine asked. "I think I shat myself."

After a second of utter, shocked silence, all four of us broke into howls of laughter. As I wrapped my arms around my belly and rocked back in forth in the passenger seat, the fine tremor that had been running through my body since the event finally ceased.

As we finally began to calm, Stony asked, "Is that what that smell is?"

Of course, that question set us off again. Tears streamed down my cheeks and I hooted uncontrollably.

Mal finally had to pull over to the side of the road to wipe his eyes because he was crying as well.

After a long while, our gales of laughter died away into intermittent chuckles and they finally quieted completely.

"Oh, I needed that," Stony commented.

I understood what he meant. The wild emotions careening through me earlier were soothed and I felt steady once again.

It seemed that laughter was an excellent outlet after an adrenaline overload.

Mal took a drink from the water bottle he kept in the console then put the vehicle into gear. Before he could pull out onto the road, I threw out a hand.

"Wait!"

He stomped on the brakes, jolting us all forward against our seatbelts.

"What is it?"

"Do you see that?" I asked, squinting as I peered out the windshield.

"There's someone standing on the side of the road, about a hundred feet in front of us."

Mal stared in the direction that I pointed. "I don't see anyone." He began to inch the van forward. "Tell me when to stop."

When we were finally close enough for me to distinguish that the figure was a man, I told him to stop.

"You can't see him, right?" I asked one more time. After I got a chorus of no's from the men in the car, I sighed. "He must be a ghost."

When I opened my door, Mal put a hand on my arm. "What are you doing?"

"I'm going to go talk to him," I replied.

"I'll go with you."

I shot him a sidelong glance. "It's not as if you can hear him. Or he can hurt me."

Mal returned my look with one of his own. "I'm still going with you."

"Fine, but don't interrupt when I'm talking to him, okay?"

He nodded in agreement.

"Let's go then."

CHAPTER

16

A S WE APPROACHED the spirit, I could see that he was very agitated, pacing back and forth in short steps, his eyes glued to us.

"Oh, thank God you stopped," he stated. "I've been trying to get someone's attention for a long time. Everyone just keeps driving past me. I need your help."

I immediately began to wonder if the man knew he was dead. His words implied that he didn't.

"What can I do?" I asked.

The man looked at me, but directed his words to Mal. "I need you to help me get back to town. I wrecked my truck."

Mal couldn't hear or see him, so he merely stood there, his hands folded in front of him, staring at a point over the ghost's head.

"Hey, man, I'm talking to you," the ghost bellowed.

"He can't hear you," I stated.

That got his attention. "Why not?"

I evaded the question, because I didn't want to just blurt out to the guy that he was dead if he didn't already know that. The one time I'd made that mistake, the woman in question had wailed and moaned for hours about her lost and wasted life. My intention to help her had floated away on a sea of ghostly tears.

"He's deaf," I lied. "I'm Zoe Thorne. What's your name?"

"I'm Hank Murphy. Listen, my truck is totaled and I need to get to town. I've got to tell the sheriff that someone tried to kill me."

Shit, the longer he spoke, the more I came to believe he had no clue that he was dead.

"Of course, Hank. I see your head is bleeding. Do you remember what year it is?"

"What does it matter?" he asked belligerently. "Someone just tried to kill me!"

"I'm just concerned that you might have a major head injury. If that's the case, we need to take you to the hospital first before we take you to the sheriff."

"It's 1996! Can we go now?"

He'd been dead for at least twenty years. I wondered how long he'd been roaming this lonely stretch of back roads, just waiting for someone to stop and help him.

The thought made me sad. I also regretted that I would have to be the one to tell him that he hadn't survived the accident.

The moon was full, the light bright enough for Hank to see my face. He must have glimpsed the remorse in my expression, because he took a step back.

"Something isn't right," he stated, shaking his head.

Simultaneously, Mal's phone rang. I had to give him credit. He didn't answer it, but he did pull it out of his pocket and shut it off. Hank's eyes dropped to the device, growing wide.

"What's that?" Hank asked, pointing to Mal's smartphone. Then he looked at us closely. "What's going on?"

I took a deep breath, mentally preparing my answer, but I never had a chance to speak.

Hank twisted his head to look behind me. "Who are they?"

I glanced back and saw that Stony and Blaine had decided to

film our interaction with Hank.

The ghost began to back up from us, lifting his hands. "Will someone please tell me what's going on?" he asked.

His voice sounded calm, but his eyes took on a wild look I recognized. He knew he was dead, he'd known all along, he just didn't want to admit it. Denial could be more powerful than evidence if the spirit was stubborn enough.

"Hank, I'm sorry. I'm so, so sorry."

He shook his head slowly. "This can't be happening. It can't."

I moved toward him, inching forward. "I want to help you. That's why we stopped."

Hank hesitated, blinking rapidly. "How long have I been…dead?" he asked, his voice cracking.

"A while," I evaded. I didn't want to upset him more than I already had.

"How long?" he barked, his voice rising.

"Twenty years," I answered. "It's 2016."

Hank's expression morphed into one I was all too familiar with. He looked defeated and grief-stricken. "My wife," he whispered. "Oh God, I never got to tell her how much I loved her. I never got to say good-bye."

"I'm sorry, Hank," I repeated, hating the apology because I knew it wouldn't help.

Nothing would help, but moving on to the next plane. Heaven or Hell, I didn't know. I couldn't remember what was out there, only that there was…something.

The lost expression faded and his eyes fired. "Someone killed me," he stated. "Someone wanted me dead. You have to find them and make them pay."

"Of course. I told you I want to help you." And I did. I wanted to help him find peace. If he did, then he could leave this world behind. "In order for me to do that, I need you to tell me what happened."

His eyes lost focus as he stared into the distance. "It was late. I was driving home from work at midnight. It was so damned dark. I heard a car coming up behind me. No, not a car. A truck. A big truck. It was loud and fast."

He paused, his eyes still locked on the trees across the road.

"What happened, Hank?" I asked softly, not wanting to break his concentration.

"They shot at me. I heard the gunshots, saw the muzzle flare. They managed to hit my back windshield. That's when I lost control of my truck. I went down into the ditch and hit a tree. It was like the world ending, so loud and violent. Then everything went black." His eyes moved back to me. "I guess I was thrown from the truck because when I woke up, I was lying on the ground in front of the mangled front end. I could see the other truck parked on the road and there was a man standing nearby. I think I reached out to him, begging him to help me. As he came toward me, I thought he was going to save me. Until I saw the rock in his hand."

I swallowed hard, knowing where the story was going.

"I don't remember anything after the first hit, and then suddenly I was standing here on the side of the road, hoping someone would stop and help me."

My heart ached with pity for this man. All these years, he'd been desperate to get help, to find the person who killed him.

"You'll find out who did this to me, won't you?" he asked.

It wasn't the first time a spirit had asked me to seek justice for them, but it was the first time I couldn't say no. I didn't know why, but the urge to give him closure, to help him find peace, it was too strong to ignore.

"Of course I will," I answered.

The relief on his face once again tugged at my heartstrings.

"My name's Henry Jacob Murphy," he stated. "But everyone called me Hank."

I grabbed my cell phone from my pocket and opened the note application. I entered his name.

"When was your birthday, Hank?" I asked.

"June third. 1971. My wife's name is Patricia Murphy. Everyone calls her Trisha."

I nodded as I took down all the information.

"If you see her…" His words trailed off as if he was searching for the right thing to say. "Tell her that I always loved her, even when I acted like an asshole."

Though I was sure Trisha knew that, I replied, "I will."

He nodded. "I'm always here," he said. "Can't seem to go anywhere else."

I wanted to reach out to him, but I knew it wouldn't make any difference. He wouldn't be able to feel my hand anyway.

"I'll find out what happened, Hank, and then I'll come back."

He looked doubtful.

"I will. You have my word."

"A person's word doesn't seem to mean much anymore," he responded.

"Mine does. I never promise something unless I intend to keep it." I paused. "So, I want to tell you this. I promise to come back and tell you everything I discover. I'll do my best to find out who did this to you, but I can't promise to carry out retribution for you. If I find out who it was, I'll go to the police and make a report, but I'm not a tool for vengeance, Hank. I never will be."

He winced, but nodded. "I understand. You have a life and I'm sure you want to keep it."

He was absolutely right. I wasn't about to risk my life or deal with any legal ramifications by chasing after his murderer. I wanted to help him, but I drew the line at vigilante behavior.

"Thanks, Zoe Thorne," he said.

Before I could reply, he disappeared, dissipating in the night breeze like smoke.

For the first time since I began speaking to Hank, I felt my shoulders relax. I took a deep breath and exhaled hard.

"Is he gone?" Mal immediately asked.

I realized that my new boss hadn't spoken once since we got out of the van and I appreciated his restraint. Looking at the way he was bouncing on his toes now, I realized that it must have been killing him to stand there in silence.

"Yes, he's gone," I answered.

"So, are we going to solve a murder?"

I stared up at him. "I guess so."

CHAPTER

17

I BARELY SLEPT after Mal and the guys dropped me off at my house. A little after five a.m., I gave up hope on getting any shut-eye and went downstairs to make a pot of coffee. Teri was quiet. I didn't even feel her presence.

As I drank my coffee, I thought about Hank Murphy and his plea for help. I wanted to find out what happened to him, but I wasn't sure where to start.

So like any other modern human being, I opened my laptop and pulled up the Google search engine.

I searched for information on how to investigate a murder. After a half hour and two cups of coffee, I realized, with a great deal of frustration, that I wasn't getting anywhere.

After drinking another cup of coffee and eating a bowl of cereal, I had an idea. I sat down at the kitchen table and typed in *how to investigate a cold case.*

I read page after page, until I finally had to stand up and stretch because of the stiffness in my back. As I raised my arms above my head, I noticed that the sun was shining brightly through my kitchen windows and glanced at the clock.

I'd been reading for over five hours and I was still in my pajamas. The coffee in my cup was stone cold and my stomach rumbled. I decided to make myself a sandwich and then take a shower before I continued my research.

Before I could do either, my doorbell rang. Curious, I walked through the house and peeked out the narrow windows that ran alongside the door. It was Mal.

Because he'd already spotted me peeking out at him, I cracked the door. "Hey, what's up? Is something wrong?"

He frowned at me. "You texted me earlier and told me to come by around ten."

It was my turn to scowl. "No, I didn't."

Instead of arguing, Mal pulled out his ridiculously huge smartphone and pulled up his texts. "Here."

My eyes narrowed as I read the message. I knew what happened.

"Come on in," I invited, opening the door. Then I turned and stomped to the staircase. "Teri, get your see-thru ass down here!"

When I faced Mal again, his eyes were on my legs, which were bare due to my short boxer-style pajama bottoms. I suddenly felt self-conscious as his eyes moved up my body to my face. In the spring and summer, I wore camisoles and girlie boxers to bed, as my room seemed to be the hottest in the house. I'd completely forgotten my lack of coverage when I'd opened the door.

"Yes, my loud-mouthed mistress," Teri answered sardonically, appearing a few feet away from me.

"Have you been messing with my phone again?"

She folded her hands in front of her and attempted to appear innocent. She wasn't very good at it.

"I have no idea what you're talking about."

I glowered at her. "Teri, you can't go around texting people from my phone! Remember what happened when you messaged that guy on Facebook?"

"He wouldn't really have cleaned your toes with his tongue. He was just lonely."

"Teri, he sent me pictures of his junk with a bow tied around it! I still have nightmares!"

"Well, it's not like Mal would do something like that," she replied defensively.

She shrugged. "Maybe, but at least he's here now and looking you over like he wants to put his hands all over you if he can only figure out where to start."

I was relieved that Mal couldn't hear her as a hot flush worked its way from my chest to my scalp.

"Don't do it again," I snapped.

"Fine," she sighed, waving a hand as she drifted up the stairs. "You should be grateful I'm trying to get you a man. It's been years, girl."

I shook my head at her words and turned toward Mal. "I'm so sorry. That text wasn't from me, it was from Teri," I stated lamely.

"I gathered as much," he answered dryly. "Did I wake you?"

"Uh, no. I've been up since five, doing research."

His eyes lit up. "On Hank Murphy?" he asked.

"Not exactly. I'm researching the best ways to investigate a cold case."

"That's a good idea," he replied, his eyebrows lifting. "I have my laptop in the car. Wanna work together? Maybe grab some lunch?"

I glanced down at my outfit. "Can you wait a half hour? I need to get ready."

"Sure. I'll go grab my stuff and do some investigating online."

As soon as he walked out the door, I bounded up the steps and into my bedroom. I tried not to think about the fact that Mal was downstairs in my living room while I was naked in my shower. It felt weird to have a man in my house, waiting on me.

I caught myself taking special effort with my hair and make-up and forced myself to go through my normal routine rather than primping. This weird attraction I felt toward Mal needed to be my little secret. We might work together, but he was paying my salary, at least until the end of the month. That meant he was my boss, even if it was temporary. In my mind, hitting on the boss was never a good idea.

Exactly thirty minutes later, I came downstairs to find Mal staring at his computer, a look of intense concentration on his face.

"Find anything?" I asked.

His head came up. "Not yet. Just some articles on the accident. I emailed you the links."

"Thanks."

"I know it's early but are you ready to eat?" he asked.

"Sure. Where do you want to go?"

"Are there any good Mexican restaurants around here?" he asked.

There were a handful of eateries in Kenna, one of which was fantastic Tex-Mex.

"Yep. I'll drive," I replied.

The cantina was downtown, sandwiched between the post office and the hair salon where Jonelle worked. When we parked and climbed out of the car, I saw my friend cutting a woman's hair at her station near the front window. I waved to her and she sent a pointed look from me to Mal.

I shook my head at her and led Mal into the restaurant. Since it was just after eleven, the place was almost empty.

After we sat down and ordered our meal from the waitress, the back of my neck tingled. I immediately recognized the feeling and discreetly scoped out the small dining room.

A man sat in the corner. He appeared to be several years younger than me, caught between the gawkiness of his teens and the filling out years to come with his twenties. As soon as our eyes met, his flicked away as if he was embarrassed to be caught staring.

"Everything okay?" Mal asked, bringing my attention back to him.

"Yeah, yeah. Everything is fine."

As we sipped our drinks, we discussed where to begin our investigation of Hank Murphy's death. Mal suggested contacting the local law enforcement. For a moment, I forgot myself and grimaced.

"Something I said?" Mal asked.

"Sorry. It's just that the sheriff isn't too...fond of me."

"I don't understand."

"Let's just say he doesn't think I'm a little eccentric like most of the town does. He thinks I belong in an institution." I couldn't believe I'd admitted that to him, but he made me feel comfortable so the words tumbled out despite my usual reticence.

Mal's eyes narrowed behind his glasses. "Has the man talked to you for more than five minutes? That's all it would take to realize that you don't have any mental issues at all."

"Unfortunately, he had to come to my rescue the first time I raised zombies in a cemetery."

Eyes wide, Mal asked, "How old were you when this happened?"

I shrugged. "It was my senior year of high school."

"So, based on what he saw in the cemetery he thinks you should be locked up?"

"Pretty much."

"That's fucking ridiculous," he argued. "I'm sure you were scared out of your mind. He shouldn't have frightened you further."

I grinned at him. "No need to get so angry on my account. I've gotten used to his attitude. A lot of people in town share it."

Mal shook his head in disgust. "I'm sorry, Zoe."

"It's just a part of my life," I replied with a shrug.

"Have you ever thought about moving?"

"Too many ghosts. The greater the population, the greater the number of spirits. Teri may get on my nerves from time to time, but she doesn't bother me much. In the city? I really would end up needing medication."

Mal nodded. "That makes sense."

The waitress returned with our food and we dug in. I could feel the disconcerting sensation of eyes staring at me.

"Look, I don't mean to pry, but there's a guy in the corner and he can't seem to stop staring at you. Do you know him?"

I shook my head. "Nope. I saw him when we came in."

"Is he local?"

"Not that I know of," I answered. I didn't elaborate that I might not know who the man was, but I did know *what* he was. I only hoped he decided to leave before we finished our meal.

Unfortunately, luck was not on my side. Mal insisted on paying for lunch, stating that it was a business expense. As we left the restaurant, I sensed the eyes of the man following me.

I thought I was going to escape unscathed, but it appeared that my luck had decided to take a vacation that day.

A few feet from the car, I heard rapid footsteps approaching from behind me. I turned to find the young man from the restaurant bearing down on me.

"Can I help you?" I asked tautly, hoping he'd take the hint from my tone of voice.

Like most of his ilk, he seemed deaf to the warning in my words. "You're different," he declared.

Mal's phone rang and he was too busy talking to hear what was happening.

I walked toward the man. "Yes, I am, but I don't appreciate you yelling it out on a public street."

He looked around, then back to me. "Oh, sorry." The man inched closer. "What are you? You seem like me, but…not."

"I'm human," I answered.

He shook his head. "No, you're not. Not totally."

I flinched at his words. "I am," I insisted.

The man entered my personal space, inhaling deeply. "You're not, but you're not like me either."

"No, I'm not a ghoul," I stated. "Now back up."

"But there's something about you. You…glow."

I hesitated then. This was the first time a ghoul had said that to me. "What?"

"You're beautiful. Like an angel. And the light you shine…"

"Hey! What in the hell do you think you're doing?"

At Mal's shout, the ghoul's head jerked back and he stared as Mal stormed around the front of the car.

"Get away from her!"

I watched, speechless, as the ghoul retreated, lifting his hands.

"I meant no harm," he said, looking at me. "I only wanted to talk to you. I'm sorry."

He tripped over the curb as he whirled and hurried off in the opposite direction. Mal moved to my side and watched him leave.

As soon as the ghoul was out of sight, he asked, "Are you okay? He didn't hurt you, right?"

"I'm fine," I assured him.

"I thought you said you didn't know him?"

"I don't," I muttered. "But I know what he is."

"What do you mean?"

I sighed. "I think it's time for your next lesson in the supernatural."

18

"SO HE WAS a *ghoul*?" Mal asked incredulously. "I'm not even sure I understand what ghouls are."

"Well, they look human enough, but they need dead flesh to survive. Most get by with animal carcasses like deer or fowl, but they occasionally need, uh, human flesh. Otherwise, they start to lose their, uh, normal appearance."

He grimaced at my words. "Where do they get it? The human flesh I mean."

"Where would you go?" I asked.

His upper lip curled. "Do they at least cook it first?"

I shrugged and sat down next to him on my couch. "I don't know and I'm not gonna ask. There are some things I don't need to know."

"So, ghouls are attracted to you? Even the females?"

"Well, I know the males are." I paused. "I don't think I've ever met a female ghoul."

Mal nodded, taking in all this information rather well. He leaned forward and rested his elbows on his knees. "So, is there anything else I need to know about you?" he asked. "Are you going to call up a vampire or resurrect someone next?" His tone was light, almost teasing.

"No. Now you know everything."

"And I'm guessing you didn't tell me about this before because you were afraid I would think the same thing your illustrious sheriff does."

I nodded.

"Well, after some of the things I've seen over the past few years, you don't have to worry about that," Mal assured me. "Most people think I'm a crackpot myself."

I smiled at him, grateful for his easy acceptance of things that my own mother refused to acknowledge. He returned the grin, shifting so that his shoulder brushed mine. His face seemed to loom closer and I realized he was leaning forward.

He was going to kiss me. I wasn't sure what to do. I wanted it. Badly. But I also knew better than to get involved with someone who paid my salary, even if it was temporarily.

My gaze dropped to his lips and thought, *What the hell. It's just one kiss.*

Before our lips made contact, Teri floated into the room. "Mal and Zoe, sitting in a tree. K-I-S-S-I-N-G. First comes love. Then comes marriage. Then comes Zoe with a baby carriage," she singsonged.

I jerked back, surprised by her sudden appearance.

Mal blinked at me. "What's wrong?"

"Nothing," I murmured, shifting back into the corner of the sofa. "I, uh, just realized that it would probably be a bad idea to, uh…" I trailed off.

"Kiss me?" he asked, mimicking my motion and settling back into his corner.

My face felt as if it were on fire, so I knew it was likely bright red. "Um, yes."

He lifted his arms so that one rested on the back of the sofa and the other stretched across the arm. "Why?"

"Well, to start, you're basically my boss now."

Mal shook his head. "Not really."

I frowned at him. "You pay my salary and delegate my assignments. That sounds like the sorts of things an employer does."

"You're not my employee, Zoe," he argued. "You're more like a…partner. Just like Stony and Blaine are my partners."

"But you don't pay Stony and Blaine," I elaborated. "You pay me."

Mal sighed. "They won't *let* me pay them because they say it doesn't feel like work and they live off their trust funds. At least for now. If we get picked up by a network, then they'll take a salary. Right now, they want me to put all the profits back into the business."

"It still wouldn't be right, Mal. We have to work together."

"Only until the end of the month," he pointed out. "This is just temporary."

At his words, my stomach clenched. I only had a short time left to work with these people who understood me and accepted me. Then it would all be over.

"Unless you've changed your mind about making it more permanent," he said.

Was that what I wanted? The last few days had gone by so quickly that I couldn't be sure.

"I need a little more time before I decide," I hedged.

Mal smiled at me. "About the job or about me?" he asked.

I stared at him, weighing my thoughts carefully. "Both," I answered.

"All right. You have a couple of weeks to decide," Mal stated. "Now, we need to get back to work."

He shifted gears so quickly and easily that I felt almost miffed. My body was still buzzing with attraction, yet he calmly picked up his laptop and went back to searching the internet for more information on Hank Murphy.

It reaffirmed my belief that it was best if we didn't get involved. I gathered that Mal, Stony, and Blaine traveled a great deal. Mal probably had a girl in every port. Well, in every town.

I got up to get a drink from the kitchen and felt Teri follow me.

"I screwed up, didn't I?" she asked. "I didn't think you were actually going to kiss him."

I stuck my head in the fridge and pulled out a soda. "It's cool, Teri. You didn't screw up anything."

"But he was going to lay a lip lock on you and I interrupted."

"It was a bad idea to begin with," I insisted, taking a sip of my drink.

"If you say so," she quipped. "If it were me, I'd still be on that couch trying to get my hands on every inch of that hunk of sexy man."

I sighed and grabbed another soda from the fridge. "Well, you're not me, Teri. I have to be smart. The only person who's going to take care of me is *me*. I can't go around playing tonsil hockey with every cute guy I meet."

"Fine, fine. I give up. You act like you're fifty years old. All you need are a dozen cats."

"Shut up," I grumbled.

Teri shook her head and faded through the wall.

With a heavy sigh, I grabbed both drinks and carried them back into the living room. If Mal could put aside the almost kiss so easily, so could I. At this point it was a matter of pride.

Besides, this wasn't about me or my hormones' insistence that they liked Mal. This was about poor Hank Murphy and his murder. He deserved justice and he'd asked me to get it for him.

CHAPTER

19

BY THE TIME Mal left for the evening, I'd spent hours online researching Hank Murphy. Unfortunately, there wasn't a lot to find because he'd died before the local newspaper started their webpage.

Mal and I decided to meet at the library the next morning and see what we could find in their archives. After that, we'd have to figure out a new game plan.

I'd just entered the kitchen, trying to decide what I wanted to eat for dinner when my cell phone rang.

It was Jonelle.

"Girl, I realize you have a glamorous new job in television, but I haven't heard from you in a week. That's not good friend behavior."

"I'm sorry," I apologized. "I've been distracted."

She laughed. "I'm not surprised. All that testosterone would distract me too. Speaking of testosterone, what's up with you and Mal going to lunch together today?"

"Nothing," I replied. "We were working and got hungry."

"Working on what?" Jonelle's voice took on a mischievous edge.

I sighed. "Not what you're thinking about. God, you and Teri are the most sex-obsessed people I've ever met."

"Please. You're just saying that because you've forgotten what sex is like. As soon as you break the seal, you'll be the same way."

Because I knew she was probably right, I changed the subject. "Something weird happened when we were coming back from The Baker Hotel last night."

I could almost hear Jonelle roll her eyes. "Oh really?"

"I saw a ghost on that deserted Farm to Market road you showed me as a short cut."

"What?"

"Yeah. I didn't see him on the way to Mineral Wells, but on the way back, he was there. Have you heard any rumors about a ghost on that road?" I asked. Jonelle was quiet for a long moment and suspicion tugged at my thoughts. "Jonelle? You knew he was there didn't you?"

"I wasn't sure because I never saw him, but I've been hearing things at the salon. Weird stuff happening, like cars dying or a patch of fog on an otherwise clear night. No one else has seen him, but they talk about how spooky it is."

"So it's not really a short cut? You set me up?"

"No, no. It is quicker to go that way, but I hoped that if the rumors were true, you'd see the ghost or whatever it was. I don't know…" she trailed off. "I guess I thought it would be nice if you could help someone who needed it."

I bit my bottom lip. "Well, that's what Mal and I were working on today. I saw him last night and we stopped to talk to him."

"So what's the story?" she asked.

"Apparently, he was run off the road in 1996 and survived the accident. Someone killed him afterwards, but did a good enough job that the police must have thought the injuries were from the wreck."

"Holy shit. That sucks. Does he have any idea who did it?"

"No. He knows it was a man, but that's about it."

"Wow, this is so cool! Talk about a cold, cold case. You're like a cross between a ghost hunter and a private dick."

"Jesus, let's not use the term *private dick* ever again, okay?"

"What? I like it. Can I call you a dame?"

"No."

Jonelle laughed. "You're spoiling all my fun." She paused. "You know what? I want to help. I'm off work tomorrow. I'll swing by in the morning with coffee and donuts and we can brainstorm."

As much fun as that sounded, this was my job at the moment and I wasn't sure that Mal would appreciate it.

"Uh, well, I have to run it by Mal first," I hedged.

"That's cool. Text me later and let me know what he says."

"Jonelle, I'm not sure he'll like—"

"Please just ask him, Zoe. Please. I want to help."

"All right. I'll ask, but don't be mad if he says no," I stated.

"I won't. I promise."

We said good-bye and hung up, but not before Jonelle asked me to talk to Mal once again.

I stared at my phone. Deciding to bite the bullet and get it over with, I texted Mal.

My friend Jonelle heard stories about Hank Murphy's ghost. She wants to tag along tomorrow. Is that okay?

While I waited to hear back from him, I felt Teri enter the living room. She perched on the couch next to me.

"So you're gonna help some guy you don't even know figure out who killed him?" she asked.

"I guess so."

Her face fell. "But you won't help me find my killer," she murmured.

I hadn't even thought about that. Abruptly, I felt like an asshole.

"You never told me you wanted me to find him." It was a shitty excuse and we both knew it. I sighed. "I'm sorry, Teri. If that's what you want, then I'll start as soon as I'm done working with Mal and the guys."

"Really?" she asked, her expression clearing.

"Yes."

She studied me. "So you're definitely quitting after the end of the month?"

I shrugged. "I don't know."

Teri just nodded and faded away without another word.

I frowned at the television after she left, unable to focus on the show onscreen. I still wasn't sure what I wanted to do.

Well, that wasn't true. I did know what I wanted. I just didn't know if it would be good for me. I wanted to keep working with Mal and the guys. I'd only recorded two episodes with them, not counting the episode they did at my house, but I loved it. It was fun and it felt…right. For once, I felt like I fit in, like I wasn't being watched with sidelong glances and judgment from my coworkers.

But there would be plenty of weird glances and judgment from other people if I continued to work with them. Could I handle that?

Honestly, I wasn't sure if I could.

Even if I decided it was worth the risk, I was sure that my mother would have a problem with it. She would make my life very difficult.

When I'd called to cancel Thursday night dinner last week, she'd seemed pleased when I told her it was for a temporary job that had the possibility of becoming permanent. I'd managed to get off the phone before she could push for details about what type of work I was doing.

I knew she would disapprove, but I wasn't sure if that was enough to dissuade me. For the first time in my life, I was doing something that I loved and getting paid for it. I was also good at it, if Mal's encouragement was anything to go by.

Our relationship wasn't the best. Was I willing to make it even more contentious because of my career choices?

And why was I worrying so much about what my mother thought? I was twenty-seven years old. It wasn't as if this job would affect my mother in a negative way. It was just a job. Why was I obsessing about her reaction?

The answer was simple. Though I knew I would always disappoint her, I couldn't help but try to win her approval. Even if it was never going to happen, I constantly felt the urge to try.

Maybe it was time to give up on that dream and start looking for one that made me happy.

My phone dinged and I picked it up to find a reply from Mal.

Yes. I'd like to knw what rumors she's hrd. Plus xtra eyes make rsrch fstr.

It took me a minute to make out all the words since Mal seemed to have an aversion for vowels in his text messages.

Great. What time should she be here?

He replied, *8 a.m. Lbry opens at 9. Brkfst b4.*

I laughed. Jonelle wasn't a morning person. She wasn't going to appreciate the hour, which she considered to be the crack of dawn.

See you then. Jonelle's bringing coffee and donuts.

SWEET. Gdnite.

I shook my head at his atrocious texting grammar. *Good night.*

I decided to head to bed. It seemed I had an early morning in store for me the next day.

CHAPTER

20

I AWOKE TO the scent of coffee. Nose twitching, I yanked the pillow off my head, wondering where it came from.

"I thought that would wake you up," Jonelle teased, waving her hand over the top of the coffee mug.

My mouth watered at the scent of the rich brew. She had gone to the next town over to Jericho Donuts. They had the best coffee and baked goods in the county.

"Gimme!" I demanded, reaching out for the cup. Then I realized that Jonelle shouldn't be here until eight. "Oh my God, did I oversleep?"

She shook her head. "Nope. I woke up at five-thirty and couldn't go back to sleep, so I decided to get the good shit. It's seven now."

"You're an angel. No, a goddess," I breathed as I sipped the delicious coffee. She'd even added the perfect amount of sugar and half and half. "Thank you."

Jonelle grinned. "I know. Now, get your ass up and showered then you can have the raspberry jelly donut I brought you."

My eyes widened. "Yes, ma'am."

Laughing, she got off the bed and left the room. I jumped up and was showered, dressed, and wearing light make-up within a half hour.

I bounded down the stairs, empty coffee cup in hand, and walked into the kitchen.

Like the good friend she was, Jonelle had the jelly donut on a plate and waiting for me. I sighed happily when I noticed that she'd purchased a huge container of coffee.

"Now I remember why you're my best friend," I joked, pouring myself another cup of coffee.

"Because you pay me?" she replied, her face innocent.

"No, because you bring me food. Otherwise, I wouldn't tolerate you."

"Ungrateful cow," she muttered.

I grinned at her as I sat down at the kitchen table and took a huge bite of the baked goody. When I finished it, I opened the box and fished out a blueberry cake donut.

"Wow, you got all my faves," I commented.

"I figured it was a good way to thank you for letting me come along."

I shrugged. "I love having you. It's just that this is my job and Mal is my boss. It felt weird to ask if my bestie could hang with us while we did work stuff. You know?"

She nodded. "Well, thank you."

"Don't thank me yet. You'll be cursing my name when you have a crick in your neck and blurry vision from staring at newspapers for hours on end."

"I still think it sounds fun."

I stopped myself from grabbing another donut after I finished the blueberry. I'd seen how much Mal could put away and I figured he'd polish off what was left.

When the doorbell rang, I let Mal in and led him back to the kitchen. He looked a bit dazed when his eyes landed on Jonelle, which didn't surprise me. Though she wasn't very tall, she was built like a pin-up and wore her long blonde hair in shimmering waves down her back. A lot of men were struck dumb the first time they saw her.

To my surprise, he shook off the Jonelle-induced trance rather quickly and settled down at the kitchen table to eat. As I suspected, he ate almost all of the remaining baked goodies.

While we finished off our coffee, Mal and I explained to Jonelle what we were looking for at the library today.

After he finished elaborating, she clarified, "So we're looking for articles on the accident, his obituary, things like that?"

He nodded. "All he told us was that he died in 1996. He was wearing short sleeves, but in Texas it could any time of year."

We piled into Mal's van and headed to the library. I was surprised at how easily the conversation flowed.

Verna, the librarian, greeted us when we arrived. She didn't seem curious about our request for newspapers in the least. She merely led us downstairs to the basement and unlocked the archive room. Her lack of interest was probably due to the fact that I came to the library often and asked for all sorts of books and periodicals. I doubted any of my requests surprised her anymore.

"Let me know when you leave so I can come back down here and lock it up, dear."

I thanked her and followed Jonelle and Mal into the little room. It was musty and the florescent light blinked several times before it finally clicked and began to brighten.

A long, narrow table sat in the middle of the room with shelves crowded around it. There was just enough space to walk around the table if no one was sitting there.

I found hooks on the wall next to the door and hung up my purse after I removed my notebook, pen, and cell phone.

We split up, walking through the cramped aisles, looking for the newspapers from 1996. The first row I examined held papers from the twenties and thirties, around the time that The Kenna

Journal was established.

"Found them." The low ceiling in the room dulled the sound of Jonelle's voice.

I made my way back to the center of the room and turned at the end of the shelves. That's when I found myself face-to-face with the spirit of Janice Marie Saint, the first librarian here in Kenna.

"Holy shit!" I cried, stumbling back.

Janice frowned at me and lifted a finger to her lips. "Language, girl. I catch you talking like that at the library again and I'll wash your mouth out with soap."

I sighed, putting a hand over my heart. "Sorry, Ms. Saint. I didn't realize you were down here."

"It's *Miss* Saint, girl. You know I never married."

Janice Marie's spirit had been wandering around the library for a long time, ever since I was a child. I always made an effort to say hello to her. When I'd gotten old enough, I'd encouraged her to move on, but she stubbornly refused. She claimed the library needed her.

Mal appeared on the other side of Janice Marie and I could see his worried expression through her opaque body.

"Are you okay, Zoe?" he asked breathlessly.

I nodded. "I'm fine. Sorry I scared you. I wasn't expecting to see Miss Saint here."

He glanced around. "Someone else is here?"

"Miss Saint used to be the librarian in the 1940's," I explained.

I could see when he comprehended my meaning completely. "Oh, I see."

I nodded. "I'll be right there."

He turned and left me.

"What are you doing down here?" Janice Marie demanded. "You better not be planning on any hankypanky with that young man. This isn't the time or place, young lady," she admonished, shaking a finger at me.

"We're not, Miss Saint," I promised. "We're here to work and look at old newspapers, nothing else."

She stared at me, her gaze fierce and piercing, as sharp as it must have been when she was alive. I wondered what happened to her that caused her soul to remain here, completely intact. That was a characteristic of violent and untimely death. I'd never asked, but now I suddenly wanted to.

"All right then," she stated. "Don't forget to let me know when you leave so I can lock up."

I shook my head as she disappeared through the wall next to me. It seemed librarians may change from time to time, but certain characteristics were ingrained in all of them.

When I returned to the table, Jonelle looked up at me. "Miss Saint?" she asked.

I nodded and picked up one of the large leather bound books that contained some of the 1996 newspapers.

"She still as peachy as ever?"

I grinned at her. "More like vinegar and salt."

Jonelle returned my smile and went back to her own book. Mal didn't look up, his eyes moving rapidly across the page he was reading.

I took his lead and settled in to read the newsprint in front of me. The editions in this binding were from June and July of 1996. I took my time and combed through each page carefully, looking for anything related to Hank Murphy, even if it wasn't about his death.

We read in silence for a couple of hours until I finally had to stand up and stretch. I walked through the maze of shelves, hoping that the movement would get the blood flowing in my legs again.

I did a few squats and felt my muscles loosen with each motion. When I returned to the table, I found that Jonelle and Mal had gotten up as well.

After another hour, I found what I was looking for. It was an accident report in July of 1996.

It was only a few sentences, but it was enough to make me think of Hank, even though he wasn't named.

Single vehicle accident on Farm to Market 457 the night of July 20th. One fatality.

I read through the paper for the following two days before I found his obituary. Henry James Murphy. Age 25. Survived by his wife Patricia Louise Murphy, nee Sneed. There was information about his achievements and his work, but the obituary was small and simple.

Reading the paragraph, I got the sense that Hank loved his simple life and his wife. He didn't want anything other than this small town, his job at the factory in Weatherford, and a home with a loving family.

Sadness swamped me. His life had been cut short and he had no idea why. There was no mention of children or other family members, so I wondered if there had been any relatives other than his wife to miss him.

"I found it," I stated, gaining Jonelle and Mal's attention. "I found the accident and his obituary."

I slid the book to the center of the table so they could take a look.

"That's it?" Jonelle asked. "That's all they wrote about it?" She sounded disgusted.

I understood how she felt, but replied, "They didn't know it wasn't an accident. I'll keep reading. Maybe there's an article somewhere after his death."

Mal's pen scratched across a page in his notebook quickly as he jotted down information.

"Keep looking," he muttered. "We need to be sure there's nothing else before we move on."

Jonelle helped me page through the rest of the newspapers from that month. The only other information about Hank's death was a short article about a fundraiser to help his wife, Trisha. It was dated a few weeks after the accident.

It was after noon by the time we righted the archive room and went back upstairs. I hadn't realized how dark it was in the basement until we stepped into the sunny lobby of the library.

"Damn," I mumbled, squinting against the brightness.

"I feel like I just stepped out of Hades," Mal commented.

Jonelle and I giggled, earning a scowl from Verna.

I approached the front desk. "We're done in the archive room. Thank you, Verna."

She didn't seem to care, but her sense of decorum required that she reply, "You're welcome."

As we walked into the parking lot, Jonelle groaned, putting a hand to her forehead. "God, I'm seeing double. That newsprint was tiny." I gave her a stern sideways glance, which made her laugh. "Okay, okay, so you warned me, but I still had fun."

"I hate to admit it, but I did too."

"Why do you hate to admit it?" Mal asked as we climbed into the van.

"Because what kind of person likes going to the library and spending three hours in the creepy basement, looking for information on a dead man?"

His eyes met mine in the rearview mirror. "My favorite kind."

Since I had no idea how to reply to that, I zipped my lips and buckled my seat belt.

"I need a drink," Jonelle sighed from the front seat. "Let's go over to Weatherford and eat at that burger joint that serves booze."

"Sounds good to me," Mal stated. "Tell me how to get there."

21

OVER LUNCH WE decided our next course of action would be to contact Hank's only living relative, his wife Trisha, and see if she knew of anyone who wanted to hurt her late husband. However, we weren't sure if she was still in the area.

The afternoon was spent at my house, where we fired up our laptops and continued our research.

Somehow, Mal managed to find Trisha's information via Facebook. She was no longer Trisha Murphy, but Trisha Dwyer, which made sense because she was only twenty-three when Hank died. Her phone number and address were in the phonebook.

"Shouldn't we, I don't know, call first?" Jonelle asked.

I looked to Mal and lifted an eyebrow. He hadn't called me before he showed up on my front porch several weeks ago.

Mal shook his head. "Probably not."

I considered our options for a moment. "Maybe you should just introduce yourself as a television producer," I suggested. "Don't mention the name of the show."

"Maybe," he responded, but he sounded distracted. "You could say that you're researching a book."

I leveled a glance at him. "She's probably heard rumors about me, Mal. She'll know I'm not a writer as soon as I introduce myself."

"Fine. Maybe I'm researching a book," he quipped.

"That might work better," Jonelle stated. "Plus, you're a handsome man. Dress in some slacks and a nice shirt and I bet you'll have her eating out of your hand."

Mal frowned slightly. "What?"

Jonelle shook her head. "Never mind."

Mal and I began to compose a list of questions for our "interview" with Trisha should she agree to speak with us. After about a half hour, Jonelle started yawning.

"Okay, that's it. I'm done for the day. I'll call you tomorrow night to see how it went," she said as she leaned down to hug me.

By the time Mal and I finished plotting how to approach Trisha it was dark outside and my entire body was stiff.

"I think that's everything," Mal stated, gathering up his laptop, notebook, and pens.

I rubbed at the crick in the back of my neck. "Thank God, I'm exhausted. Hey, where were Stony and Blaine today?"

"They're editing the latest episodes of the show."

It surprised me that Mal let them handle it alone. After being in such close proximity for the last few days, I was beginning to realize that Mal was a bit of a control freak. *The Wraith Files* show was his baby and he struck me as the type that would take excellent care of anything he loved that much.

"You look surprised," he commented.

"I guess I am," I admitted. "I just got the impression that you would be in charge of something like that."

He shook his head. "No way. Stony was a film major in college and Blaine was an art history major. They're better qualified to handle that side of the process. If I tried to butt in, it wouldn't look as great."

And now I had something else to admire about Mal. Not only was he handsome and intelligent, he understood his strengths and weaknesses and he didn't have any hang ups about them.

I lamented the fact that my conscience refused to ignore the reality that he signed my paychecks. I liked him, more and more each day, but I would not be financially dependent on a man I was dating or sleeping with. I needed the security of my independence, in knowing that I could take care of myself if things didn't work out. Despite the things Jonelle and Teri said, regardless of their belief that I was too rigid and uptight, it was a principle I wouldn't compromise.

And for those reasons, it was highly probable I would never have anything more than a professional relationship with Mal because I was beginning to seriously consider extending my contract with the show.

I watched as he finished packing up his things.

"I'll be here to pick you up at four tomorrow. Maybe we'll have better luck catching Trisha at home closer to the end of the workday."

I nodded and walked him out.

"Thanks for your help today," Mal said as he walked out my front door. "This has been an exciting development."

"Hey, it's my job now," I replied. "It's also the first time I've considered helping a ghost figure out who murdered them. It's exciting for me too."

Before I closed the door, he leaned a shoulder against the jamb. "So have you given any more thought to that kissing thing?"

His sudden shift of subject threw me off balance and I ended up blurting out, "Yes."

"And?"

I shook my head. "Still not a good idea."

"Damn. Well, let me know if you change your mind." He grinned. "It might be fun."

I bit back a smile because I didn't want to encourage him.

"Maybe. Or it might be a train wreck in the making," I replied.

Mal shrugged. "That could be fun too."

This time I couldn't stop the smile that curved my mouth. "I don't even want to know in what context you would find a train wreck entertaining."

"Hey, it would definitely be interesting. See you tomorrow, Zoe."

"Night, Mal."

I shut the door behind him, locked it, and leaned my forehead against it. Somehow his subtle flirtation was a great deal more effective than the blunt overtures that Stony and Blaine used.

Or maybe it had more to do with the person doing the flirting.

Either way, I needed to make a decision and soon.

THE NEXT AFTERNOON I stepped out on my porch and locked the door as soon as Mal pulled up in front of my house.

I didn't want to admit it, but I was nervous. I'd never done anything like this before. I hated confrontation of any kind. I would face it if I needed to, but I preferred to avoid it. Probably from years of being on the receiving end of my mother's sharp tongue.

Our spontaneous arrival at Trisha Dwyer's house could very well end badly.

I tried to keep up with Mal's small talk as he drove, but it was a struggle. My focus was on what would happen when Trisha opened the door. If she opened the door.

"You okay?" Mal asked.

"Yeah."

A few minutes later, he asked again, "Are you sure you're okay?"

I glanced at him. "Yeah, I'm sure. Why?"

He shrugged. "No reason except that your left leg is bouncing and the rest of your body is so tense it might as well be stone."

Why did he have to be so observant?

"Okay, so maybe I'm a little nervous," I admitted.

"A little? You're wound up so tight that you'll shoot to outer space if you fart."

I choked as I gasped and laughed simultaneously. Without thinking, I smacked his arm. "Oh my God, don't say stuff like that to me!"

Mal guffawed. "The look on your face was priceless!"

I laughed until tears ran down my cheeks. When I finally stopped, my nerves had calmed as well. I wiped my eyes with a tissue I dug out of my purse.

Mal gave me a few moments before he asked, "So why are you so nervous?"

"I hate confrontation," I answered with a shrug. "Something about women screaming at me sets my teeth on edge."

"Same here," he muttered. "If it helps, I do cold visits like this all the time about haunted spaces and most people can be stand-offish, but I've encountered very little yelling."

"Good to know."

Mal smiled. "I promise, if she starts screaming or being nasty, we'll leave. We can find out what we need to know another way."

"Thanks."

We drove the rest of the way to Trisha's house discussing what we would say and do. Mal suggested that he introduce me as his assistant, which would allow him to do most of the talking. It also decreased the likelihood that I would be on the receiving end of Trisha's wrath should the interview go sideways. Mal didn't mention it, but I understood that was his intention.

I probably should have insisted that it wasn't necessary, but I appreciated his consideration.

He turned into a driveway and I felt my heart rate kick up.

"You ready?" he asked.

"Yeah."

We got out of the car together and were met on the porch by a woman who appeared to be in her mid to late-forties. Her light brown hair was lightly streaked with grey and lines were beginning to deepen around her eyes and mouth.

Her harsh features were those of someone who'd led an unhappy life. I could also see the echoes of the loveliness she once had, but time and bitterness had erased it.

She had a cigarette in her left hand and lifted it to her mouth as she moved to the top step. "Can I help you?" While her words implied hospitality, her tone and body language clearly stated that we weren't welcome here.

Mal stopped at the base the stairs. He smiled up at her from the bottom step, but didn't move any closer. "Hello, my name is Malachi Flemming. I'm a producer for a reality television show and I'm looking for Patricia Murphy Dwyer."

Her expression remained suspicious, but she also seemed interested. "I'm Patricia Dwyer. Why do you want to speak to me?"

"Well, we're in the area filming with local residents for a documentary about small towns and someone mentioned that your first husband had died around twenty years ago. We were hoping that it would be possible to include an interview with you and maybe some of your late husband's friends."

His words surprised me. I thought he was going to introduce himself as a writer. Either way, it was too late to do anything about it now.

Her eyes narrowed. "Why would you want to include something like that in a documentary on small towns?"

"We're trying to include a broad spectrum of stories, from the incredible success to unbearable loss. We want to demonstrate that small towns and big cities have all of those things in common."

She studied Mal carefully as she sucked on her cigarette. "Fine," she answered, exhaling a stream of smoke. "Come on in."

We climbed the steps and followed her inside. The house was meticulously tidy, no dust on the furniture, knickknacks perfectly arranged. Still, the house reeked of smoke and ashtrays were scattered on all of the tables.

"Have a seat," Trisha invited. "My husband, Steve, won't be home for an hour or so."

"By the way," Mal said as he sat on the sofa, "This is my assistant, Zoe. Do you mind if she records our interview?"

Trisha's eyes flicked to me. "I guess."

I took out one of the digital recorders that Mal kept to document electronic voice phenomena and turned it on. I stated the date, time, and that we were interviewing Mrs. Trisha Murphy Dwyer before I placed the recorder on the coffee table.

For fifteen minutes, Mal asked her general questions about how she met Hank and how old they were when they married. Somehow he coaxed her out of her surly mood. He even had her smiling and laughing.

Mal asked her about their friends and relatives. I was amazed at how skillfully he broached the subject of anyone who might not have had the best relationship with Hank. He said he would like to avoid anyone who might not represent Hank in a way she would approve.

That's where we hit a wall. Trisha insisted that everyone loved her husband and that he hadn't made a single enemy in his short life.

It wasn't long after that she glanced at the clock on the wall and stood. "Well, I've truly enjoyed speaking to you about my first husband. It's been a long time since I've been able to talk about him at length with anyone. But my current husband will be home soon and I need to get dinner started."

I gathered the digital recorder and my notebook and followed the two of them outside. Mal thanked her for her help and shook her hand. Trisha didn't even spare me a glance.

Once we were in the car and on our way back to my house, Mal glanced at me. "See that wasn't as bad as you thought it would be, right?"

I shook my head in amazement. "You are too much."

"I'm going to take that as a compliment," he answered.

"It kind of is," I quipped. "But I'm also wondering now if you are leading a double life as a con artist."

Mal laughed. "No, I've just learned to read people quickly over the years."

"Uh, that's pretty much the same thing a con artist does, Mal," I quipped.

"I guess you're right." He chuckled quietly. "Well, I'm hungry now. Wanna grab some dinner?"

I glanced at my watch and saw that it was almost five-thirty. "I'd love to, but I already have plans tonight."

"Hot date?" he asked lightly.

I huffed out a short bark of laughter. "Not exactly."

The only thing hot at my parents' house for Thursday night dinner was the food and occasionally my mother's temper.

"Well, then I guess I'll drive you home."

CHAPTER

22

"HOW'S YOUR NEW job going?" my mother asked casually as she flipped the fried chicken.

"Fine," I answered. "I've got until the end of the month before my temporary status is up, but they're interested in hiring me full time."

My mother's reaction was not at all what I expected. She dropped the tongs on the counter with a clatter. "What?"

I looked up from the potatoes I was mashing with butter. "I said that my temp status is up at the end of this month and they want to hire me on for full time work."

She scowled at me fiercely. "Full time?"

"Yeah."

My mother shook her head. "I can't believe this. I thought you'd given up all this nonsense years ago."

I felt a sinking sensation in the pit of my gut. "What nonsense, Mom?"

"This ghost crap!" she snapped. "I thought you'd finally outgrown it, but now you're looking to make a career out of it!"

I gaped at her. "How did you know what I was doing?"

"Oh, don't insult my intelligence! Kenna is a small town. People talk. Now that you taken up with those...those...*wraith* guys," she sneered, "It's all anyone wants to talk about when they see me.

It's embarrassing and it has to stop."

As I watched my mother rant, I realized that nothing I did or said would ever satisfy her. I'd always held out hope that eventually she would see the efforts I made and finally appreciate them.

But that was never going to happen.

Because my mother explained exactly what the problem was when it came to our relationship; I embarrassed her. The epiphany stung. No, it hurt like a mule kick to the chest. My own mother felt humiliated by me, by the choices I made. By the job I held. Everything about me was a reason for ridicule in her eyes.

"Well, I'm sorry that I embarrass you, Mother," I stated levelly. "That was never my intention. Even as a child when I tried to tell you about the people only I could see and hear. Even when you screamed at me in the street, telling me to stop lying. Even when I cried because you punished me for refusing to keep quiet."

Her face paled at my words.

I suddenly noticed my tight grip on the potato masher and pried my fingers loose. After I wiped my hands on a dishtowel, I walked over to the hook where I hung my purse when I came to visit.

"But what I won't apologize for is wanting to work with people who don't make me feel like a freak because of what I see. People who appreciate my abilities and what I can offer."

My mother scoffed. "You mean those weirdos with the Internet show? I'm sure they're mothers are very proud."

I stared at her for a long moment, still feeling the reverberations of the pain that sliced through me at her scorn. "Maybe. Maybe not. But I've finally realized that *nothing* I do will make you proud, Mother. It wouldn't matter if I were a doctor or a great teacher or if I won the Nobel Peace Prize. You would always find fault with me." I fished my keys out of my purse. "But none of that matters any longer. I'm twenty-seven years old and it's time that I stopped worrying about how you'll feel about my decisions. I need to make choices that make *me* happy."

I opened the back door and glanced over my shoulder one last time. "When you're ready to make peace with that, I'll listen."

My mother didn't say a word as I walked out the back door, letting the screen slam shut behind me. She didn't call out as I marched to my car and climbed inside.

She didn't even watch me back out of the driveway from the kitchen window.

It wasn't until I parked in my own garage that the tears came.

I climbed stiffly from my car and walked into the house in a daze. Immediately, Teri materialized in the kitchen.

"Zoe, what's wrong?"

I waved a hand at her. "Just give me a sec," I mumbled.

I dropped my purse on the kitchen table and trudged into the living room to collapse on the couch. I hated that my mother and I couldn't seem to get along. After twenty-seven years, I should be used to her harsh words and short temper, but I wasn't. It still hurt.

I'm sure a psychologist would have a damn good time explaining how my intense dislike of confrontation stemmed from my antagonistic relationship with my mom. Even though I understood it, it didn't solve the problem.

"Zoe?" It was the first time in the two years I'd been living in this house that Teri's voice sounded hesitant. "I don't think I've ever seen you cry." I felt the cold touch of her hand on my shoulder. "What's wrong?"

I inhaled deeply, drying the last of the tears as they fell from my eyes. "Oh nothing unusual. Just a fight with my mother."

She frowned. "I've never seen you so upset over a disagreement with your mom."

"Well, let's just say I won't be welcome at Thursday dinner

anytime soon," I whispered.

Teri was silent for a moment. "I'm sorry, Zoe."

"It's okay," I answered, my breath hitching. "It was a long time coming."

Once I'd calmed down, I went into the half bath under the stairs and washed my face with cool water. Teri was hovering by the door when I came out.

"Maybe you should call Jonelle," she suggested. "She'll know how to make you feel better."

"I just need some time to myself, Teri. I'm not ready to talk about it yet."

She nodded and her image shimmered.

"Teri," I called.

She stopped and looked at me.

"I mean it. Don't text Jonelle and tell her to come over, okay? I want to be alone tonight."

Teri sighed audibly. "Fine, I won't."

After she vanished, I moved to the couch, stretched out, and grabbed the remote. I just needed to switch off my mind for a while.

The doorbell rang about an hour later and I immediately assumed that Teri had gone against my instructions and texted Jonelle.

"Dammit, Teri," I muttered, rolling to my feet.

But when I looked out the window, I saw my father standing on the front porch, his hands in his pockets.

"Dad?" I asked as I opened the door.

"Hey, sweetie. Can I come in?"

"Of course."

I turned off the TV and we sat on the couch, facing each other in an uncomfortable silence.

My dad sat on the edge of the cushion, his elbows resting on his knees. "I, uh, I'm not sure what to say, Zoe."

"I'm guessing Mom told you what happened?"

"Her side of it, yes," he paused and looked at me, his expression apologetic. "But I'd like to hear what you have to say too. I know your mom can be…difficult."

"Well, you know I'm working temporarily for a show on YouTube, right?"

Dad nodded. "Yeah, your mom mentioned it. Some ghost hunting show?"

"Yeah. They investigate reports of hauntings and paranormal events." I laughed a little. "At first I thought it would be silly, but it's actually kind of fun. And Mal, my boss, he pays me well."

My dad rubbed his hands together. "What do you do on the show?" he asked.

"I speak to the spirits that we encounter," I admitted quietly. "Like a medium."

Dad sighed. "Your mom said as much." He rubbed a hand over his forehead. "Zoe, honey, are you absolutely sure that this is something you want to do?"

My heart sank at his words. Dad always seemed to believe in my abilities. He never questioned me or chastised me the way my mother had.

He reached out and covered my hand with his own. "Please don't look at me like that. I'm not angry or telling you that you shouldn't. I just want to be sure that you've thought this through. You haven't talked about your…" he hesitated, searching for the right word, "Gifts for years. I thought maybe you'd stopped seeing things. To hear that you were working with this group, well, it was a surprise."

"It just seemed easier not to talk about it," I stated. "Especially since it seemed to upset Mom."

My father nodded. "I understand." He looked down at his

work-roughened hands. "Do you know why it upsets your mother, Zoe? Your gift?"

I always wondered why my father referred to my abilities as a gift, especially since my mother seemed to disagree so vehemently. I shook my head in response.

"When your mother was young, she was a lot like you," he stated.

"What do you mean?"

He sighed. "Well, she saw the things that you see."

I gaped at him. "What?"

"Your mother, she used to see spirits. For as long as she could remember."

"Used to?" I asked.

"She can't any longer," he answered.

I shook my head in disbelief. "I don't understand."

"You were too young to remember Glynnis when she passed away, but your mother's mother—" Dad rubbed his hands over his face. "She wasn't a very nice person, Zoe. When Sarah tried to tell her what she saw, Glynnis swore she was possessed by Satan himself. The things she did to your mother, they," he cleared his throat, "They were horrible."

My entire body felt cold at his words. "What happened, I mean, why did she stop seeing?"

"She didn't want to see them anymore. She wished that the gift would disappear and it finally did. To your mother, it was a relief because she thought it meant your grandmother would stop hurting her."

I winced at his words. "If Glynnis hurt her because of what she saw, why is she so angry with me?"

My father reached out and placed his hand over mine. "Because it scares her, Zoe. She doesn't understand why she could see and hear the things she did or why you do either. Growing up, all she heard was that her abilities were from Satan and that she was going to Hell. Can you blame her for being terrified?"

I couldn't.

"Dad, I can't just sit back and let her talk to me like that anymore," I explained.

He nodded. "I know, sweetie. Honestly, I'm surprised it took you this long to put your foot down. I just didn't expect it to be about this. Like I said, you haven't talked about the spirits you see in years. I thought that perhaps you'd stopped seeing them as your mother had."

"If you're not upset with me, why did you come?" I asked.

My dad's face fell. There was no other way to describe it. "Because, baby, your mother was in tears when I got home, so I knew it had to have been a horrible fight. I wanted to check on my girl."

My eyes filled with tears. "I'll be okay." I sniffed. "I'm just glad that you're not mad at me."

Dad reached out and pulled me into a hug. "I love you, Zoe. You're my favorite daughter."

I had to laugh, even as tears trickled down my cheeks. "I'm your only daughter," I replied.

"Yeah, but you're still my favorite."

"I love you too, Daddy."

Dad released me. "Now, I'm not making excuses for your mother. I've talked to her several times over the years about how she's going to drive you away if she doesn't ease up. I only wanted you to understand why she gets so upset."

I nodded. "I do."

"Well, go get your old man a beer and we'll sit and talk for a bit before I go home. I want to know all about this new job."

CHAPTER

23

T HE NEXT DAY, the chiming of my cell phone woke me up from a dead sleep. My eyes felt puffy and my head ached as though I was hung over, even though I'd only drunk one beer.

I flailed as I fought my way out of the blankets and snatched up my phone.

"Hello?" My voice was hoarse and rough.

"Zoe?"

I shoved my hair out of my face. "Yeah, it's me."

Mal chuckled. "Sorry. I didn't recognize your voice for a second. Did I wake you?"

"No, I was just contemplating my plans to take over the world on the backs of my eyelids."

He laughed again. "I see you're just as witty first thing in the morning as you are any other time."

I sat up and leaned back against the headboard. "So what's up?"

"Oh, I just thought you might want to keep working on Hank Murphy's case today," he commented. "Stony and Blaine finished all our episodes up to date and want to help us with this."

My eyes widened at the thought of the two of them "helping".

"Okay, what exactly did you have in mind?" I asked.

"Well, if you didn't mind, I thought we could meet at your

house and see what we can learn from the list of friends that Trisha gave us yesterday. I figured that maybe one of Hank's friends might know something she didn't."

"What time?" I asked, squinting at the digital clock next to my bed.

"In an hour?"

That would give me just enough time to brew a pot of coffee and get ready. "Sounds good. Bring breakfast."

"Uh, what am I supposed to bring?" he asked.

"The cantina downtown serves breakfast. I want a Roberto's bowl."

"Hang on, hang on. I'm gonna write this down. You said Roberto's bowl, right?"

"Yeah. It's one of their best breakfast dishes."

"All right. Breakfast coming right up. We'll see you in an hour."

I hung up and rolled out of bed. I needed to shower and dress, but first, coffee.

Exactly an hour later, my doorbell rang. And rang. And rang.

I hurried through the living room and peeked out the window just as Stony rang the bell for the fifth time.

"What the hell, Stony?" I asked.

"Outta the way, woman. This shit is HOT!"

Stony pushed past me and ran for the kitchen. Mal and Blaine followed at a more sedate pace.

"Hey, Zoe," Blaine greeted me.

"Hey, guys," I responded. "What's up with Stony?"

"Oh, nothing. I just have first degree burns on my forearm," the man in question replied as he emerged from my kitchen, a bag of frozen peas held to his arm. "They didn't warn me that they heat those refried beans to the same temperature as molten lava."

He removed the peas and showed me the patch of bright red

skin on his inner arm. I grimaced in sympathy.

"Damn. Sorry, Stony. If it's any consolation, I appreciate the sacrifices you made to bring me breakfast. Very chivalrous of you."

His eyes narrowed. "Are you making fun of me?"

"No way," I answered, doing my best to look innocent.

"Well, if you feel that badly, there is one little thing you could do for me…" he trailed off suggestively.

"Okay, so I was making fun of you," I quipped.

"Dammit!"

I laughed at his disappointed expression. "Stony, if you really thought I'd say yes, I don't think you'd ever talk to me this way."

He blinked at me rapidly. "Why do you think that?"

"Because you talk to every other woman the same way, whether they're twenty-five or sixty-five," I answered.

"Well, shit, there goes all my fun," he grumbled.

I stifled a laugh. "How about you talk to me the way you do Blaine and Mal?"

"Blaine?" Stony asked incredulously.

"Good point. Talk to me the way you talk to Mal," I insisted.

"All right," he sighed. "You're the boss."

"Are we done setting Stony straight?" Blaine asked. "Because I'm starving and that food smells amazing."

We gathered around the kitchen table and Mal passed out food as I poured coffee and orange juice. The atmosphere was familial as we ate breakfast.

"Oh God," Stony moaned. "I'm moving here. This is the most delicious thing I've ever eaten."

I grinned as he rolled his eyes in mock ecstasy. The food was fantastic as usual.

Once the empty containers were cleared away, Mal asked Stony and Blaine to search for more information on Hank Murphy and his wife online. When we spoke to Trisha yesterday, she gave us a list of names and numbers of friends we could contact. Mal suggested we split it evenly and start calling people in hopes that someone could give us more insight on Hank's life.

By my third phone call, I was beginning to wonder if maybe Hank had been confused when he died. It was just as Trisha said; everyone who knew Hank loved him.

The final name on my half of the list was Sharon Kemper. When she answered, I went through my spiel about researching Hank Murphy for a documentary on small town life. Sharon seemed excited at the prospect of appearing in a film, even if it was an independently financed documentary. She was also a bit of a gossip.

I learned more about Hank and Trisha's sex life than I needed to and that they'd had a shotgun wedding because Trisha was pregnant.

"Bless her heart, she lost the baby a few weeks later. Almost died too, the poor thing," Sharon said solemnly. "She never could get pregnant again after that, no matter how much they tried."

I decided a change of subject was in order. "How was their marriage when Hank passed away?"

Sharon paused for so long I thought she'd hung up.

"Sharon?"

"I'm here." She took a deep breath. "Will this be off the record?" she asked.

My heart skipped a beat. She knew something, I could sense it. "Absolutely."

"Well, I'm pretty sure Hank didn't know, but Trisha was screwing around with his best friend. Had been for about six months before he died."

"Wow."

"Yeah, I couldn't believe it. Hank was one of the best men I've ever known, why Trisha would risk that for Steve, I'll never know."

"Steve?" I asked, thinking the name sounded familiar.

"Oh, Steve Dwyer. She's married to him now. Has been for nearly twenty years. They got hitched, let's see, eighteen months after Hank passed. Couldn't bring myself to go to the wedding, knowing that she'd been cheating on such a fine man and marrying the guy so soon after her husband's death."

I realized I had stopped taking notes as Sharon spoke and quickly began to scribble the information in my notebook.

"I had no idea," I murmured automatically when Sharon paused.

"Well, of course not, dear. It's not something that Trisha would want to advertise. No one blinked an eye when they hooked up after Hank's death though. People thought it made sense that it would happen since he claimed that Hank would want him to take care of her." Sharon made a sound of disgust. "Karma's a bitch though. I think they've been making each other miserable since a year or two after they got married anyway. Don't know why they never got divorced."

I had an idea. If they planned Hank Murphy's murder together, neither of them could walk away from the marriage without risking the other turning them in to the cops.

"Well, I really appreciate the information, Sharon."

"And this is just between us?" she asked.

"Of course."

After she disconnected, I slowly lowered my phone to the table and looked at Mal.

"What is it?" he asked.

"I think I know who might have wanted Hank Murphy dead and why."

24

M AL STARED AT me, shock plainly written on his face. "Trisha Murphy was having an affair with her husband's best friend, Steve Dwyer?"

I nodded. "At least according to Sharon. If we could find at least one other person to corroborate, that would help."

Mal looked at his list of names. "I have two more people on my half of the list. If neither of them know anything, maybe we can call the others again."

An hour later, Mal got off the phone with the last man on Trisha's list, Bill Collins.

"Collins knew that Dwyer and Trisha were having an affair. He found out the week before Hank died and intended to tell him, he just didn't have a chance."

Mal rubbed his hands over his face. "Now, we just have to figure out if Dwyer acted alone or if Hank's loving wife was in on the murder."

"How are we going to do that?" I asked.

"I'm not sure," he answered.

"I feel like we're stumbling around in the dark here, Mal. Neither of us are detectives. How are we supposed to prove that any of this happened? It's been twenty years and the crash was written off as a horrible accident, not a homicide. No law enforcement official in their right mind is going to listen to us."

"Are you saying we should give up?" he asked.

I wanted to say yes, to tell him that this was useless and we should stop wasting our time, but my promise to Hank stopped me. I had given my word that I would try to get him justice and right the wrongs done to him.

"No," I sighed. "I'm just lost as to what we should do next."

"Maybe we should see if we can get our hands on a copy of the accident report," Mal suggested.

"I tried, but the state archive doesn't hold reports after five years."

"What about the local sheriff's office?" he queried.

I shrugged. "I don't know, but I do think we'd have a hell of a time getting a copy. The sheriff hates me, remember?"

"Let me see what I can do," Mal stated, picking up his phone.

I lifted my hands in surrender. "That's fine. While you're making calls and likely getting shot down, I'm going to take a quick walk and stretch my legs. All this sitting is making my body stiff."

Blaine and Stony didn't look up from their screens as I rose from my seat. Both wore ear buds and their heads were bobbing in time with whatever music they were blasting.

I took a quick walk around the block, soaking in the warmth and sunshine of the late spring day. I realized I hadn't gotten any exercise for several weeks and I needed it. I wasn't used to inactivity and all the web searches, reading, and television meant my ass had been glued to the couch far too often.

My mood was much better as I bounded up the steps to my house. When I entered, I found Mal staring down at his phone where it sat on the table in front of him.

"How'd it go?" I asked.

"Well, I can get a copy of the accident report," he replied, his tone even. "But I have to wait until someone sifts through twenty years worth of files because all the paperwork between 1995 and 1997 was *misplaced*."

I bit my bottom lip to keep from laughing at the look of consternation on his face. "It is a small town, Mal. Things aren't always run as efficiently as they are in a larger city."

"I said I would be willing to come down and go through them myself, but I'm not allowed."

"So all we can do is wait, right?"

Mal sighed and leaned forward, resting his forehead against his palms. "Yeah."

"Well, while we're waiting, why don't we focus on something else? Are there any more sites you want to film while you're here?"

"Several." Mal looked up at me. "But there's not much time left in your contract."

I took a deep breath. "If it's okay with you, I'd like to continue working on Hank's case until it has run its course."

"It could take weeks," he stated.

"I know."

"Are you saying you want to work with us permanently?" he questioned.

"Will you be angry with me if I say I'm still not sure?" I countered.

"No. Are you still unsure?"

"A little," I answered. "This is a completely new career path for me. I never thought about being on camera before now. It was never a consideration for me. It's—" I paused, searching for the right thing to say. "It's unnerving."

I hated to admit a weakness to Mal, but I wanted him to understand that I wasn't a flake.

"I understand, Zoe," he assured me. "Take your time. Help us for another few weeks."

"Thanks."

"What'd I miss?" Blaine asked, pulling an ear bud out of his ear.

I grinned at him. "Nothing. Just me telling Mal that y'all are stuck with me for a few more weeks."

"Awesome!"

Stony flinched and looked up from his computer. "Dude, why are you yelling?" He removed his own headphones.

"Zoe is staying with us for a few more weeks."

"Fan-fucking-tastic!" He turned to Mal. "So what's next, boss?"

SEVERAL HOURS LATER, I booted the men out of my house. They had taken over the kitchen, then the living room, and were quickly eating through all the food in my fridge and pantry.

If I decided to work with them on a permanent basis, I would have to set some boundaries.

However, once they left, the house felt too quiet. Teri was nowhere to be found and there was nothing that captured my attention.

My mind kept wandering back to what happened at my parents' house the night before. I felt much better after talking to my father, but it was difficult to break a lifetime habit of reaching out to my mother and apologizing for whatever I'd said to upset her. I caught myself staring at my phone, contemplating calling her.

But I couldn't do it. If I caved and gave in to my urge, none of the issues my mother had with me, or that I had with her, would be resolved.

Finally, I couldn't sit still any longer. I snatched up my cell phone and dialed.

"Jonelle? You busy tonight?"

CHAPTER

25

I WOKE UP the next morning with a vicious headache, the taste in my mouth made me wonder if I'd licked the floor at Birdie's, and my stomach lurched.

I was lying on my stomach, but I wasn't in my bed. Cautiously, I opened one eye and realized that I was stretched out, face down, on Jonelle's couch. The room was blissfully dim and there was a can of Sprite on the coffee table in front of me with two ibuprofen tablets sitting on top.

When I moved to sit up, I flinched as the ache in my head became unbearable for a split second. I held myself very still and waited for the flash of pain to pass. Lifting my right hand slowly, I picked up the can and dumped the pills into my left palm. Now that I was upright, the sickening sensation was no longer relegated to my stomach. I had a bad feeling that if I moved to fast, the twisting and turning in my gut would get nasty very quickly.

I hissed when I cracked the top on the can. The sound seemed to echo in the living room. With great care, I dropped one tablet into my mouth and washed it down with the fizzy soda. I waited for several minutes, wanting to be sure that my stomach wouldn't reject either before I took the next.

Once the pills were down, I hauled myself to my feet and made my way down the hall to the bathroom. The shades were drawn in there as well, a fact for which I was extremely grateful.

I avoided looking at myself in the mirror, knowing that I wouldn't want to see my own reflection if I looked half as rough as I felt.

I washed my face with cool water and rinsed my mouth out with the mouthwash that Jonelle kept by the sink. I also borrowed a comb. She kept a vat of Barbicide in her bathroom anyway, so I knew she wouldn't mind.

Still moving stiffly, I made my way back into the living room and heard the sounds of Jonelle moving around in the kitchen. When I came around the corner, she glanced up and chuckled.

"Damn, girl. I don't think I've seen you look this bad on a morning after since you graduated from college."

"Tell me about it." I eased myself down into one of the chairs at her dining table.

"Here, drink this. It'll help," she commanded, setting a glass in front of me.

"Uh, this better not be a Bloody Mary," I warned. "I'm pretty sure my stomach couldn't tolerate any more alcohol this morning."

"No, it isn't the hair of the dog that bit you. It's that tomato and vegetable juice blend you hate."

I grimaced at her. "Seriously? You just said I hate it, so why are you giving it to me?"

"It's either that or eating a banana. Which do you prefer?"

"Neither," I groaned, resting my aching head in my hands.

"It'll help balance out your electrolytes and stuff," she insisted. "It's a trick I learned from a nurse friend of mine. When you plan to drink a lot, or you already have, eat or drink something high in potassium. Tomatoes have a lot of potassium, so….drink up."

Gingerly, I lifted the glass, willing to drink almost anything if it would help with this heinous hangover. I struggled not to gag after the first sip. "Why'd you let me drink so much anyway?" I asked.

Then I thought for a moment, my memories hazy. "Wait a minute, you didn't let me. You actually encouraged me to get wasted!"

I moaned and clutched my head when my voice grew louder.

"Why would you do this to me?" I whispered.

"Because you needed it," Jonelle answered, setting a cup of hot tea in front of me. "You've been wound up tight since you lost your job months ago and after that fight with your mom, you needed to cut loose and forget about responsibilities and family obligations for a night."

I drank more of the red juice, pleased that there was only half a glass left. Gathering my courage, I drained it and shoved the glass away from me, sputtering and shaking.

"That's probably true," I admitted, "But you know I don't like to drink enough to make myself sick and I am definitely sick as a damn dog this morning."

"Okay, you're right. Once we got started, I lost track of how many tequila shots we did, so your hangover is on me."

"Tequila?" I asked. "You let me drink tequila? You know that's a bad idea. I always end up doing stupid shit." Then I took a moment to truly look at her. "And why in the hell aren't you hung over?" I snapped.

It was true. Jonelle's eyes were clear and sparkling and she looked well rested. While I, on the other hand, probably looked like a piece of road kill she'd scraped off the asphalt.

She shrugged. "I'm used to it."

I groaned and lowered my head to the kitchen table. The cool wood felt wonderful against my throbbing head.

"Did I do anything I'll regret last night?"

"You mean besides kissing half the men in Birdie's?" Jonelle retorted.

"Please tell me you're joking," I demanded, lifting my head to stare at her balefully.

"I am," she chuckled.

"Bitch," I muttered.

"Yep. Now, the bitch is gonna make you breakfast. How do you want your eggs?"

"In the trash," I replied, lowering my head back to the table.

Half an hour later, Jonelle had bullied me into eating some scrambled eggs, sausage, and toast and drinking another small glass of tomato juice. I was beginning to feel much better.

Sipping my hot tea, I asked, "Thanks for taking care of me this morning. And listening to my drunken ramblings last night." Now that the fog around my mind was clearing, the things I'd said and done last night were much clearer.

While I hadn't done anything humiliating, I had been in tears at some point.

"You're welcome," Jonelle said. "God knows you've done it enough for me in the past."

She studied me for a few seconds and I could tell she was gearing up to say something.

Finally, she spoke. "You were talking a lot about your mom last night. Not just that she's upset with you for taking the job with the YouTube show, but that she used to see spirits the same way you do."

I nodded. "Yeah, my dad told me about it, but I still don't understand. She knows what it's like to see and hear things no one else does, yet she insisted that I was making it all up."

"Abuse changes people, Zoe," Jonelle replied, touching my arm. "It sounds like your grandma was a piece of work, physically and mentally abusing your mom. I mean, what sort of mother tells their child that they're possessed by evil or Satan or whatever when they're six years old?"

I nodded. "I know, Jonelle. It's just difficult for me to reconcile all that information in less than twenty-four hours."

"I understand."

We drank our tea in silence for a while before Jonelle said, "You also mentioned something about working for Mal permanently, and how that could be bad because he has a really nice ass and you want to kiss him."

"I don't remember that," I accused.

Jonelle grinned. "This was a conversation we had right around the time you passed out. I didn't think you would. So I take it you have the hots for your new boss, huh? Why didn't you mention this before?"

"Because I knew you would tell me to go for it," I answered. She opened her mouth to reply but stopped when I lifted a hand. "It's a bad idea and you know it, Jonelle. He signs my paychecks. I refuse to be financially dependent on a man I'm dating."

She sighed. "Yeah, that's a good point. Are you sure you really want this job? I mean, you can find a job anywhere, but handsome, sweet, and funny men who can pay their own bills are harder to come by."

"I love this job, Jonelle," I responded with a laugh. "For the first time, I feel like I fit in somewhere."

"But that's also why Mal is perfect for you," she argued. "He knows about your talents and he accepts you for who you are!"

"Not happening, Jonelle," I stated. "I like Mal a lot, but this job is special."

"Maybe Mal is too."

My head was beginning to throb again. "Jonelle, I've made up my mind."

She huffed. "I don't understand why you seem so determined to be alone. Commitment isn't a disease you know."

I didn't point it out, but her tendency to go through men was just a different way of ensuring she wasn't committed either. Jonelle had her reasons, just like I had mine. Arguing with her about it would only serve to create strife between us.

"Can we talk about something else?" I asked.

Jonelle smiled at me. "Sure."

I got up to clear the table, carrying the dishes to the sink.

"And thanks for not pointing out that I can't commit either, Zoe."

I glanced back at her. "I have no idea what you're talking about."

She smiled at me, but still looked sad. "We're quite a pair, huh?"

"Two of a kind, which is almost too much awesome for this little town to handle."

She grinned at me, the sorrow fading from her expression. "True. Speaking of awesome, I need to get to work. My first appointment is in twenty minutes and I still have to drop you off at home."

"I can walk."

Jonelle scoffed. "Looking like something the cat dragged in? No way. Someone would alert the sheriff to let him know that a wild woman was wandering around town. This way the only people to witness your walk of shame will be Preston and that invisible demon you call a resident ghost."

"Fine. Let me get my purse."

CHAPTER

26

TWO DAYS AFTER my wild night with Jonelle, I got a call from Mal.

"They found the report," he stated as soon as I answered. "Wanna go up to the sheriff's office with me to pick it up?"

I hesitated. I tried to avoid the sheriff as much as possible because the dislike that rolled off him in gigantic waves was extremely off-putting. Though he had a damn good poker face, the man's emotions could fill a room. I could never tell what he was thinking due to his expression but rather by the atmosphere that surrounded him.

"C'mon. We'll be in and out."

"All right. Pick me up in half an hour."

When he rang the doorbell thirty minutes later, I almost stuck my head out and told him I'd changed my mind. Then I took a deep breath and squared my shoulders. The longer I worked with Mal and the guys, the greater my certainty that this was a job I wanted to keep. If I did, I would have to get used to dealing with people who might not like me because they thought I was a kook or crazy.

On the ride to the station, Mal kept up a steady stream of conversation as though he sensed my nerves. Knowing how observant he was, it shouldn't have been a surprise that he noticed.

After building it up in my head, our visit to the sheriff's department was a bit anti-climactic. We walked inside to the front desk and Mal stated his name and that he needed to pick up a copy of an accident report from 1996.

Within five minutes, we were back in his car and on our way to my house.

"That was easier than I expected," I commented.

"Yeah, well it is an election year," he responded cryptically.

I twisted my head to gape at him. "Are you saying what I think you're saying?"

"I realize you don't care for the illustrious sheriff, but it seems most of his deputies think he's great. When I contributed a nice sized chunk to his campaign fund, well, it took a lot less time to find the report than they initially thought it would."

"Are you saying you *bribed* them?" I asked incredulously.

"Not bribed," Mal replied defensively. "More like provided incentive."

I shook my head. "Great. Now the sheriff will have a reason to lock me up if he finds out."

"Oh, I'm sure he knows what happened. Don't worry so much."

I didn't say anything else, but Mal didn't know Sheriff Lamar Daughtry like I did.

Back at my place, Mal carried the file into the kitchen while I poured each of us a glass of sweet tea. I winced when I saw the pictures he took out of the folder first.

"Wow, they gave you the entire file, didn't they?" I asked.

Mal flipped through the paperwork, skimming the information. "It appears so. I guess they didn't think they would need it any longer."

I sat down and gingerly picked up one of the pictures from the scene of the accident.

"God, poor Hank," I murmured.

Mal nodded. "Poor Hank indeed."

I forced myself not to stare at the pictures of Hank's body, but instead focused on the other details of the photo. I wasn't sure what I was looking for, but instinct told me that the clue we needed would be in the photos.

"Hmmm, it seems that Deputy Lamar Daughtry was first on scene. Is this the same man as Sheriff Daughtry?"

I sighed. "Yeah."

"I wonder if he'd let me interview him," Mal mused.

I sincerely doubted it, but then again, Mal was good at convincing people to do the things he wanted. If anyone could get through to the brusque sheriff, it would be him.

A small detail caught my attention in one of the photos, but I couldn't make it out clearly. I pushed back from the table and searched through the junk drawer until I found my magnifying glass.

When I looked at it through the glass, I realized why it was bothering me. Lying about a foot from Hank's head was a large rock. In the pictures it appeared to be covered in a black liquid, but I had a feeling it was blood. Hank Murphy's blood.

"Hey, will you look at this?" I asked Mal. "I want to be sure I'm not imagining things."

Mal took the magnifying glass and leaned down over the photo. "What am I looking for?"

"There's a rock to the left of Hank's head. Do you think that's blood?"

He studied the picture for a few minutes. "It might be. Hang on."

Mal sifted through the other photos until he found another shot of the scene from a slightly different angle. He scrutinized it closely.

"I think it is. Take a look."

This shot had been taken at a different angle, the scene lit up by headlights or floodlights, I wasn't sure which. The substance on the rock was clearly dark reddish brown. I was almost certain it was blood after seeing the second picture.

I lifted my head and looked at Mal. "Do you think it means anything?"

Mal shrugged. "It could just be blood spatter from the accident. Or it could be the murder weapon."

"Hank said that the man was carrying a rock. That's a big one. It would do a lot of damage."

Nodding, Mal looked at the picture again. "Yeah, but I'm pretty sure that they didn't keep it as evidence," he muttered.

"Probably not, but maybe the sheriff will remember it."

Mal sighed. "We can hope, but I doubt it. This was twenty years ago."

I leaned back in my chair and crossed my arms over my chest.

"What?" Mal asked.

"Think that campaign contribution will buy you thirty minutes of the sheriff's time?"

"Only one way to find out," he replied with a grin.

CHAPTER

27

"THIS IS A bad idea, Mal," I repeated for the fourth time in the last twenty minutes. When I suggested he go see the sheriff, I'd meant alone, not with me in tow.

He sighed. "You're worrying over nothing."

"Uh, remember the cemetery and the zombie, Mal?" I pointed out.

His eyes narrowed as he turned to me. "Why would you bring that up?"

"Because you said I was worrying over nothing then too," I pointed out.

When the receptionist's head lifted at my words, I realized my voice had risen.

Leaning closer to Mal's ear, I hissed, "He'll take one look at me and tell us both to get lost."

"At least we'll have tried, right?"

It was my turn to sigh, because he was correct. I'd made a promise to Hank. I needed to stop looking for excuses to give up and focus on following through.

"All right, but you're buying me ice cream after this is over," I insisted. "I'm gonna need it."

Mal chuckled. "I'll buy you an entire gallon. Whatever flavor you want."

"Good."

The receptionist picked up the phone when it buzzed, her eyes moving to us.

After she replaced the handset, she called out, "The sheriff can see you now."

We followed her back to Sheriff Daughtry's office. I felt the same trepidation I did when I was called to the principal's office in elementary school. I tried to ignore the sensation, but it wasn't working.

The last time I'd had a run in with Lamar Daughtry was the night of the cemetery incident in high school, when my so-called friends had abandoned me miles from town.

When he found me, I'd been standing in the middle of the graveyard, shaking and nearly incoherent, surrounded by zombies. The following ten minutes were fraught with tension. At the time, Daughtry was still a deputy, working under his father. His dad, Jeremiah Daughtry was the first African American sheriff in our county, and he was a damn good man. At least that's what my father always said. I was only seventeen so I didn't pay attention to county politics because they didn't matter a whit to me.

Lamar, his son, was a shoo-in as sheriff when his dad retired at the end of the year. I'd seen him around town, but never spoken to him. He'd always been polite, but distant. At the time, I didn't think I'd ever been so relieved to see another human being in my life.

When he approached, the zombies had stepped in front of me, jostling with each other.

At the time it scared the hell out of me, but after what happened with Mal at the cemetery recently, I realized they were protecting me from a perceived threat.

"What in the hell is going on here, Zoe Thorne?" he'd asked quietly.

I was so terrified that my brain struggled to comprehend his question.

"Zoe?"

It never occurred to me to wonder how he knew my name, even though we'd never met before.

"I-I don't know," I stammered. "I was out here with some f-f-friends and these things," I gestured around me, "Just appeared out of the ground."

"Where are you friends now?" His voice was still calm and soft, but I could feel the weight of his emotions pressing against me.

The zombies shuffled forward again, moving toward him, and I heard him draw his sidearm.

"Okay, Zoe, I know you're scared, but I need to you to calm down. Can you do that for me?"

I wrapped my arms around myself and rocked back and forth. "I don't know what's happening. I don't understand."

"Zoe, you have to calm down. I think that your fear is affecting whatever in the hell these things are."

Somehow his deep, accented voice pierced through the veil of terror that had fallen over me and I blinked.

"It is?" I asked.

At my question, the zombies stopped moving forward. They remained still even as Lamar moved around them and walked toward me. His gun was still in his hand, but resting at his side.

"I know you're upset, Zoe, but I need you to focus for me."

I nodded my agreement, my gaze locked on his dark brown eyes. He was younger than I thought based on his voice, maybe in his early thirties.

"I want you to look at those…things and tell them to go back to where they came from. Can you do that?"

I took a shaky breath. "I think so."

"Give it a try," he commanded gently.

I turned toward the corpses standing peacefully in front of me. "Go back to where you belong," I stated.

They shifted, but didn't move.

"Say it like you mean it, Zoe," he encouraged.

"Go back to where you belong!" I repeated. This time I felt a snap of power behind my words, as if their effectiveness was increased by my intention.

Slowly, the three zombies had trudged back to their graves and climbed inside. Lamar stood with me as the dirt began to refill the holes by itself.

Once the sound of rushing earth died away, the calm, cool exterior he'd presented earlier disappeared.

He grabbed my elbow and dragged me out of the cemetery. "I don't know what in the hell you were thinking, Zoe Thorne, but I can promise you that if you ever pull a stunt like this again, I will find a way to have you thrown into an institution for the rest of your natural life."

There was something about his tone, about the way he said those words that made me believe down to my bones that he meant them. Since that night, I'd avoided Lamar Daughtry like the plague. I didn't want to give him even the smallest reason to follow through on his threat.

Now, I was about to walk right into the lion's den and give him all the ammunition he needed.

Sheriff Daughtry got to his feet as we entered. He smiled at Mal and shook his hand. Then his eyes landed on me. His smile didn't fade, but I sensed a distinct brittleness to his expression and I knew he was forcing himself to maintain it.

"Please have a seat," he requested, indicating the chairs in front of his desk. After we settled in, he folded his hands across the blotter on his desktop. "What can I do for you two today?"

His eyes were directed toward Mal, but I got the impression his words were meant for me.

Mal removed Hank Murphy's file from his laptop bag. "Thank you for agreeing to see us, Sheriff. We're working on a documentary about..."

Sheriff Daughtry lifted a hand. "Son, I know who you are and what you're really doing in Kenna, so please don't insult me by trying to lie. You're some kind of ghost hunter." His hard brown eyes flicked to me. "And for some reason you've decided to investigate the death of Hank Murphy. I have no idea why."

I struggled not to fidget beneath Sheriff Daughtry's piercing stare. He knew exactly what we'd been up to in regards to finding Hank Murphy's killer. I kept my gaze steady on Sheriff Daughtry's, refusing to look away first even though I really wanted to hide beneath the chair in which I sat.

Mal seemed unaffected by the sheriff's cold reception. "You see, sir, we have reason to believe that Hank Murphy's death may not have been an accident."

Finally, those hard brown eyes moved away from me and landed on Mal. "Excuse me?"

Mal removed the pictures from the file and the magnifying glass he'd borrowed from his bag. Placing them on the desk, he pointed to the rock in the photo. "If you look, Sheriff, there is blood on that rock, yet it's at least a foot from Hank Murphy's body."

To my surprise, Sheriff Daughtry humored him and studied the rock in the photo. "That could be spatter from where he landed. Or maybe he rolled over after he was expelled from the car. There are several reasons that his blood could have ended up on that rock."

"Perhaps," Mal responded, "But we have reason to believe that foul play was involved. For example, did you know that Trisha Murphy was having an affair with her husband's best friend, Steve

Dwyer?"

Sheriff Daughtry didn't bat an eye. "That's unfortunate, but that doesn't mean that this was anything but a tragic accident."

I inhaled sharply. "I saw Hank Murphy, Sheriff."

"Excuse me?" he asked.

"I saw Hank Murphy on that farm to market road," I reiterated.

"Zoe, if you're referring to the crash, it was twenty years ago. You would have just been a child."

I cleared my throat. "You know that's not what I'm talking about. I saw Hank last week on the side of that road and he told me he'd been murdered."

The sheriff frowned fiercely at me. "Zoe." My name was a warning.

One that I ignored. It was as if the fear left my body and all that was left was me. The real me. A strong, outspoken woman who wasn't afraid of the threats made by a young sheriff's deputy a decade ago.

"Lamar, you know what I'm capable of. You've seen it with your own eyes, so please don't insult me by treating me like I'm crazy. I *saw* Hank. I spoke to him. He told me what happened that night. How someone fired a gun at him and ran him off the road. He also said a man climbed out of the other truck and came towards him with a rock in his hand. He can remember being hit once in the head before everything went dark. What happened to him twenty years ago wasn't an accident. Someone wanted to kill Hank Murphy and they went to a lot of trouble to make it appear as something other than murder."

The frown on his face faded, but his expression became a cold stone mask of anger.

"Who do you think you are, talking to me that way?" he asked harshly. "I was there that night and I can tell you that I saw no evidence that it was anything other than what it was; a horrible single car accident."

I shook my head. "Even after finding me in that cemetery ten years ago, you still can't acknowledge that not everything in this world can be explained with logic and science. There is more to this life than that."

The sheriff slammed his hand on the desktop. The loud noise made me jump. "Zoe Thorne, that is enough!"

"I'm not a scared teenager anymore, Lamar," I snapped back, shocked at my own audacity. "A murderer has walked free for twenty years and, if you ignore us and what we're sharing with you, they may very well be free until their dying day!"

"Even if you were right, there is no evidence. Because there was no foul play suspected, no evidence was collected. That rock you pointed out—gone. Any tire tracks, footprints, anything that might help us figure out who did it—gone. There is not much we can do."

"So that means you do nothing at all?" Mal asked.

The sheriff rose from his chair. "I think it's time for you to leave."

Shaking, I also got to my feet and let Mal lead me to the door.

Before he could open it, the sheriff called out, "I don't want to hear about you two going around and stirring things up, do you understand? This is the end of the matter, or you and I will have a problem."

When neither of us responded, he continued, "By problem, I mean I will find a reason to arrest you and throw your asses in jail. Do you understand?"

Mal and I both nodded.

"Then get the hell out of my office."

Without another word, Mal and I left.

CHAPTER

28

M AL GRABBED MY hand as we walked out of the station and I was grateful for it, because I wasn't sure my legs were going to hold me.

This was the reason I hated confrontation. After all was said and done, my body felt weak and shaky. I couldn't believe the things I'd said to the sheriff. I wondered if he would do as he'd threatened all those years ago. God, my mother would have a field day if the men in white showed up at my house with a straightjacket.

After we climbed in the car, the tremors began in earnest. My chest hurt and I felt as if I couldn't pull enough air into my lungs. My breaths sounded gasping and as painful as they felt.

"Zoe?" Mal's voice sounded far away. "Oh my God, Zoe. What's wrong?"

"He saw me ten years ago, in the cemetery," I choked out. "The first time it happened. The first zombies."

Mal's hand wrapped tightly around mine. "I'm here, Zoe."

"H-h-he said that he would have me committed to a mental institution if he ever caught me doing something like that again," I whispered in a harsh rush, the words hurt as they were yanked from my throat. I'd already told him all this, but the enormity of what I'd just done hit me harder than I expected.

"For fuck's sake," Mal muttered. His arms came around me, pulling me close across the console of the van. He tucked my head into the hollow of his shoulder and held me close.

I managed to keep from crying, but each breath I took sounded as if it was heaved from my lungs while I fought for control.

"No wonder you think the sheriff hates you."

I huffed out a bark of laughter. "Think? I know."

"I don't think that's hate, Zoe. I think he fears what you can do because it can't be explained."

"Either way, I've always been too scared to push him. Until now."

"Hey, listen," Mal pried me away from his chest and cupped my face. "I will never let him do that to you, Zoe."

His eyes filled my vision and I was mesmerized by the golden flecks in the brown of his irises.

"How could you stop him?" I whispered.

His face was so close to mine. I could feel his breath against my mouth and knew his lips were only scant inches away.

"You forget who my family is, Zoe. Even if he managed to get you into an institution, it would only be a few hours before I could have you out again. My father's man eating lawyers could accomplish that easily."

I didn't believe that claim for a second, but I did trust that he wouldn't allow me to be locked away to rot over Sheriff Daughtry's vendetta.

"You promise?" I asked.

His response wasn't verbal this time. I trembled as his mouth sealed over mine. The kiss was sweet. Reassuring.

But it had been so long since a man had held me, kissed me, that I felt overwhelmed.

My mind reeled as the unexpected sensations assailed me. When his tongue brushed my upper lip, I instinctively opened my mouth. Mal gathered me closer, his tongue tangling with mine. He tasted like the mints he'd popped on the drive to the sheriff's office.

The whoop of a siren tore us apart. I panted, leaning back against the passenger door and staring at Mal as the cruiser took off out of the department parking lot.

I lifted a shaky hand to my lips, my fingers touching the swollen tissue. My mind was completely blank.

Mal stared at me, his brown eyes moving over my face, taking in the nuances of my expression. I felt as though my thoughts were being dissected.

"Uh, I'll, uh, take you home," he mumbled.

Wordlessly, I nodded and reached for my seat belt.

When Mal pulled into my driveway, he made no move to get out of the van. I took that to mean that whatever had passed between us would remain unspoken.

I unbuckled my seatbelt and opened the door.

"Zoe."

I glanced over at him, unsure of what to expect.

"We will talk about that kiss sometime soon. Just not today."

I nodded shortly and stepped out of the van. Mal waited until I was inside the house before he drove away.

Teri was waiting for me in the living room when I dropped my keys on the table in the foyer.

"How'd it go?" she asked.

"About as well as I expected."

She grimaced. "That good, huh?"

I trudged to the sofa and plopped down on it. "Oh yeah. The high point was when Mal kissed me."

"What?" she screeched. "He kissed you?"

I sighed, throwing an arm over my eyes. "Yeah."

"How was it?" she asked, nudging me with an icy hand.

"A bad idea," I stated.

"Okay, fine. Maybe it was a bad idea, but how was the kiss itself?" she pushed.

I dropped my arm away and turned my head to look at her. "Fucking amazing."

She grinned, a delighted expression on her face.

"But we can't do it again."

She scowled at me. "Why not?" Then she shook her head. "Never mind. It'll be some lousy excuse."

"There's nothing lousy about choosing to think with my brain instead of my hormones," I retorted.

"Until you end up old and alone," she snapped back. "At least you'll have your principles."

Then she disappeared.

CHAPTER

29

LATER THAT NIGHT, I got a text from Mal.

Intrvwing Dwyer tmrro. Wll fill u in.

I glowered at the message. So now I was out of the loop? I didn't think so. Sheriff Daughtry might have put the fear of God into me a decade ago, but I wasn't seventeen anymore and I had people who would help me if he tried to follow through on his threats.

I dialed Mal and waited as the phone rang.

"Hi, Zoe. Are you feeling better?" he asked.

"Much. What I'd like to know is why you're going to talk to Dwyer without me?" Before Mal could respond, I continued. "I know I lost it today after we talked to Daughtry, but I'm not going to live in fear of him any longer. I won't give him that sort of power over me again."

I waited for Mal's answer, but when he didn't speak, I asked, "Well?"

"Uh, just waiting to make sure you're done before I say anything," he replied.

I took a deep breath. "Yeah, I think I'm done."

"Well, you see, I thought Dwyer might be more inclined to talk to me if I approached him alone. From what I understand, he's been a loner since his best friend, Hank, died. He also goes to the local honkytonk a couple times a week after work. Doesn't talk to anyone or dance with anyone. He just sits at the bar and drinks. I thought that might be the best time to make contact."

"Oh."

I could hear the smile in Mal's voice. "That's it? *Oh?*"

"Well, now I understand your reasoning. It's just…after today, it felt like you were taking me out of the loop because you didn't think I could handle the pressure."

He chuckled. "You're doing better than most people would, Zoe. I don't think less of you for getting upset this afternoon. Sheriff Daughtry is intimidating and I doubt he's in the habit of making idle threats. He would have scared the pants off me when I was seventeen too."

"Yeah, well he still scares me and I'm twenty-seven."

Mal and I chatted for a while, but he didn't bring up the kiss he'd planted on me earlier.

Neither did I.

THE NEXT EVENING I was watching television and trying not to obsess over how Mal's interview with Steve Dwyer was going.

Around nine-thirty, my phone dinged. I glanced at the screen. It was from Mal.

R u up?

I was surprised to hear from him. I figured he'd be at the bar until late. **Yes.**

His reply was quick. **I'm cmng ovr. Do u hv frzn ps?**

What in the heck was he talking about? **Have what?**

FROZEN PEAS.

I had no idea why he might need them. Still, I did have a couple bags in the freezer.

Yes.

B thr in 5.

When I let him in a few minutes later, my mouth fell open.

"What happened to you?" I asked, shutting the front door behind him.

"Oh, I ran into Dwyer's fist with my face a few times. Nothing serious."

Mal's left eye was swollen nearly shut and his cheek glowed, the flesh a bright reddish purple.

"Dear God, how many times did he hit you?" I asked, leading him into the living room.

Mal collapsed on my sofa and leaned his head back. "A few."

"Hang on. I'll be right back with the peas."

I hurried into the kitchen and grabbed the biggest bag of frozen peas I had.

I brought it back into the living room and settled it over Mal's face. He flinched and exhaled on a hiss.

"Jesus, that feels horrible and wonderful at the same time," he sighed.

"Want to tell me exactly what happened?"

"Well, I followed the plan I went over with you last night. I asked someone to point Dwyer out to me and sat down next to him. We chatted for a bit. It was a simple conversation."

"Okay, Mal, I don't know if you realize this but a 'simple conversation' usually doesn't end with you getting punched in the face."

"Well, he might have slugged me when I asked him if Hank

knew that his best friend was fucking his wife before he died," Mal admitted.

"You didn't."

Mal held the peas to his eye as he nodded. "Sure did." He closed his good eye and resumed his prone position. "Then, while I was lying on the floor, I asked him if Trisha knew that he killed Hank with that rock or if she was just an innocent party."

I sank down onto the couch next to him. "Oh my God. What did he say?"

"Nothing," Mal answered. "But his face turned white and, honestly, he looked like he was the one who'd been punched." He reopened his good eye and turned his head so he could see me. "He did it. There's no doubt in my mind. His reaction when I asked him that question was practically an admission of guilt."

"Oh my God," I repeated.

"Yeah, I think that's what I said when I realized that he really was guilty."

"What are we going to do?" I asked.

"There's nothing we can do." Mal sounded defeated. "There's no proof. Unless Dwyer or Trisha confesses, we have no legal recourse. The sheriff isn't willing to help us so…"

I flopped back onto the cushions and stared at the ceiling. "So no justice for Hank Murphy. We know who killed him and why, but because all the evidence was missed or ignored twenty years ago, there's nothing we can do."

"Pretty much," Mal said.

"I don't like that solution," I stated.

"I don't either, but there's not much else we can do."

We sat in silence for a long time.

"God, I need a drink," I groaned. Just a few days ago, I'd sworn not to drink again, but after tonight's epiphanies, I wanted one.

"Me, too. Got anything stronger than beer?"

I glanced over at him. "Whiskey, vodka, or tequila?"

He removed the peas from his eye. "Seriously?"

"What?"

"Nothing. Whiskey, please."

When I returned with his drink, I brought the bottle.

"Does this mean you won't be working with us any longer?" Mal asked as he took the glass I offered him.

I poured myself a small amount of the amber liquor and sipped. "No, it doesn't," I replied. "I think I made my decision within a few days of working with Blaine, Stony, and you, I just wasn't ready to admit it."

Mal smiled. "So you're going to be a permanent part of the team?"

"Yeah, I think I am."

"Well, at least there's some good news tonight," he said, lifting his glass. "Welcome to the team, Zoe Thorne. We're happy to have you."

I clicked my glass against his. "Thank you."

CHAPTER

30

AFTER ONE DRINK, Mal thanked me for the peas and the whiskey. He left after instructing me to meet him in the morning at the hotel where he and the guys were staying. He explained that Blaine and Stony would want to officially welcome me to the team.

I wasn't sure if I wanted to know what that included, but I assured him that I would be there.

Once I was alone, I picked up my phone and texted Jonelle. She was a night owl, so I knew she would still be awake.

I have a new job.

My phone rang a few seconds later.

"You quit the show?" she yelled in my ear.

"Of course not! I told Mal that I wanted to work with them full time."

"Oh, good. I thought that you'd decided to quit after all."

"No. I just decided to quit questioning myself and do it."

"I'm glad. We should celebrate! Tomorrow night?"

Jonelle was always looking for a reason to party, but in this case, I agreed. We should celebrate.

"That sounds like fun. Birdie's?"

"Hell no, woman! We're going over to Weatherford to one of

the nice places. This is a party that deserves more than sticky floors and sixties crooners."

I laughed. "All right, but no tequila and no trying to hook me up."

"C'mon!"

"I mean it, Jonelle. I want to drink to my new path in life, not find a man or deal with another massive hangover."

"Good point," she replied with a sigh.

"Am I picking you up?"

"Zoe, seriously. This is your celebration. I'll be the designated driver. Or I'll see if I can hire an Uber."

A giggle escaped my mouth. Kenna was such a small town that hiring an Uber car was damn near impossible.

"Good luck," I said.

"Smart ass."

"Okay, so I'll see you tomorrow night. I have to go to bed because I'm supposed to be at Mal's hotel tomorrow morning at ten."

After we disconnected, I headed upstairs to get ready for bed. As I lay in my bed, staring at the shadows on my ceiling, I waited for the fear to come. I was making a huge change in my life. I should be terrified.

But I wasn't.

In fact, I was so excited that I wasn't sure I could sleep. In the last three weeks, I realized that the choices I'd made over the last few years had been safe ones. While they hadn't made me miserable, my choices hadn't made me happy either.

For the first time since I graduated college, I was genuinely happy. I didn't have to hide anymore.

So with the happiness, I was also going to gain freedom.

MY FIRST OFFICIAL day as a full-time employee with *The Wraith Files* was almost exactly like the first. The only difference was Stony insisted on putting moonshine in my coffee.

Apparently Stony's uncle had a still in his barn and he liked to make his own booze. To be honest, it was really good. I could barely taste it, which also meant it was likely lethal, so I placed my hand over my coffee cup when Stony tried to add more.

We spent the rest of the day going over the episode that they filmed at my home, looking for editing errors and other issues. The episode would go live on YouTube next week.

I probably should have been ashamed of myself, but I laughed uproariously when Teri sprayed Marcy in the face with water. Though I saw the clip before, it still cracked me up.

Though I tried to pay attention to the flow and camera angles, it looked fine to me. Despite their tendency to exhibit goofball behavior, Stony and Blaine were consummate professionals when it came to the editing and production of the show.

After the final viewing of next week's episode, Mal presented us with a list of locations that would be ideal for filming. Most of the buildings and homes weren't in Texas. I don't know why, but I hadn't considered how much traveling I would have to do with Mal and the guys.

The realization was a pleasant one. I'd always wanted to travel but rarely had the time or the money. Now I would be able to travel for work.

I was also relieved to find that Mal expected our input when it came time to determine the itinerary. Though he was definitely the leader of the group, he expected us to collaborate on all the important decisions.

The day ended at four in the afternoon, which worked out great. I had plenty of time to get ready for my night on the town with Jonelle.

I went home and took my time getting ready. I even painted my toenails. By the time Jonelle rang the doorbell at six, I was ready to go.

When I opened the door, I found four grinning fools on my porch.

"Surprise!" Blaine cried. "We're here to take you out and debauch you."

I laughed. "I can see that." I glanced at Jonelle. "I take it you texted Mal."

"I might have," she replied innocently. "But only to make sure you got off work on time to go out."

"Whatever." I rolled my eyes.

Jonelle found all sorts of reasons to party and her philosophy was *the more, the merrier*. Of course she would contact Mal, Stony, and Blaine.

"Let's go," Stony demanded. "I'm starving."

As Stony and Blaine led Jonelle out to the van, I turned to Mal. "You guys didn't have to come. I know you have a lot to do for the release of the next three episodes."

Mal shook his head. "No way. It's just been the three of us for so long. This is a big step. We should celebrate it." He paused. "Also, I needed to get Stony and Blaine out of that hotel. I think they were going stir crazy. I actually caught Blaine having a conversation with himself in the mirror this morning. An argument, actually. With himself!"

I had to laugh because I could imagine it.

"Well, I'm glad you got him away from the hotel before the situation became dire."

Mal took my hand as we walked down the sidewalk toward the van. I didn't say anything as he laced his fingers with mine. We still hadn't talked about the kiss we shared.

Honestly, I wasn't sure what I would have to say anyway. The kiss had been singular and completely out of character for me.

And now that Mal was my boss for the foreseeable future, I couldn't allow the experience to be repeated. It was in our mutual best interest.

CHAPTER

31

I T WAS NEARLY midnight before we piled back into the van and headed back to Kenna. The evening had begun unexpectedly and I had a blast. It had been a long time since I'd gone out with a group of friends and not felt like the fifth wheel.

We started with dinner at a local steakhouse that Jonelle knew I loved. I ate a delicious ribeye and drank good red wine. Then we moved to a local bar that usually had a great live band several days a week.

Mal, Stony, and Blaine insisted on buying all the rounds, despite my attempts at refusal. When the music went from slow and mellow to lively, Stony and Blaine took turns dancing with Jonelle and me.

Finally, I had to give up. My feet were beginning to hurt and I was incredibly thirsty.

A stunning woman in her mid-forties snagged Blaine before he could follow me off the dance floor and insisted that he dance with her. As I walked back to the table and plopped down next to Mal, I noticed that Stony and Jonelle were deep in conversation as they danced.

"I think something's going on there," Mal stated, tilting his beer bottle toward our mutual friends as they danced.

"I think you're right." I sighed. "I just hope Stony doesn't get his heart broken."

Mal looked at me with surprise. "Shouldn't I be the one saying that to you about Jonelle?"

I shook my head. "No. Jonelle insists that she isn't ready to settle down, so she'll probably see Stony while y'all are in town and that'll be that. No harm done, no feelings hurt. At least on her part."

"Then they're a matched pair. Stony likes to keep things simple."

I released a small laugh at his words. "I don't even know what that means."

"Me either," Mal admitted.

"I think they'll be fine either way," I assured him.

As the hour grew later, the music took on a more mellow turn.

Mal turned to me and held out his hand. "We haven't danced yet. What do ya say?"

I tried to ignore the tremor in my knees as I put my hand in his and let him lead me onto the dance floor.

His arm wrapped around my waist, pulling me close. In my wedge heels, I was only a few inches shorter than him, so our bodies lined up almost perfectly. My thighs brushed his as we swayed and my breasts pressed against his chest with each breath I took.

The sensations were light and tantalizing. The longer we moved, the more attuned I became to every subtle motion of his hips and shoulders. I wasn't sure who moved first, but the space between us disappeared as the first song segued into the second.

I could feel the stubble along his jaw as it brushed my cheek and I tried not to think about the short distance between our lips. All I needed to do was turn my head.

When Mal spoke, his words proved that his mind had taken the same path as my own.

"We never did talk about that kiss the other day," he murmured, his voice little more than a low rumble in my ear.

"No, we didn't," I replied.

"Think we should?"

I had to clear my throat before I could respond. "Do you think we should?"

I sucked in a deep breath as his mouth brushed my ear when he answered, "Probably." His lips touched my neck, just below my ear lobe and I shivered. "Or maybe we should forget talking about it and do it again."

It was difficult to concentrate on the conversation as he nuzzled my neck. My head fell back and I hummed low in my throat.

"That sounds nice," I whispered.

Suddenly, another couple jostled us, too busy necking to even notice that they'd almost plowed us over.

I exhaled harshly, grateful for the interruption. It had broken the trance that had fallen over me while I was in Mal's arms.

I stepped back and looked up into his face. "You need to stop doing things that like," I stated.

"Things like holding you?" he asked, his arms tightening around me slightly.

"I'm serious, Mal."

He loosened his grip on me. "Okay, let's go back to the table and talk."

His hand curled around mine and he led me back to our seats. As soon as Blaine saw the expressions on our faces, he got up and headed toward the bar, presumably to get another drink.

Mal held my chair out for me and then twisted his around so that we faced each other when he sat. He wasn't wearing his glasses tonight and I could see his gorgeous brown eyes clearly.

"Tell me what's going on in that beautiful head of yours," he invited.

I lost my train of thought for a moment when he called me beautiful, but managed to get myself together. Though I wanted to just tell him that I couldn't get involved with my boss and let that be the end of it, he deserved the entire truth. Even if it made me uncomfortable to reveal so much of myself.

I took a deep breath. "I'm sure you've figured out by now, that I don't have a lot of friends. Just Jonelle."

He nodded, but didn't speak. Mal was an excellent listener, probably because he seemed to intuit when he should talk and when he should be silent.

"I worked at my last job for four years and couldn't count a single person in my office as more than a passing acquaintance," I explained. "I felt like an outsider, even on my last day. Probably because I couldn't completely be myself with anyone there. If I'd tried to tell them about my abilities, they would have immediately assumed I was crazy or on drugs." I paused to gather my thoughts. "This job, with you and the guys…it's special to me, Mal. Not only do you know about my gifts, but you accept them with an open mind and encourage me to use them. For the first time, I can be myself outside the walls of my home without worrying about someone calling a psychiatrist or giving me odd, judgmental looks. And I don't want to do anything to risk that. Now that I have this, I don't want to give it up."

Mal took my hands in his. "Zoe, even if you and I didn't work out, we're both adults. I'm sure we could be professional."

I had to laugh. "It's easy to say that now, Mal. As much as I like you, we barely know each other. For all you know, I have all kinds of odd quirks and habits. Or maybe you'll drive me crazy. Either way, I don't think there's any way we can keep that from spilling into the show, into your work."

He squeezed my hands. "Who says it'll go bad?"

With a shrug, I answered, "It might not, but I'm not sure I'm willing to risk losing the one place I can be myself for a 'maybe'." I realized how that sounded and immediately tried to explain. "Please don't misunderstand me, Mal. You're wonderful, but there's always so much unknown in any relationship that I'm afraid—"

"Hey, Zoe, take a breath. I may not agree with you, but I understand everything you're saying. I'm not going to terminate your contract just because you don't want to date me." He grinned at me. "In fact, I'd say you should be in charge here because you seem more mature than any of us."

I smiled at him. "I'm glad you understand."

"And if you change your mind in the future, well, I'm around."

Laughing, I pulled my hands free. "Oh, so you're going to wait around, pining for me."

He seemed to consider my words for a moment. "Okay, maybe not."

"Hey, why are you people sitting down?" Jonelle asked breathlessly as she came up to the table. "Less talking, more drinking and dancing!" She whirled around and pointed to Stony. "Buttery nipples for everyone, sir! On the double!"

He gave her thumbs up and headed toward the bar.

Mal and I didn't have a moment alone together the rest of the night, which was probably for the best.

By the time we all piled into the van, all of us were buzzing, except for Mal. He stopped drinking after two beers when it became clear that Blaine and Stony were going to engage in a shot challenge.

I leaned back in the front seat and listened to Stony and Jonelle whisper to each other in the back, their conversation punctuated by soft snores from Blaine. I was just about to drift off when I heard the first pop.

Drowsy, I wasn't sure what I'd heard until the second and third shots sounded.

"Those are gunshots," I told Mal, sitting straight in the seat.

His eyes were shifting between the side mirror and the road. "I know. There's a truck coming up on the left and I can see the muzzle flash from their window."

Another shot rang out and I heard a ping as it hit the side of the van.

"Oh my God, they're shooting at us!" I flattened myself down against the console and looked toward the back of the van. "Everyone get down on the floor. Someone is shooting at us!"

I heard scuffling as they did as I said.

"What the hell is going on?" Blaine asked sleepily.

"Get on the floor!" I yelled, fear making my voice sharp.

The van swerved as another shot hit the side. It was too dark to see the entry points of the bullets, but I prayed no one had been hit.

"Everyone hang on," Mal bellowed right before he slammed on the brakes.

My body was thrown against the seatbelt and I gripped the console tightly. I couldn't see what was happening, but Mal floored it and the van shot forward.

"Stay down," he barked when I started to lift my head.

Suddenly, the entire van shuddered as the front end made contact with the other vehicle. Tires squealed and metal screamed. Or maybe it was me screaming, I couldn't be sure.

The van shimmied wildly and, for a terrifying moment, I thought we were going to flip over. Mal fought with the wheel, but we skidded off the road, coming to a rocky halt in the ditch.

"Stay down," he commanded me, unbuckling his seatbelt.

In the shadows, I could see him reach beneath the front seat and gasped when the moonlight glinted off the gun he pulled out.

"Call nine-one-one. If they shoot me, I want all four of you to make a run for it," Mal commanded. "Do not get yourselves hurt trying to save me."

Before any of us could argue, he was out of the van.

I lifted my head to peek over the dashboard. The truck that had been following us was parked in the middle of the road. No one got out. It just sat there, motionless.

"Oh fuck this," Jonelle muttered. "Stony, I need the light from your phone."

I couldn't tear my eyes from Mal's back as he crept toward the truck, keeping his body low in the ditch. "Jonelle, please tell me you didn't bring your gun tonight," I pleaded as I fumbled with my bag for my phone.

"Of course I brought my gun. It's like that credit card commercial says, never leave home without it."

"You are not going out there," I argued. "You've been drinking. You could hit Mal by mistake."

I finally found my cell in the depths of my purse and pulled it out. With shaky hands, I lifted it and called nine-one-one.

"Nine-one-one, what's your emergency?"

"We're on Farm to Market 457, about five miles west of Weatherford. A truck fired shots at us and ran us off the road. Please send police as soon as possible."

"Okay, ma'am. I'm dispatching an officer to your location as we speak. Where is the shooter now?"

I swallowed and watched as Mal climbed out of the ditch, directly behind the truck. When the reverse lights came on, he lifted the weapon and pointed it at the vehicle. Before he could pull the trigger, the brake lights blazed as the driver put the truck in gear and peeled off.

"Ma'am? Are you injured? Can you tell me where the vehicle is now?"

As I watched the truck disappear around the curve I answered,

"Heading east on 457, toward Kenna. And no, I'm not injured." I twisted my head to look toward the back of the van. "Are any of you hurt?" I asked.

"Just a little bruised from getting tossed around," Stony answered. "We should be fine."

I screamed as the door next to me flew open. Clutching my phone to my chest, I wheeled around and saw Mal standing in the open door. "Oh my God, you scared me to death!" I yelled.

He glanced at the phone in my hand. "Did you call nine-one-one?"

I nodded.

I heard a distant voice saying "Ma'am? Ma'am? Can you answer me please?" and realized that the 911 operator was still on the line.

Lifting the phone to my ear, I stated, "We're fine. My friend opened the passenger door and scared me, that's all."

"Help will be there in just a few minutes. Please stay on the line."

We waited in tense silence until we heard the sirens, then Mal moved around and replaced the gun beneath the front seat.

"They're here," I told the operator. "Thank you."

As the officers pulled up on the side of the road, I hung up the phone and climbed out.

The night was definitely not ending the way I thought it would.

CHAPTER

32

APPARENTLY, IT WAS a slow night in the county because four deputies responded to our call for help.

We all gave our statements, but Mal was the only one who got a good look at the vehicle. He managed to identify the color, make, and model, but only got the first three letters on the license plate. After they spoke with each of us, the deputies studied the bullet holes in the side of the van. One was level with where Blaine's head would have been. We were incredibly lucky that no one was hurt.

As we waited for them to tell us we could leave, another squad car pulled up and I watched as Sheriff Lamar Daughtry climbed out. He stared at me as he walked toward his deputies, and I could see his expression due to the flashing lights from the cruisers. It was stony and forbidding.

I wondered if he would find a way to blame me for the situation and arrest me.

When he saw the sheriff's arrival, Mal moved directly to me and put an arm around my shoulders. I leaned into him, too shaken to care if the gesture made me seem weak.

"It's okay," Mal murmured into my ear.

Jonelle moved to my other side and took my hand. She knew all about the night in the cemetery. She hadn't been with me because we hadn't started hanging out until a few months later, but I'd told her the story.

After speaking briefly to his deputies, the sheriff came over. He paused when he saw the protective way Mal and Jonelle were surrounding me and I thought I saw him flinch. I chalked it up to a trick of the red and blue flashing lights.

"You know, I find it interesting," he stated, "That yesterday I get a complaint from Steven Dwyer about some guy that matches your description accusing him of murdering his best friend and tonight y'all get run off the road by a vehicle that not only matches the description of his, but has a license plate with the first three letters that match his."

Mal's body stiffened next to me. "What?"

"Steve was very upset when we spoke yesterday and I told him I would look into it," Sheriff Daughtry continued. "Then tonight you call me with this crazy story."

Jonelle bristled at his words. "Crazy story?" she asked loudly. "It's crazy all right, but it's also exactly what happened!"

The sheriff ignored her and looked first at Mal, then at me. "What did I tell you about bothering anyone with your stupid suspicions? And now you're trying to drag a good man's name through the mud."

I gaped at him in utter shock. "Are you saying that we *made this up*?" I asked. "Did you even look at the bullet holes in the van?"

"Well, Mr. Flemming here and your friend Jonelle are licensed to carry concealed weapons." He gave them each a hard look. "Are either of you carrying tonight?"

"Yes," Jonelle answered grudgingly.

"My weapon is under the driver's seat," Mal replied.

Sheriff Daughtry shrugged. "Either one of you could have fired those shots."

"For God's sake, why?" I asked, my voice rising.

"Because you think that Steven Dwyer is guilty and I refused to believe you."

Mal tucked me behind him, whether to protect me from the sheriff or keep me from kicking him in the balls, I'm not sure. "I'm not an idiot, Sheriff Daughtry. Surely you found some of the spent bullets in the van. Compare them to my gun and to Jonelle's. You'll see that they weren't fired from either."

Daughtry leaned closer. "You bet your ass we will," he growled. "I won't have you coming into my town and causing trouble just because you don't like the way I do things."

"What are you going to do when you realize that we aren't making this up?" I asked him softly, stepping around Mal. "Are you going to ignore it the way you tried to when Mal and I came to you? Or are you going to do your job?"

"I always do my job," he snapped.

"Then be my guest," Mal said, sweeping a hand toward his van. "Tear the damn thing apart, find all the bullets and compare them. Then we'll see."

"I'll need you to surrender your weapons," the sheriff shot back.

"Mine is in the van under the front seat, as I told you."

"Mine is in my purse," Jonelle explained. "I'll be happy to give it to one of your deputies."

It was nearly two in the morning when the sheriff finally released us. Stony insisted on going home with Jonelle 'for protection'. Initially, Mal demanded that he and Blaine stay with me but changed his mind when he found out I only had one guest bed.

I hugged Jonelle good-bye. "I'll call you tomorrow."

"I'm sorry tonight ended like it did," she stated.

"Not your fault. I'm glad you're okay."

She squeezed me tighter. "Me too."

Mal, Blaine, and I were packed into the back of a cruiser and driven to my house. By the time I made the guest bed and put blankets and pillows on the couch, it was after three and I could barely keep my eyes open.

"Okay, you two, I'll let you MTV Deathmatch for the bed. I need some sleep. You know where the kitchen and bathrooms are. Make yourself at home."

I trudged upstairs and managed to go through the motions of washing my face and brushing my teeth. The only reason I bothered to put on pajamas was because I had two men in my house, otherwise I would have been too tired to care.

Despite the strange and frightening events of the night, I was asleep as soon as my head hit the pillow.

CHAPTER 33

I COULD HEAR someone moving around downstairs when I woke up and, for a horrifying split second, I thought the person who tried to shoot us was back. Gasping, I sat up in bed, clutching the blanket to my chest.

Fear washed away the last dredges of sleepiness and I reached for my phone. Then I remembered that Mal and Blaine had stayed the night.

Sighing in relief, I flopped back against the mattress. I lay there for a few moments, waiting for my heart to return to its normal rhythm.

The scent of coffee drifting into the room got me moving. I rolled out of bed and headed into my bathroom for a shower.

Twenty minutes later, I came down the stairs to find Blaine still asleep on the couch, snoring. He didn't stir as I walked past the sofa. I found Mal in the kitchen, pouring two cups of coffee.

"Hey," he greeted.

"Morning." I grabbed the half and half out of the fridge and walked over to the counter.

"Thanks," he said as he took the carton from me.

I added sugar and then half and half to my cup as well. "Thank you for making coffee."

He smiled. "After the night we had, I figured we could use it."

"Yeah. It's weird though, I went right to sleep and slept hard."

"Well, you didn't sleep long. It's only nine."

I shrugged. "Once I woke up, I couldn't go back to sleep. Especially when I smelled the coffee." We sat at the kitchen table together. "You didn't sleep long either," I pointed out.

Mal shrugged and drank more coffee. "I don't sleep much anyway."

"Well, what do you want for breakfast?" I asked. "I can throw something together."

"You don't need to cook for us," he argued.

"No, but I'm hungry and it's almost impossible to cook for only one person."

He laughed. "Okay."

I perused my fridge and realized I was going to need to grocery shop soon. I did have bread, eggs, and milk, so I decided to make French toast.

As I mixed the eggs and milk with cinnamon and vanilla, I asked Mal, "How long do you think it'll take for the sheriff to run the ballistics test?"

He shook his head. "I'm not sure. They probably don't have a facility here and they'll have to send the weapons to Fort Worth or Dallas. It could be a couple days. It could be a couple weeks."

I tried not to let the worry show on my face, but Mal, ever observant, noticed it anyway.

"You'll be safe, Zoe. I'll make sure of it."

"It's not just that," I explained. "I'm worried that Sheriff Daughtry is going to let his personal feelings toward me prevent him from doing what he should."

Mal shook his head. "I don't think so. But I do think he wants to get all the facts."

I hummed in the back of my throat, but didn't respond.

"Zoe, this will all be resolved, one way or another. We can call someone else for help if the sheriff refuses to do his job," Mal reassured me.

"Someone shot at us last night, Mal! Who's to say we survive long enough to do that?"

He got up and came over to me, putting his hands on my shoulders. "We will. I'll make sure of it."

"Do you think that it was Dwyer in the truck last night?"

Mal nodded. "I'm almost positive after what the sheriff said."

"How did he know where we were?" I asked.

"I'm betting he followed me here from the bar the night he hit me. He's probably been watching us for a few days, trying to figure out how much we really know and trying to decide what he should do. I think last night wasn't planned. It was sloppy and he was taken by surprise when he realized I was armed. He saw an opportunity and, since it worked on Hank twenty years ago, he tried to kill us the same way."

My skin chilled at his words. Dwyer didn't care that his actions could have killed five people, three of which knew nothing about this situation.

"But for all he knew, Jonelle, Stony, and Blaine weren't in-volved."

"Murder doesn't have a statute of limitation, Zoe. I think he's afraid of what we might know and he wants to be sure that we can't share it if we haven't already."

I shook my head. "What a dick."

Mal released my shoulders and went back to the table. "I can't argue with you there."

"So what do we do in the meantime?" I queried.

Shrugging, Mal answered, "Work and wait. Unfortunately, we can't leave until the sheriff returns our van, so we're stuck filming here. I'll need a ride into Weatherford to rent another van for a few days." He glanced at me. "Do you mind?"

I shook my head and went back to cooking the French toast.

"One other thing," he stated. When I looked up, he continued, "I'll be staying here until Dwyer is arrested."

"You don't have to do that," I argued. "I have my shotgun and I'm angry enough to use it on Dwyer if he shows up."

"I'm still staying," he insisted.

"You don't have a gun right now," I pointed out.

"Yes, but I can take care of myself without it, too."

I sighed. I had to admit, at least to myself, that the idea of having him here assuaged most of my fears. "Fine."

"I'll help with the cooking and cleaning," he promised. "And I'm not a complete slob."

I laughed. "I'm holding you to that."

"Coffee," Blaine moaned as he stumbled into the kitchen from the living room. "Must. Have. Coffee."

Grinning, I poured him a cup. "Do you want some French toast?" I asked.

Blaine squinted at me. "Are you an angel from Heaven?" he mumbled.

I chuckled as I flipped the last piece of bread in the egg mixture. "Nope. Just cooking breakfast. Mal made the coffee."

Blaine responded with a grunt as he collapsed into a chair at the kitchen table.

"Sorry about Blaine," Mal apologized. "He's not a morning person."

"I can see that," I quipped.

By the time I set a plate of French toast in front of him, Blaine's eyes were mostly open.

"Will you marry me?"

I laughed. "No way. I'm saving myself for Tom Hiddleston."

"Okay, you and Tom wanna adopt a grown son?"

"You're older than me, Blaine," I chuckled.

"So?"

Shaking my head I went back to the stove to make myself a plate. By the time I sat at the table, Blaine had finished his.

"Seriously, I'm handsome, independently wealthy, and reasonably hygienic. Are you sure you won't marry me?" Blaine asked.

"Nope. I don't care about money and there's no such thing as reasonably hygienic."

Blaine sighed. "Fine. I'm going to take a shower then."

"Uh…"

Mal grinned at me. "Stony brought us clothes. Don't worry. Blaine won't be walking around your house naked."

"Okay, that's good. There are clean towels under the sink," I called to Blaine as he dumped his dirty dishes in the sink.

He lifted a hand in acknowledgement as he left the kitchen.

Teri materialized right behind Mal's chair. "Did he say he was going to take a shower?"

I glared at her and gave my head a small shake, telling her without words not to do what I knew she was thinking.

"Don't you look at me like that. Do you know how long it's been since I've seen a naked man? Thirty years!"

"Teri," I warned.

"Fine, fine. I'll look but I won't touch okay."

Before I could reply, she disappeared. Shit.

I sighed and found Mal looking at me, his fork poised in mid-air.

"Was Teri in here?" he asked.

I nodded. "How do you think Blaine feels about spectral voyeurs?"

Mal burst into laughter. "What he doesn't know won't hurt him."

"If you say so," I agreed mildly. I had a feeling that Teri would figure out how to make her presence known somehow.

A few minutes later, an ear-piercing male yell came from upstairs. "Oh my God, who's grabbing my ass?"

I tried. I really did. I managed to contain the laughter until I glanced at Mal. Then retaining any sort of dignity was impossible. I howled and cackled until tears ran down my face.

There was no way life would ever be boring with this odd trio.

Unfortunately, my good mood was dampened when my phone rang and I saw my father's name on the screen. He'd probably heard about what happened last night. He had friends in the department and some of his work buddies sometimes listened to the police scanner. Like it was a hobby.

I hadn't thought about calling him when I got home this morning because I was so exhausted I could barely function. Though I doubted that explanation would fly when I shared it with my father.

Taking a deep breath, I answered the phone, "Hey, Dad."

"You're alive," he declared baldly.

"I'm sorry, Dad. Really. It was so late when the sheriff released us from the scene that I came straight home and went to bed."

"You should have called me."

"I know. I'm sorry."

My father exhaled and said, "Don't ever scare me like that again, baby. And if something *does* happen, please call me as soon as it does."

My heart hurt, the sharp ache caused by guilt and remorse. "I will. I promise."

"I love you, Zoe."

My eyes began to burn as the memory of last night returned, the fear and knowledge that my life might well end. "I love you too, Daddy."

He cleared his throat, but when he spoke, his voice was still rough. "Now, I want you to tell me what happened."

I sniffed and took a moment to gather my composure, then I did as he said.

CHAPTER

3|4

AFTER HEARING ABOUT what happened, my father wanted me to move back home with him and my mother, but I refused. I didn't want to put my parents in danger.

"Zoe, I want you home where I can make sure you're safe."

"Dad, Mal is staying with me. I promise, I'll be fine."

"Honey, I have a shotgun and a thirty-eight. You'll be safer here with me," he argued.

"Mal has a gun too, Dad. I'm not moving home and putting you and mom in danger." I didn't mention that the gun in question was currently in the possession of the sheriff's department. For all I knew, Mal had another weapon stashed away. "And you bought me a shotgun when I got the house, remember?"

He paused after that. "Okay, well, I feel a little bit better knowing he's armed too, but does he know how to shoot?"

"He's licensed to carry a concealed weapon. He had to take a class."

My dad sighed and I knew that he was going to let the argument go for the moment. "Okay, but if anything else happens, I won't take no for an answer. You'll be moving back into your room until the sheriff gets it straightened out."

I hadn't mentioned the things that the sheriff had said to me, or his accusation that Mal, our friends, and I were making this up.

My dad was usually a laid back guy, but if he heard about what the sheriff had said, he would lose his temper. I didn't want to think about what he might say or do if that happened.

I also didn't want to think about what my mother would say if my dad got arrested. She would definitely blame me, and our relationship was so tenuous right now that I doubted it would survive something like that.

In the end, I decided it was best not to mention the sheriff's allegations to my dad and focus on reassuring him. I also promised to check in daily.

Now, all Mal and I could do was wait.

Three days after the accident, Mal got sick of biding his time, expecting the sheriff to get back to him. He'd called and left message after message, but no one called us back. He was still staying with me and Stony and Blaine were staying with Jonelle.

"If we're stuck here, we might as well work," he finally declared.

The work consisted of filming promo footage of me and assembling bits and pieces from the episodes to add to the intro for the show now that I was a permanent addition. Jonelle insisted on doing my hair and make-up for the trailers and teasers that Mal wanted to film.

When she saw the first episode of me on camera, she turned to me and said, "From now on, you need to wear makeup when you film."

"I did!"

"Wear more," she stated.

It took several days of intense work to get it all finished, but once it was done, I was pleased with how it looked.

Mal also took the time to show me the show's social media pages and group email account. When he found out I didn't have any personal pages of my own, he insisted that I set them up so that viewers could contact me if they wanted to.

I didn't complain too much because Jonelle had been on me for several years to set up a Facepage or Instashoot account or whatever the heck they were called. She willingly helped me create the accounts and set up my first few posts. Then I discovered a website called Pinterest and promptly spent the next three hours looking up recipes and decor ideas for my house.

By the time we completed everything, it was time for the episode they shot in my house to go online.

I decided that everyone should come over and watch the show on my smart TV. I would cook dinner and we would relax.

Between work and the silence from the sheriff's office, the last week had been hectic and tense. We all needed to blow off steam.

By six o'clock on the night the show was to go live, everyone was crowded around my kitchen table. Even Teri had joined us, despite the fact that I was the only one who could see or hear her. As I often did, I found myself acting as a sort of translator between her and Jonelle, and eventually the others.

It was fun. We ate, drank, and laughed. It was how I always wanted family dinners to be at my house growing up.

As an after dinner treat, I'd made chocolate cake with vanilla ice cream and suggested we eat dessert in the living room while we watched.

Jonelle, Stony, and Blaine headed into the living room and Mal helped me gather the bowls of cake and ice cream.

"You know, we don't usually watch the show the night it's scheduled to go live," he mentioned casually. "We've watched it so many times during the screening process that we're sick of the footage."

"Are you saying you think this was a stupid idea?" I asked, wondering if Stony and Blaine felt the same.

He studied my face for a moment. "I don't think any idea you could have would be stupid, Zoe. This has been fun, I just didn't want you thinking that you had to do something like this every week. You might not be tired of it yet, but you might feel differently in a few weeks or months."

I shook my head. "No way. We worked hard on these episodes. We should celebrate them."

Mal smiled at me. "Have I mentioned lately that I'm glad you're working with us?" he asked.

"Nope. But I believe you might have pointed that out several times yesterday," I quipped.

"Well, I am glad."

Until recently I hadn't realized how foreign the feeling of happiness was to me. It had been so long since I was genuinely unfettered and happy that I'd forgotten the sensation.

In the last few weeks, my eyes had been opened and I wanted to hold onto this feeling for as long as possible.

As we ate cake and ice cream, I pulled up the YouTube app on my smart TV and found the episode.

"Y'all ready?" I asked.

There was a chorus of agreement and I started the show. My heart raced as the opening credits played and I saw myself on-screen. It was strange to be watching myself on TV.

As Mal began his introduction for the episode, my doorbell rang. Without thinking I got to my feet and moved to answer the door.

Before I took more than two steps, Mal's hand curved around my elbow and he pulled me to a stop.

"Let me answer the door," he insisted.

I nodded my agreement and stood behind him as he glanced out the side window.

"You have got to be shitting me," he muttered under his breath, unlocking the door and throwing it open. "Good evening, Sheriff Daughtry. What can I do for you?"

The sheriff didn't seem surprised to see him. "I'd like to speak to you for a moment," he declared.

I followed Mal out onto the porch. Sheriff Daughtry's eyes flicked to me, but he didn't say anything about my joining them.

He removed his hat and rubbed the back of his neck. "I received the preliminary results from the ballistics test and neither of the weapons you had on the scene matched the spent rounds." He looked as though he had something else to say, but he stopped speaking.

"Is that all?" Mal asked.

The sheriff took a deep breath. "I...well, I went to Steven Dwyer's residence today and he appears to be gone. When I contacted his employer, they told me that they hadn't seen him since last week."

"Really?" Mal asked.

"He hasn't been into work since the day you were run off the road," he commented.

"What a coincidence." Sarcasm dripped from Mal's words.

"Look, I had to consider every possibility on the scene that night. You come to me, accusing an upstanding member of the community of murder without proof, and then a few days later you're shot at and run off the road by a vehicle that matches the description of his vehicle. It was suspicious," the sheriff replied defensively.

"Of course it was. There's no reason that we could have been attacked because I confronted Dwyer with the fact that I knew he committed murder."

I glanced away from the sheriff's face because the exasperation so clearly written in his expression made me want to laugh.

Sighing heavily, the sheriff continued speaking without responding to that statement. "I wanted you to be aware that we're actively looking for Steven Dwyer. No one has seen his wife since last week either, so we believe they may be together."

"In other words, we should watch our backs?" Mal asked.

"I only wanted to notify you that you'll be able to pick up your weapon at the sheriff's department in two days and that you should be aware that we have yet to make contact with Dwyer."

"Thank you, Sheriff. I'm assuming that Zoe and I are on our own when it comes to protecting ourselves," Mal replied.

I could practically hear the sheriff's teeth grinding at the antagonistic attitude that Mal was exhibiting. "I'll arrange for deputies to drive by Ms. Thorne's house and the hotel several times a day."

"I'm sure that will be very effective."

I hid my snort of amusement behind a cough before I said, "Thank you, Sheriff Daughtry. I appreciate your concern for our safety."

The sheriff's dark eyes narrowed as he weighed my words and the sincerity behind them.

"If you have any questions, please call the department and leave a message. I'll get back to you," he assured us. "Y'all have a good evening."

As he walked out to his car, Mal muttered beneath his breath, "Yeah, just like he *got back to me* on the last six messages I've left for him."

He had a good point.

Mal turned and looked down at me. "It looks like I'll be staying here for a little while longer. That okay with you?"

I shrugged. "Sure, as long as you don't try to make me work twenty-four hours a day. Oh, and you pick up your socks and put the toilet seat down."

Chuckling, Mal wrapped an arm around my shoulders and led me back inside the house.

"I haven't left the toilet seat up since the unfortunate incident of 2010."

"Sat down when the seat was up, didn't you?" I asked smugly.

Mal shuddered. "It was the worst ten seconds of my life."

CHAPTER 35

I WOKE UP later than usual the next day. Probably because my body tensed at every little sound or creak, as my anxiety-ridden brain interpreted the noises as the furtive footsteps of a psychopathic murderer.

When I came downstairs, I could hear Mal talking to someone in the kitchen. My feet stopped abruptly as I entered and saw who sat at the table across from him.

"Hey, Zoe," Mal greeted me. "Your mom didn't want me to wake you. We've been getting to know each other."

My mother folded her hands on the tabletop. "Yes, we have."

While my mother preferred to use many words to get her point across, she could also do a damn good job with just three or four. I wondered what she was doing here. When I hadn't heard from her after I'd nearly died, I assumed that meant we were no longer on speaking terms. Period.

"Uh, hi, Mom. How are you?"

"I'm doing well, thank you."

Mal brought me a cup of coffee. I thanked him as I reached for it and took a sip. It surprised me to discover that he'd added half and half and sugar, exactly how I liked it.

I glanced at him with wide eyes, but he was already heading toward the living room.

"I'll give you two a little privacy," he stated.

Bemused, I watched him leave the kitchen. He knew that my relationship with my mom wasn't the best, I'd mentioned it in passing more than once, yet he'd waltzed out of here without a care in the world.

Apparently, he would protect me from a threatening sheriff but not an overbearing parent. Then I frowned when I realized that I expected him to protect me at all. I decided to worry about it later because right now, I had a bigger problem sitting to my left.

I sipped my coffee again and my eyes darted to my mother. I knew I should say something, but I had no idea what.

As the silence between us grew longer and longer, I finally blurted out the first thing that came to my mind. "I'm not sleeping with Mal."

From her withering glare, I realized that was exactly what she was thinking after finding Mal in my home so early in the morning.

"I didn't say you were," she answered primly. "Though it's probably best if you don't since you do have to *work* with him now."

The tone of voice she used when she said "work" made the nape of my neck prickle with irritation.

"Are you here to lecture me about my career and relationship choices?" I asked, focused on keeping my words even and calm.

My mother sighed. "No, I'm not." She paused, toying with the handle of her coffee mug. Finally, she cleared her throat. "I'm here to apologize."

Convinced I'd hallucinated the last statement, I asked, "What?"

The look my mother flashed me was scathing. "I said I'm here to apologize."

"Uh, okay. I wasn't sure I heard you correctly," I explained.

When I didn't speak again, her lips pursed tightly, as though she'd just eaten something sour. "I'm sorry."

I wasn't sure if she was apologizing for everything that had happened between us in the last few years, or just for the fight we had a couple of weeks ago, but it didn't matter. My mother *never* apologized. At least not to my father or me.

She probably never would again.

"I'm sorry that I lost my temper," I replied.

She blinked at my words and I realized that she hadn't expected me to reciprocate. I tried to remember the last time I'd apologized to my mother for anything and couldn't think of a single instance. It was a similarity between us that made me uncomfortable now that I was aware of it.

Mom tilted her head in a sharp nod. "Apology accepted."

And just like that, it was over. I wondered if she would be able to bite her tongue when she thought I was making the wrong decision.

We drank our coffee in awkward silence for a few minutes before my mother spoke again.

"Malachi seems like a very nice young man," she commented. "Not at all what I expected."

Intrigued, I asked, "What did you expect?"

"Just…someone a little less mature, I suppose."

"You mean you expected him to be a total loser who still lived with his mom, right?"

A smile tugged at the corners of her mouth. "Maybe."

"He studied history at Baylor. The other two men on our team studied film and art history at Baylor. They met their freshmen year. They're very intelligent, even if they are a bit eccentric."

My mother studied my expression. "You look so happy just talking about them. Happier than I've seen you look in a long time."

I nodded. "I am. I wasn't necessarily unhappy before, but I didn't enjoy my job the way I enjoy working on the show."

"I, uh, watched the episode last night. I must admit it was interesting. Especially when that odd medium woman was sprayed in the face with the shower. I'm just glad that your…resident ghost didn't pull a similar prank on me."

I struggled to keep the shock from showing on my face. My mother admitted not only that Teri was real but that she was glad she hadn't done something mean to her.

"Well, Teri wasn't pleased with how the medium was, um, representing her. Or that the medium was a complete fake and con artist."

"She did seem a bit over the top," Mom admitted.

"A bit?"

My mother chuckled. "More than a bit." She got up and refilled her coffee cup. "I'm looking forward to watching the first episode with you in it," she stated.

I couldn't believe that my mother intended to keep watching the show. Then I remembered what happened during the first episode.

"Um, Mom, I might need to warn you about the next show." When she didn't speak up, I continued, "We filmed it in the cemetery in Springtown, the one with the glowing headstone," I began. "And, well, something happened while we were there."

Her eyebrows lifted. "Do I really want to know?"

"Probably not, but I don't want you to get an unpleasant shock," I admitted.

"I think I know," my mother replied, bringing her coffee cup back to the table. "It never happened to me, but I could always feel them when I went to a graveyard as a child. The dead."

I blinked rapidly. My mother's complete change in attitude was throwing me for a loop. Just a few weeks ago, she would have had a coronary if I mentioned feeling a connection to the dead, much less raising a zombie.

"You did?"

Nodding, she took another sip of her coffee. "It was an odd sensation. It was like their souls were watching from a distance, just waiting for a chance to talk to me."

"I know exactly how that feels," I said. "It's the same after the sun sets, only stronger. It's as if they can reach out then. Sometimes they do, you know, come to talk to me."

"Their spirits?" my mother asked.

I shook my head. "Not quite. It's like an echo of their personality is there, but it's faint. But sometimes the newer graves, they…" I trailed off.

Her eyes widened and she put a hand to her throat. "They what?"

I bit my bottom lip, not sure how to break it to my mother that I was some sort of zombie commander.

"Let's just say, the bodies sometimes come to visit me."

"Come to visit you?" she asked, an odd expression on her face.

"Well, the graves open up and then the body climbs out," I explained in a rush. "You might call them zombies."

"Oh my God," she whispered.

"That never happened to you?" I asked.

She shook her head, lifting her hand from her throat to cover her mouth.

"It only happens after dark," I said quickly.

"I've never been to a graveyard after dark," my mother admitted.

"It's not my favorite thing." I glanced at my mother. "I want to ask you something, but I'm afraid you won't want to answer."

"You can ask me," she replied, "but I can't promise that I'll want to talk about it."

"Do you ever miss it?" I asked.

"Miss what?"

"Being able to see spirits, talk to them."

My mother hesitated, staring down into her cup. "It's been a long time, Zoe. I haven't seen a ghost since I started high school. At the time I was incredibly relieved because it meant that your grandma would stop punishing me." Her eyes flicked to me. "Your dad told you about your grandma, right?"

I nodded.

"I was glad that it was gone. I have been for years."

I wondered if that was why she freaked out when she realized that I inherited her ability, but I didn't ask aloud. I could tell that my mother had a difficult time discussing this and the peace we'd established was too new for me to test it just yet. I wanted to be able to talk to my mother.

She smiled, but it seemed sad. "I thought that your life might be easier if I could discourage you from using your gifts, because I honestly felt mine was better. But lately I've begun to wonder if that was true."

"I used to think my life would be less challenging if I didn't have these gifts," I replied. "But for the past few weeks, I've been glad."

"I know this may be hard to believe, honey, but I've always wanted you to be happy. I just didn't think about the fact that your version of happiness wouldn't be the same as my own."

My throat tightened at her words, but I didn't want to be sad. This was a first for my mother and me. We were communicating.

"Oh my God, Mom," I gasped.

Eyes wide, she straightened, "What's wrong?"

"We sound—" I paused for effect. "Normal. Quick, tell me I'm making a poor life choice."

She stared at me for a moment then she laughed. "It's not that unusual for us to get along is it?"

I didn't answer verbally, just lifted an eyebrow.

"Well, too bad. I think I like being normal with you," she replied.

"Okay, but let's keep it to a minimum until I get used to it. It's a little scary."

My mother shook her head. "Well, on that note, I have to be going. I have an appointment at the salon." She rose and carried her mug to the sink, rinsing it out before she stuck it in my dishwasher.

I wanted to laugh as I watched her because there were five mugs sitting around the sink that I hadn't bothered to put in the machine. Some things never changed.

I waved to her from the front door as she climbed into her car and drove away. A chill raced up my back making me aware of Teri's presence behind me.

"I thought I heard the voice of Satan. How is your mother?" she asked.

Smiling, I shut the door and faced her. "Different. I think the exorcism took this time."

Teri scowled at me. "Aw man, does this mean I have to be *nice* to her when she comes over?"

I glared at her. "Teri, she can't see or hear you."

"Yeah, but the next thing you know you're gonna make me stop moving her car keys or putting bugs in her purse."

"Oh my God, don't you dare!"

"See what I mean?" she asked, crossing her arms over her chest. "It's started already."

CHAPTER
36

LATER THAT AFTERNOON, I was stretched out on the couch, reading a Regency romance, while Mal worked in my kitchen.

I'd never realized how much work filming a YouTube show could be until Mal moved into my house. He was constantly on the computer or the phone, scheduling shoots, editing scripts, or doing any number of things that needed doing.

I tried to stay out of his way, but it was beginning to drive me a little nuts. Though he was professional, he was completely disorganized and he could be a great deal more efficient. I just had to figure out how to broach the subject with him.

"We have to talk," Mal said, coming out of the kitchen.

I lowered my book to look at him. "About what?"

"It's easier if I just show you," he replied. "Come take a look at something in the kitchen."

Frowning, I replaced my bookmark and followed him into the kitchen. I shook my head at the state of my table. There were notebooks, papers, and other miscellaneous items everywhere. I shuddered to think what the desk in his home office might look like.

"What am I looking at?" I asked.

"This," he answered, pointing toward the computer screen.

It was the number of subscribers to our channel on YouTube.

"Wow, we have one hundred thousand YouTube subscribers?" I asked.

"We didn't."

"I don't follow," I stated, confused by his words.

"Zoe, since the show aired last night with all the promo information about you and next week's episode, we've gained fifty thousand followers."

"What?" I asked incredulously.

"Since announcing that you joined the show and posting that short clip of you from next week's episode, we've grown by fifty thousand subscribers."

"That can't be right." I shook my head. "Maybe you misread the numbers before or something."

Mal gave me a pointed look. "We've been hovering just above fifty-two thousand for months. Nothing I did seemed to help us grow. Now that you've joined the show, our subscriber numbers have doubled. It's amazing! People are already talking about you on the social media pages."

I felt the blood drain from my face. "They're talking about *me*? What are they saying?"

He shrugged. "The usual. That it's cool you can see ghosts. That they're glad there's a girl in the group now." He cleared his throat. "And maybe a few comments about how hot you are," he mumbled, his voice dropping almost to a whisper.

"What?" I cried, sitting down in front of the laptop and reading the comments on the YouTube video. My cheeks felt hot as I toggled over to *The Wraith Files* Facebook page and started reading the posts there.

"Oh, my God," I muttered, propping my head on my hands. "I can't believe this."

Mal patted my shoulder. "Hey, don't get so upset. It's a good thing."

"A good thing?" I asked, my head popping up. "Have you *read* some of these comments? One guy wants to do something unspeakable to my…my…I can't even say it!"

Mal blanched. "Yeah, well there's always a few weirdos." He leaned around me, his hands flying over the keys on the keyboard. "I think I'll just block him right now though, because that really was nasty."

"Am I going to end up with a stalker? Because I can't have a stalker, Mal. My stress level is too high at the moment with a murderer trying to kill us yet police can't find him. A stalker would drive me right over the edge!"

Mal squatted down beside me, putting a hand on each of my shoulders. "Breathe, Zoe. Take a deep breath. You will not have a stalker. These are just trolls."

"Trolls? Do they live under a damned bridge?"

He shook his head and sighed. "It's a term used to describe someone who makes outrageous and derogatory comments on social media posts. They don't really mean it."

"Then why would they write that?"

"To elicit a response. A strong response. Please try not to let them get to you. I'll delete any wildly inappropriate comments. I promise."

I took a deep, shuddering breath. "Okay, okay. You're right. It's the Internet, people post things they would never say otherwise, right?"

Mal nodded.

"I still think I need a drink," I muttered.

"Well, it's after noon, so I don't think we'll go to Hell for drinking a couple beers."

A few hours later, after three hard ciders and a lot of deep breathing, I was feeling much better about the situation.

"Am I going to be a celebrity?" I asked Mal as we lounged on my sofa and watched television.

I was feeling a little giddy as I popped the cap on my fourth hard cider, otherwise I never would have asked.

"Maybe," Mal answered.

I burrowed deeper into the couch cushions, my shoulder bumping his. "I'm not sure I want to be a celebrity," I grumbled. "The *paparazzi* sucks."

Mal laughed. "I don't think you'll have to worry about the *paparazzi* unless a network picks up the show."

I twisted my head around so I could stare at him with wide eyes. "A network? Like who?"

Shrugging, he replied, "I'm not sure. My agent is talking to almost everyone...Bravo, Syfy, A&E, AMC, and a bunch of others. There wasn't a lot of interest before, but with the amount of attention the latest episode is getting, we may finally get somewhere."

I gaped at him. "Bravo? Syfy? Those are all huge networks you're talking about!"

"Yeah, but there's no guarantee they'll want us."

"Okay," I nodded as I spoke. "So, no freaking out yet?"

"Not yet," he stated.

We watched TV for a little while longer, until I could barely keep my eyes open.

"All right, I have to go to bed," I declared, shoving myself to my feet. While I didn't stumble, it was a near thing. That hard cider had gone straight to my head.

"Don't forget that we have to go pick up my gun at the sheriff's department tomorrow," Mal called out to me as I trudged up the stairs.

I waved a hand in acknowledgement, but kept climbing without a word. After my sleepless night yesterday, I had no trouble falling into a deep, dreamless slumber.

CHAPTER

37

"FOR FUCK'S SAKE, of all the nights for you to sleep like a drunken sailor on shore leave," Teri muttered.

My face felt cold, as though someone had held ice against my cheek for too long.

"Goddammit, Zoe, wake the fuck up!" she yelled.

My eyes popped open and I sat straight up in bed. Before I could yell at her for scaring the shit out of me, she lifted a finger to her lips.

"Shhhh, there are people in the house. You have to get out of here."

Still feeling foggy from sleep, I fought my way free of the blankets on my bed.

"That's fine, Zoe. Don't worry about being quiet. You want them to know you're awake and trying to escape," she spat sarcastically.

I didn't respond verbally, but shot her a withering glare as I crept toward the bedroom door.

"What are you doing?" she asked. "You need to go out the window and go over to Preston's. He's home. I watched him jerk o…I mean, get dressed earlier."

I grimaced at her slip. There were some things a person just didn't need to know about her neighbor.

"What about Mal?" I whispered as quietly as possible.

She shook her head. "He fell asleep on the couch. They had him tied up before his eyes were open all the way."

"Who?"

Teri shrugged. "I'm not sure. Her name's Trisha, that much I heard."

My heart began to pound in earnest. It had to be Trisha and Steven Dwyer. On bare feet, I padded down the hallway to the mouth of the stairs, Teri trailing behind me.

"Zoe, seriously, you need to leave!" she cried out behind me.

I squatted down and peeked around the railing. I could see Mal's jean-clad legs and bare feet and the top of Trisha Dwyer's head. It was definitely her.

"Steve, we need to go get the girl," she insisted, her voice little more than a hiss. "She could have woken up."

"I know, Trish, but I need to make sure this guy is tied up before I go upstairs for her."

Trisha sighed loudly, but didn't argue anymore.

Moving carefully, I backed away from the stairs on my hands and knees. When I knew I wouldn't be seen, I climbed to my feet. I wanted to go downstairs and help Mal, but that would be stupid because I knew nothing about self-defense and I was unarmed. The shotgun I'd bragged to Mal about was hidden in the coat closet by the front door. My best bet was to do as Teri suggested and climb out my bedroom window. Preston was a tough, muscular firefighter. He could help me, or at least act as a deterrent so I could call the police.

Instinctively, I avoided the boards in the wood floor that squeaked, and went to the window. It had been a long time since I'd tried to open it. As I tugged on the sash, it got stuck about an inch from the bottom.

I gritted my teeth as adrenaline flooded my body in response to this new obstacle. Carefully, I lowered the window then tried again. The sash made it up three inches before it stopped, but now it was completely stuck. I couldn't close it or open it further.

As I fought with it, the window squeaked. Sucking in a sharp gasp, I stood perfectly still, waiting to see if Steve and Trisha would come pounding up the stairs.

Nothing.

The only other window in the room had more than a twelve foot drop straight to the ground. This one opened up over the roof that stretched out over the back porch. The distance from the roof to the ground was a lot smaller.

I was going to have to force the window open and make a run for it. I didn't have time to waste. Steve was going to finish tying Mal up any second and come for me.

I pulled in a breath and yanked up on the window with all my might. Wood squealed and shrieked as the glass flew up, crashing into the top of the window frame.

Without waiting for a reaction from the intruders, I threw my leg over the window sill, realizing too late that I should have stopped to put on shoes. There was no time now.

As I shimmied out the window, I could hear footsteps thundering on the stairs.

"Dammit."

At Steven Dwyer's curse, I slipped and slid down the pitch of the roof, gasping as the rough shingles cut into my bare feet and legs.

"Trisha, she's going out the back."

When I reached the edge of the roofline, I crept over to the border that hung above the back porch. I lowered myself over the edge, my toes brushing the top of the wooden railing.

I let go too quickly and lost my balance, falling backward into the shrubs around my house.

I barely felt the sharp twigs as they bit into my legs, tearing my flesh. Scrambling to my feet, I rounded the back porch and headed toward the front of the house. Maybe if I could get in view of my neighbors and start screaming, it might draw enough attention to scare off Steve and Trisha.

I made it three steps before an enormous weight hit my back, knocking the breath out of me as it crushed me to the ground.

I tried to suck in air to scream, but my lungs refused to work. Hard, rough hands grasped my arms and flipped me over onto my back.

In horror, I stared up into Steven Dwyer's enraged face. He must have been handsome once, but the excessive drinking and misery from his marriage had ruined his looks, just as they'd ruined Trisha's.

"Bitch," he snarled, pulling his arm back.

Before I could lift my hands to protect my face, his fist descended and the world exploded into a flash of multi-colored lights, followed by darkness.

CHAPTER 38

MY CHEEKBONE THROBBED where it was pressed into the carpet of my living room. I couldn't hold back the moan that spilled from my throat. My head hurt so badly that I wanted to cry.

I tried to lift a hand to my face to check my cheekbone, but it wouldn't move. Opening my eyes into thin slits, I tried to take stock of my surroundings.

Then the memories came rushing back.

My eyelids flew open and I found myself face to face with Mal. His brown eyes were focused intently on me.

"Oh God, Zoe, I thought you were dead," he whispered, his voice so quiet it was nearly soundless.

I tried to speak but my mouth was so dry that my tongue felt glued to the roof of my mouth.

"I don't understand what you're waiting for," Trisha Dwyer bitched. "They know everything and we just broke into their house. If we leave them alive, they'll tell the sheriff and our asses are in jail for the next twenty years to life."

My eyes widened at her words. Mal's expression mirrored mine.

"Well excuse me for hesitating to kill two innocent people, Trisha," Steve barked.

"I don't understand why you're stalling. You've done it before.

How hard is it to do it again?"

"You forget that the only reason I did it before, Trisha, is because *you* told me that Hank beat the shit out of you when you told him you were pregnant with my child and you were leaving. You told me that he said he'd kill you before he let you leave. That you lost the baby. Our baby." There was a short silence. "But it was all a fucking lie, wasn't it? You just wanted that big, fat life insurance policy."

"Shut the fuck up," she snapped.

"For the last eighteen years, you've made my life nothing but misery, Trisha, so excuse me if I'm not pissing myself with joy at the idea of killing two more people because you fucking want me to!" he roared.

"Keep your voice down, Steve! Do you want the neighbors to call the cops?"

"I just don't understand why you didn't do the same thing to me, Trisha. Couldn't you find another dumb redneck to do your dirty work?"

There was no response. Mal and I stared at each other in utter shock and terror.

"You couldn't, could you?" Steve asked with a bitter laugh. "But you tried, didn't you?"

Suddenly, I felt something cold around my ankles, working at the rope that Dwyer had used to tie my legs. I couldn't see her, but I felt Teri's presence at my back. As the ropes loosened, I sighed in relief.

Teri, I mouthed to Mal. He looked confused but I didn't have time to explain.

"Steve, you know we don't have a choice. This will be the last time. After these two are gone, we can leave. You don't have to stay with me. It'll all be over," she wheedled.

"Hurry, Teri," I breathed.

"I'm hurrying, I'm hurrying," she muttered. "Do you know how hard I have to concentrate to touch these fucking ropes?"

A few seconds later, the ropes around my wrists fell away. Mal watched incredulously.

"Knife. Right pocket," he whispered.

I nodded my understanding, glancing up to see that Steve and Trisha's backs were to us. I wouldn't get a better opportunity to free Mal.

Quickly, I slid my hand into his pocket and pulled his pocketknife free. I opened it, praying that it wouldn't click or make any other sort of sound.

God was on my side because it opened soundlessly. It cut through Mal's bonds easily.

As he rolled into a sitting position, he nodded toward the front door. Steve and Trisha were still talking, but their voices were quieter now.

I rose to my feet and ran toward the front door. In that moment, fear had driven away my ability to think clearly. Otherwise, I would have yanked the shotgun out of the closet and taken aim at the couple from Hell.

"Steve! They're getting away!" Trisha yelled.

I glanced back over my shoulder in time to see Dwyer lift his arm, a pistol gripped in his hand and aimed right at Mal.

"No!" I screamed, watching helplessly.

Just before Steve pulled the trigger, Teri appeared at his side, shoving at his arm with both hands.

The shot went wide, embedding itself into the wall. Mal didn't hesitate. He lunged forward, grasping Steve Dwyer's wrist with one hand as his other fist plowed into his nose.

Even from across the room, I could hear the crunch of the bones as the older man cried out in pain.

I saw Trisha fumbling with her pocket and realized she was

armed as well. There wasn't time to run for the coat closet. Terrified and desperate, I grabbed the first thing I saw, which was one of the antique brass bookends on a table beside me.

"Trisha!" I yelled.

When her head whipped around, I hurled the heavy object at her from just a few feet away. She didn't have time to evade and the bookend caught her in the shoulder.

Crying out, she stumbled and fell to the floor. I dashed over to her, landing on her back in the same manner in which Steven had taken me down earlier. I heard the wind go out of her lungs in a rushing groan.

Before she could recover, I drove my hands into her shoulder length hair, grasping two handfuls. I bashed the side of her skull against the hardwood floor, flinching at the hollow thunk. She flailed beneath me and I did it once more, my stomach turning at the sound of her head hitting the wood.

This time, her body went still beneath me.

I quickly dug through her pockets and ran my hands around her waist, finding a small revolver tucked into the front of her jeans.

A pained groan filled the air and I straightened, lifting the gun as I rose. Though I didn't own a handgun, my father made sure I knew how to use one. Just in case, he'd said. After this was over, I was going to thank my father for his paranoia.

It was unnecessary though, because Steven Dwyer collapsed at Mal's feet in an unconscious heap.

Mal stared at me, startled. "I thought you didn't have a hand-gun," he declared.

"It's Trisha's," I replied, lowering the weapon to my side.

"Do you even know how to shoot one of those?" he asked.

"Just because I don't own one doesn't mean I'm clueless. My daddy taught me how to shoot when I was a kid." I glanced down

DON'T WAKE THE DEAD   241

at Trisha's unmoving form. "I suppose one of us better call nine-one-one before they come to."

"You do it." Mal held out a hand. "I'll take the gun and watch these two."

I didn't argue. I didn't want to have to shoot one of them if they woke up and tried to finish what they started.

I ran upstairs and grabbed my cell phone off my nightstand. Teri appeared next to me, tears on her ghostly visage.

"I thought you were going to die," she said brokenly. "I don't think I've been so frightened since I died."

"I'm fine," I soothed her. "Thanks to you. You saved us, Teri." I felt tears fill my own eyes. "I'm so glad you were here."

"Me too," she responded, moving toward me.

Though it tingled like hell, I let her wrap her arms around me. She couldn't feel the contact, not really, but we both needed the comfort of an embrace, even if it was an incomplete one.

"Okay, I have to call the police before those two psychos wake up," I stated, stepping back. My arms and back burned from the cold touch of her energy.

"Can I hang out in your room tonight?" she asked. "After they all leave."

I usually banned her from my bedroom, especially when I was sleeping or dressing, but in this case I would definitely make an exception.

"Absolutely."

CHAPTER

39

THE REST OF the night was a clusterfuck of epic proportions.

A horde of sheriff's deputies descended upon my home. Their squad cars roared up the street, sirens screaming and lights flashing. There were at least six parked around my house, even on my lawn, and several more on the opposite side of the street.

It looked as though every deputy on duty, and even quite a few off duty, had shown up for this call.

If it hadn't been too little, too late, the level of response might have impressed me.

The sheriff himself was one of the first to arrive on scene. By that time, the first deputy on the scene, Deputy Klausen, had called for two ambulances. One for Trisha Dwyer and one for me.

I tried to convince him that I was fine, but he'd merely walked me to the mirror in my foyer so I could see my reflection. At the sight of the red and purple bruising on the left side of my face, extending from my hairline to my chin, I stopped arguing. My cheekbone didn't ache. It *hurt*. The pain increased with each beat of my heart.

My head was pounding and my stomach didn't feel so hot either. As soon as the deputy saw the expression on my face, he guided me to my couch, wrapped a blanket around me, and went in search of something for me to drink.

He returned with a glass of ice water and a bucket.

"What's the bucket for?" I asked blandly.

"In case you need to puke."

I stared at him in consternation. "Why would I need to do that?"

He squatted down in front of me. "I'm pretty sure you have a concussion, Ms. Thorne. Nausea is a common symptom. I thought you might prefer not to run for the bathroom."

Faintly, I nodded, because he was right. My stomach was queasy and I was in no shape to make a mad dash to the bathroom under the stairs if I needed to vomit.

"Could you call my parents please, Deputy Klausen?" I asked softly. "My dad's work buddies listen to the scanner and I don't want one of them to call him with this news."

"I'll have them meet us at the hospital."

I nodded and gingerly leaned back on the couch. I felt someone else sit next to me and turned my head to peek from beneath my lashes. It was Mal.

"Hey," I greeted him, my voice little more than a whisper.

Now that the adrenaline was fading, I could barely stand to talk, the sound of my own voice turned the ache in my skull into excruciating pain.

"Your head hurt?" Mal asked, his voice just as quiet.

"Yeah."

He didn't say anything else, just reached out and curled an arm around my shoulders, pulling me against his side so that my uninjured cheek rested against his chest.

We remained like that until the ambulance arrived.

FOUR HOURS LATER, my headache was better but it was threatening to return to its former glory because of my parents.

"Baby, you need to be home with us so we can keep an eye on you," my father insisted. "The doctor said as much."

"No, he didn't," I argued, keeping my voice low. "He said that someone needed to wake me up every so often. That was it. Mal is going to stay with me tonight. He can do it."

The expression on my father's face would have made me laugh on any other night. Tonight, however, it meant more arguing and I didn't have the energy for it.

"Dad, I'm hurting and nauseated. I'm going to be miserable for at least twenty-four hours. I'd like to experience that misery in the comfort of my own bed, okay? If you guys want to stay with me so you can be sure I'm taken care of, so be it. I just want to go home."

"Zoe," my dad began.

"We'll go home and pack a bag. We'll meet you and Mal at the house," my mother stated, hooking her hand around Dad's arm. "Come on, Jimmy. I need to pick up a few things at the supermarket before we meet them and it'll be opening soon."

I winced at her words, realizing that it was fast approaching six a.m. I just wanted to pop a few pain pills and sleep for a week. Which sucked because the doctor didn't want me to take anything stronger than Tylenol. I also knew that my mother would be waking me up every hour on the hour to make sure I hadn't slipped into a coma, even though the doctor had explained that I needed plenty of rest.

An hour and half later, Mal carried me from the car into the house.

"I can walk," I insisted. "You're injured too. You shouldn't be carrying me."

"I'm not arguing with you about this while you're hurt. So just be quiet."

"Mal—"

"You saved my life, Zoe. I'm carrying your ass into that house and sleeping on the couch for the next few days until you're feeling better. Then we can argue about what you can and can't do for yourself."

I sighed heavily and rested my sore head on his shoulder. I honestly didn't have the strength to argue anyway. The stress and pain had taken their toll. All I wanted was a dark, cool room, a big glass of water, and rest.

"Thank you," he murmured.

"You're lucky I'm too tired to argue," I yawned.

I was fighting sleep as he carried me upstairs and laid me on my bed. My mother didn't speak as she began to help me change my clothes.

"Can I get a glass of ice water?" I asked. "I'm really thirsty."

"Of course, honey," she replied softly.

I curled up beneath the blankets as she left the room, my eyes drifting shut.

"Here you are, Zoe. You need to wake up and drink this so you can take your pills."

I pried my eyelids open and stared blearily at her. "Okay."

I swallowed a couple of Tylenol down with several large sips of water, the frigid liquid soothing my sore throat and dry mouth.

"Thank you," I murmured.

"You're welcome, sweetie," she answered.

I felt the bed shift next to my hip and her cool hand brushing my hair gently from my forehead. It felt wonderful and reminded me of the few times I was sick as a child. My mother always managed to make me feel better just by stroking my hair.

"Zoe," she whispered.

"Yeah, Mom."

"I don't think I could stand it if something happened to you," she breathed. "I love you, baby."

"Love you too, Mama," I replied, turning over onto my side.

Then I stopped fighting and let sleep come.

CHAPTER

40

A HAND TOUCHED my shoulder, waking me from the light doze I'd fallen into.

"Already?" I sighed.

"How are you feeling? Is the headache better?" my mother queried in a low voice.

"Mom, I've told you every hour for the past six that I'm okay. My headache is easing off and the nausea isn't bad as long as I don't move. Can we do this in say, another three hours?" I tried to modulate my tone so that I didn't sound bitchy, but I was exhausted so I wasn't sure that I succeeded. I knew that she had to be as tired as I was and I appreciated that she was concerned, but I knew the best thing for me would be uninterrupted sleep.

She paused. "I'll give you two. If you're doing okay after that, then we'll go for three."

Grateful for the compromise, I said, "That's fine."

"Do you need anything?"

I cracked one eyelid to see my mother hovering over me with Teri floating behind her. "Sleep."

She shook her head. "Fine," she replied with a sigh.

I waited until the door clicked shut before I nestled deeper into the bed and let myself drift off.

When my mother woke me a few hours later, I genuinely felt

better and my stomach had settled almost completely. I could hear the faint sounds of men talking downstairs, but I was too tired to try and eavesdrop. Teri was still standing against the wall, keeping silent watch.

The next time I woke up, I did it on my own. The sun was rapidly setting, the room was dark, and I realized I'd slept the day away. Teri seemed to have abandoned her watch.

Moving slowly, I sat up and swung my legs over the side of the bed. Immediately, my bladder protested. I needed to pee quite badly.

My legs were shaky and weak as I slowly made my way to the bathroom. Once I'd used the facilities and washed my face and hands, I felt a lot better.

Until I looked in the mirror.

I couldn't help it. I started to cry when I saw my face. Though the doctor said that it was a miracle no bones were broken, there was massive bruising and swelling. The entire left side of my face was purple with splotches of black. My left eye was swollen nearly shut.

Seeing the damage that Steven Dwyer had done to my face with one punch, it hit me how lucky I was to be alive and the tears kept falling. If Teri hadn't been able to stop Steve from shooting Mal or I hadn't reacted quickly enough to stop Trisha from pulling her gun, we might both be dead.

I lowered myself onto the edge of my tub and sobbed until there were no tears left. I cried for everything that Hank Murphy had lost, and the relief that I hadn't lost my life as well.

As the storm of emotion ebbed, I rose and staggered to the sink. Grabbing a washcloth, I turned the tap on cold and dampened the material so I could wipe the remnants of my crying jag from my face.

Once that was done, I pulled my hair back into a loose ponytail and went into my bedroom to get dressed. I was just pulling on a pair of light cotton pajama bottoms when my mother stuck her head inside.

"You're up." She seemed surprised.

"Yeah. All I needed was a few solid hours and I feel a lot better."

She came into the room and shut the door behind her. "Do you need help?"

"Nope," I answered. "I'm a little stiff, but I can manage." I walked into my closet and found my oldest, softest t-shirt and a comfortable cotton bra. As I changed, I asked, "What time is it?" I hadn't looked at the clock when I got up.

"After seven," she replied. "Are you hungry? I made chicken soup and homemade rolls for dinner."

At her words my stomach rumbled loudly.

"My stomach says yes," I declared as I emerged from the closet to find that my mother had neatly made my bed and picked up my clothes from the floor. "Mom, you don't have to clean up after me," I insisted. "I can do it."

"You can do it tomorrow or the next day when you're feeling better. Today, I'll do it."

I sighed but didn't argue because I wasn't sure how my head would feel if I had to bend down.

"Thanks for making dinner," I commented as I walked down the stairs behind her.

"It's no trouble at all. I thought your stomach might not tolerate anything heavier."

She was probably right.

As the living room came into view, I saw Mal and my dad sprawled in chairs on opposite ends of the couch and heard the sounds of a football game. My dad's eyes scanned me as I came down the last few steps.

"You're moving better," he stated, getting to his feet.

"I feel better," I responded.

He walked to me and pulled me in for a gentle hug. "What did I tell you about scaring me like that again, Zoe?"

I sighed. "I didn't really have much choice."

His arms tightened around me. "I know, but I don't like knowing that my little girl was in danger and I wasn't here to protect her."

I didn't have to look up to know that he was probably giving Mal a hard look over my head.

"Well, it'll please you to know I'm thinking about getting a dog and maybe a stun gun."

"The dog sounds great, but I think you should keep that shotgun I gave you in the bedroom instead of the coat closet," he argued.

"Yeah, I realized that when I woke up and figured out that people were in my house."

At my acknowledgement, my dad sighed and released me. "Lesson learned the hard way, I guess. Your mom has had that soup simmering all afternoon and smacked the hell out of my hand when I tried to sneak a roll, so how about we go eat?"

I nodded. "Sounds good." I glanced at Mal as my parents disappeared into the kitchen. "How are you feeling today?" I asked him.

"I'm fine," he answered. He reached out and ran a finger lightly down the left side of my face. "You look like you went ten rounds with a heavyweight champ."

Though his touch didn't hurt, I flinched as it reminded me of the state of my face.

"Did I hurt you?" he asked, jerking his hand away.

"Not my face, no. Just my vanity."

He grimaced. "Sorry. I didn't mean to bring up a painful subject."

"Well, the doctor said that I don't have any permanent damage, just a couple weeks with a very colorful face, so I really shouldn't be so sensitive."

"I still think you look great," Mal responded, earning a scornful look from me. "What? I like my women rough and tumble."

Despite my sensitivity about the bruising, I laughed. Mal always seemed to know exactly what to say to cheer me up.

"You're strange," I stated.

Mal shrugged. "What can I say? I have peculiar preferences."

Shaking my head I took a step toward the kitchen, only to have Mal's hand curve around my arm.

"Thank you for saving my life," he said quietly.

"It was only partially me. Teri's the one who shoved Dwyer's arm when he was about to shoot you."

Mal nodded. "I'll have to thank her too." He pulled me into a hug. "But I did notice that you jumped Trisha Dwyer even though she was obviously armed. I appreciate it. If you hadn't..." he trailed off.

I wrapped my arms around him, offering him comfort because I had a feeling he hadn't had a chance to process what happened. It was likely that he was experiencing the same overwhelming emotions I had in my bathroom earlier; the relief, the fear. We'd come too close to dying.

"So, what does one do to thank a ghost for saving their life?" Mal asked as he released me from the hug and stepped back.

I considered him for a moment. "Well, you could give Teri a little show later. She thinks you have a nice ass."

For the first time since I met him, Mal seemed speechless. "Huh?"

"You know, a striptease," I continued. "Teri is always lamenting that she hasn't been close to a naked guy in thirty years. It'd be the highlight of her decade."

I bit back a grin as a red flush worked its way up Mal's neck and face.

"Uh, maybe, well, I'm not sure…" he stuttered.

Laughing, I waved a hand. "I'm teasing you."

The blush began to fade from his cheeks and he looked cha-grined. "Oh."

"Though if you wanna sleep naked in the guest room some-time, I'm sure she'd be satisfied."

I laughed as the bright crimson color returned to Mal's cheeks and left him standing in the living room as I went in search of dinner.

CHAPTER

41

AFTER DINNER, I convinced my parents that I would be fine on my own for the night. The nausea had disappeared completely after two helpings of my mother's chicken soup and three yeast rolls smothered in butter, and while my head still hurt, I could handle the dull ache. As long as I didn't move too quickly, then the pain spiked once again.

It took Mal promising to look in on me several times during the night before my parents would even consider leaving. As much as I loved them, I needed peace and quiet in order to rest and heal.

Once I explained that I would have an easier time resting without people around, my father finally caved but insisted that he and my mom would come over the next day to make sure I was healing properly.

I took what I could get and agreed.

As my mother gathered their overnight bag and her purse, she said, "Oh, I forgot to tell you. The sheriff came by earlier today hoping to take your statement. I told him you were in no condition to talk and that he should return tomorrow. He'll be here around ten."

I bit back a sigh. I hadn't given the sheriff a single thought since I'd been released from the hospital early that morning. I knew I would have to talk to him and the sooner I got it over with, the better.

"Thanks, Mom."

She nodded sharply. "He tried to convince me to let him talk to you today, but I told him that you were in no shape. I know your daddy thinks highly of him, but that man is a bit of a bully when he wants his way."

I chuckled. "I have to agree with you there," I stated.

My dad sighed. "I said he was a good sheriff, that's all. We need somebody in office that won't pander to the well-to-do folks and stand up for all the citizens of the county."

"That may be true, Jimmy," my mother snapped, "But he was there at the hospital last night and I know for a fact that the doctor told him it would be at least twenty-four hours before Zoe would be well enough to speak with him. He ignored the doctor's orders!"

My dad frowned. "That ain't right."

Before my parents could descend into dissecting Sheriff Daughtry's actions, I stated, "Well, I'll be well enough to talk to him tomorrow and I'd like to get this over with so I don't have to think about Trisha and Steven Dwyer anymore."

They immediately stopped talking about Daughtry.

"Of course, baby," my father said. "We'll get out of here so you can go lie down and we'll see you tomorrow, okay?"

"Thanks, Daddy," I stated, rising up on my tiptoes to kiss his cheek. I gave my mother a kiss as well. "Thanks for everything, Mama."

My mother's hands clasped my forearms as she looked intently into my eyes. "I would do anything for you, Zoe, and it would be my pleasure."

I blinked, surprised at the vehemence behind her words, but she let go of my arms before I had a chance to formulate an appropriate response.

"We'll be back around noon with lunch," she stated, following my dad out the front door.

As soon as they were gone, I glanced at Mal. "Do you wanna talk or watch TV?"

"TV. I'm talked out. The sheriff took my statement at the department earlier today."

"If you change your mind, I'm happy to listen," I offered.

Mal put an arm around my shoulders and led me back to the sofa. "Maybe when you're not swaying on your feet."

I sighed as I sat back in the cushions. "Good point."

"What do you want to watch?"

Since my head was still a little fuzzy, I shrugged. "You pick." I hesitated. "Um, just nothing gory or violent, okay?"

"No problem."

To my utter shock, he chose *Gilmore Girls*.

"You watch this?" I asked.

"Uh, hell yeah. Lauren Graham and Alexis Bledel? They're hot and funny."

I pulled a blanket over my legs and snuggled into the corner of the couch. The last thing I remember was Lorelai asking her parents to help her pay for Rory's tuition.

I woke up as Mal hit the top step of the stairs. "Hey, you shouldn't be carrying me. I'm heavy," I complained.

"Nah," he replied.

He sounded a bit out of breath, so I knew it was a lie.

"Put me down. I can walk," I demanded sleepily.

"Too late now. I've already got you upstairs and two steps from your room."

"Fine," I conceded.

He deposited me on my bed. "I'll see you in the morning. Do you need anything before I go to sleep?"

"No, thanks," I replied.

Mal left the room, turning off the overhead light as he went. Despite sleeping most of the day, I was tired. Apparently, concussions were exhausting.

I awoke to find Teri hovering over me, my face ice cold.

"They're here," she whispered.

My blood curdled at her words. Even though I knew the answer, I still asked, "Who?"

"A man and a woman. They're coming for you, Zoe. You have to run."

Heart pounding, I threw back the covers and leapt to my feet. Before I could move, the bedroom door burst open, slamming against the wall. Steven Dwyer was framed in the doorway.

I watched in horror as his arm lifted and revealed a pistol clenched in his fist. Frozen in fear, I couldn't move as he pulled the trigger. Agonizing pain burned through my left temple.

Then I was falling. And falling. The floor seemed hundreds of feet away. As it rushed up to meet me, I screamed.

"Zoe!"

Crying out, I knifed up, my hand clapping over my left temple. I cringed back from the dark shadow that loomed over my bed.

The lamp next to my bed clicked on, illuminating Mal's form. Without thinking, I dove into his arms as tears streamed down my face.

"Sh," he whispered. "You're okay. It was a nightmare."

I clutched at him, burying my head against his shoulder. My body heaved with the force of the sobs torn from my throat.

Mal held me and rocked me, murmuring comforting nonsense in my ear.

It took a long time for me to calm down. Once I did, Mal handed me a tissue from the box on my nightstand.

"A dream about last night?" he asked.

I nodded as I wiped my eyes and blew my nose.

"Do you want to talk about it?" he invited.

"Not really," I replied. "But will you stay with me until I fall back asleep?"

"Of course," he replied simply.

Mal climbed into bed next to me and pulled me against his side so that my head was pillowed on his shoulder. As I curled up against him, I realized that this behavior might be sending the wrong message if I wanted to keep our relationship professional.

Mal's hand stroked my hair and I decided that I would address the issue tomorrow. For tonight, I would take the comfort I needed however I could get it.

CHAPTER

42

THE NEXT MORNING wasn't awkward at all. Mostly because I woke up alone.

I could smell coffee brewing and bacon frying. I gasped after I glanced at the clock. It was a few minutes after nine. Knowing Sheriff Daughtry, he would be here early.

My body felt stiff and sore as I climbed out of bed, worse than the day before. I remembered my father's warning, that the second day would be the worst and grimaced.

I avoided the bathroom mirror as I hobbled through the door and went straight to the shower. Dropping my clothes on the floor, I stepped under the steamy spray and hissed as the hot water pounded on my achy muscles.

Moving as quickly as I could manage, I washed my hair and body. I gingerly washed my face, trying to avoid the bruised side. The scratches on my legs and arms stung, but I needed to feel clean. I hadn't had a shower in two days.

When I was done, I stood beneath the spray and let the hot water soak into my neck and shoulders. Aware that time was passing, I sighed and leaned down to turn off the flow. I could have stood beneath the spray for hours, but I didn't want Sheriff Daughtry to conduct my interview in my bathroom. Knowing him, he would try.

After I toweled off, I perused my dresser for wardrobe choices. Finally, I gave up and grabbed a bra, panties, and my favorite pair of yoga pants. I'd worn and washed them so many times that they were softer than anything else I owned. I tugged a loose t-shirt over my head and pulled my hair from beneath the collar.

Because I had a feeling the whir of the hair dryer would probably make my headache return, I left my hair wet and twisted it into a loose braid to keep it out of my face.

When I appeared in the kitchen, Mal looked up from the plate he was filling with eggs and bacon.

"Good morning. I was just about to wake you up with breakfast in bed."

"Want me to go back upstairs and wait?"

"Nah. The sheriff will be here soon. He'd just make me drag you back down," he replied. "Now sit down and let me serve you."

"Okay, just this once."

Once again I felt the nagging sensation that my interactions with Mal were veering into dangerous territory, especially when he poured me a cup of coffee and brought a plate of food to the table for me.

"Do you treat all your employees this way?" I teased.

"Well, you're my only employee, so I'm not sure. I'll get back to you." He brought another plate and cup of coffee to the table and sat next to me. "How are you feeling this morning?"

I picked at my eggs. "Better. The headache is almost gone."

"I meant your emotions, Zoe. That was a wild nightmare. I thought you were going to wake up the neighbors."

I shrugged. "I don't know how I feel. I'm trying not to think about it. I almost felt as though I were living through it again. It was...terrifying."

Mal put his hand over mine. Before he could speak, the doorbell pealed. With a sigh, Mal glanced at his phone.

"Well, it seems the sheriff believes in being early. It's a quarter to ten." He got to his feet. "Eat a little breakfast. I'll stall him in the living room."

I managed to choke down a few bites of egg and toast before Mal returned with the sheriff in tow. Mal frowned pointedly at my partially full plate.

The sheriff rocked back on his heels when he saw me. "My God, Dwyer did one hell of a number on you."

I scowled at him, trying not to flinch as the expression made my face hurt. "Yeah. I'm lucky to be alive."

Daughtry's jaw tightened at my words, which told me that my jab had been a direct hit. He knew that Dwyer was dangerous, yet he hadn't protected Mal and me.

"Well, Dwyer confessed to everything. The plot to kill you and Mal, the murder of Hank Murphy, and Trisha Dwyer's participation in both crimes," he declared.

"Really?" I asked. "Why?"

Daughtry accepted a cup of coffee from Mal. "Thanks," he muttered before he sipped. Then he deigned to answer my question. "Apparently, Hank's death was of Trisha's design. She claimed that her husband threatened to kill her and beat her up when she told him she wanted a divorce. Dwyer thought he was protecting her from a potentially dangerous situation. In reality, she wanted to escape a messy divorce and get the insurance payout."

I shook my head. "Jesus."

The sheriff took another sip of coffee. "Yeah, she's a piece of work."

"So what's going to happen?" I asked.

"Well, I'm going to have you tell me what happened that night, in detail. Then you'll sign the statement. The judge has already denied them both bail since they're considered a flight risk after they dropped off the face of the Earth last week. When their trial comes around, the DA will probably want you both to testify. Hopefully, they will both be locked up for the rest of their lives." Sheriff Daughtry shook his head. "It's sad. I think Dwyer truly loved Trisha when he killed Hank. He thought he was saving her. Over the years, he's come to realize that she played him and probably never loved him. Neither of them could leave because they couldn't be sure the other wouldn't rat them out."

"I'd say they made their own beds," Mal stated firmly.

Sheriff Daughtry nodded. "Yeah, they did. But Dwyer made his bed from the lies he was fed from a woman he loved." He removed a digital recorder from his pocket. "If you're ready, Zoe, we can get this done and you can get some rest."

His attitude towards me was almost gentle. Maybe there was one positive effect of the bruises covering the left side of my face.

He started the interview by asking me to state my name, the date, and a bunch of other information. Then he launched into questions regarding the terrifying night that Trisha and Steve Dwyer tried to kill me. While I answered, he jotted down short notes on a legal pad in front of him, occasionally stopping me mid-sentence to clarify something I'd said.

By the time we were done, I was shaking. Reliving that night, especially after the horrific dream I'd had a few hours ago, was torture.

Sheriff Daughtry's voice was soothing and quiet as he asked me if everything I'd stated was true. When I agreed, he asked me to read the statement and sign it. My signature was little more than a large Z followed by a bunch of squiggles because the tremor in my hand was so strong I could barely hold the pen.

Once that was done, Sheriff Daughtry stopped the recorder and collected the machine.

"Thank you for talking to me today, Zoe. I know it was difficult, especially since you're still not feeling well, but the longer we waited, the more likely you would forget important details. Especially since you have a head injury."

My brows lifted at his words. It had only been two days, but I remembered every single second of that experience in vivid accuracy.

Mal walked the sheriff out and returned to the kitchen, looking annoyed. "I know that interview probably ruined your appetite, but you need to eat." He poured me a glass of orange juice and pushed my plate closer to me. "Drink that and eat a slice of toast."

"Yes, Mother," I grumbled.

He chuckled. "I need you to get better so we can get back to work."

"Oh, so all this nurturing is motivated by greed, huh?"

He shook his head. "You're obviously feeling more like yourself if you're making smart ass remarks."

"Um, not well enough to make my own food, if that's what you're getting at."

Mal didn't answer, but he did laugh.

As he began to clean up the breakfast dishes, my mood darkened. We finally knew what happened to Hank Murphy and the culprits would be spending the rest of their lives in jail.

"We need to talk to Hank," I declared. "I just don't know what to tell him. Is it worth it to crush his spirit after he's already dead?"

"He's waited twenty years, Zoe. He can wait a few more days until you're well."

I shook my head. "That's exactly why I don't want to wait, Mal. He's been on that road, alone, and waiting for decades. He deserves to know what happened to him."

Mal shut off the water and dried his hands, moving over to the table. "Maybe, but you need rest. Plus, you're not allowed to drive for at least a week."

"I thought you could drive me."

"Not happening," he answered with a shake of his head.

I sighed and tried a different tact. "Tomorrow."

Mal just kept shaking his head.

"Either you drive me or I call Jonelle. She'll do it."

Mal eyed me. "Fine. I'll drive you tomorrow night, *if* you put your feet up all day today."

I wanted to roll my eyes, but that would have made my head hurt, so I settled for making a face at him. "I wasn't planning on running a marathon, Mal."

"That's the deal, take it or leave it."

"I'll rest today," I agreed grudgingly.

"Good. Starting now," he demanded. "Finish your toast and juice then go lie down for a little while."

"Now, you really do sound like my mother."

Mal ignored my jab and went back to washing the dishes.

I began to wonder if my mother was rubbing off on him. God, I hoped not. One of her was plenty, even if her attitude was changing.

CHAPTER

43

THE NEXT EVENING, I dressed in cutoff shorts and a t-shirt and pulled my hair into a ponytail. I came downstairs to find Mal standing by the front door, his keys in his hand.

"So I don't have to call Jonelle for a ride?" I asked.

"Nope. I'll drive you."

I was glad that I didn't have to argue with him. Though I was feeling more like myself, I was still tired. The only reason I was so determined to speak to Hank was to give him peace.

He'd been waiting for help for twenty years and he deserved to move on. Especially since the woman he'd been waiting for had been the one to plan his murder.

As Mal drove toward the isolated area, I tried to figure out what I would say to Hank. I'd been wracking my brain for the last two days, but how did someone tell a man that the woman he loved wanted him dead?

"What's wrong?" Mal asked.

I glanced at him. "Nothing, why?"

"Zoe, your left leg hasn't stopped bouncing since you got in the car. Something's bugging you."

Okay, so Mal was beginning to see right through me. "I'm just not sure what to say to Hank. I've never broken someone's heart before."

"Hey, what about mine?"

"Your what?"

"My heart. You broke it when you turned me down flat."

"Not helping," I replied.

Mal grinned. "Okay, so you didn't break my heart. Just my ego. I'll probably survive."

"Seriously, Mal. What do I say? I'm not great with people at the best of times, and this is definitely not a better time."

"Tell him the truth, Zoe, as kindly as you can. That's all anyone could ask of you in this situation. There's no 'easy' way to break this kind of news to someone. But as you said, Hank needs to know so that he can move on."

I nodded. "You're right."

I took deep breaths to help calm my nerves as Mal turned down the Farm to Market road. As we drove I saw the faint glow of Hank's figure in the distance and felt my own heart ache.

I wondered how long the last few weeks had seemed to him. Had they felt like an eternity or had they passed in the blink of an eye? Did time seem shorter now that he'd been alone for so long?

Suddenly, my nerves calmed. I might be here to deliver painful news, but Hank Murphy would be able to let go and move on after this.

Hank stood perfectly still as Mal parked and we climbed out. His eyes widened as he took in my face.

"What happened to you?" he asked me.

"We found out who killed you and they took exception to that."

"They? There was more than one person?" he asked.

I nodded.

"Did the police arrest them after they hurt you?"

"Yes." I took a deep breath. "Hank, you knew the people that hurt you. You knew them very well."

"Who?"

"The man that killed you was Steven Dwyer," I replied. "But he wouldn't have done it if it hadn't been for the encouragement of someone else close to you."

Hank sighed, closed his eyes, and dropped his head forward. "Trisha."

"I'm sorry?"

He lifted his head and looked at me, his eyes sad and hollow. "I knew that Trisha was screwing around with someone. I just didn't expect it to be Steve and I definitely didn't expect her to want me dead." His eyes shifted to the left side of my face. "Did Steve do that to you?" he asked.

I nodded.

"Will they pay for what they did?"

"Yes," I replied. "Steve confessed to killing you and breaking into my house. He also implicated Trisha in both crimes. They'll be going to jail for a very long time."

"So my murderers have been brought to justice?" he asked.

"They have."

Hank heaved a huge sigh. "After all these years, it's over." His shoulders sagged. "I can't believe it."

"I'm so sorry, Hank," I apologized.

He smiled at me, but it was full of sorrow. "What do you have to be sorry for, Zoe? You didn't do any of this."

"I hate giving you hurtful news," I confessed. "You didn't deserve any of this."

"Neither did you," he replied. "Thank you for helping me, Zoe. It's finally over."

"You're welcome, Hank."

He cocked his head to the side. "Did you hear that?"

"I'm sorry?"

"Someone's calling my name," he stated, twisting around.

I didn't hear anything.

"There it is again," he repeated. "Don't you hear that?" he asked again, facing me.

"No, I don't," I replied. Although I was beginning to understand what was happening.

"Do you see that light?" Hank asked, his voice full of awe. "It's beautiful."

He was moving on.

"It's time to go, Hank," I answered.

He looked at me. "What do you mean?"

"You're being called. It's time to move on and leave this place behind."

The sadness faded from his expression. "It's really over, isn't it?"

"It is. I hope you'll be happy, Hank."

He smiled at me, his eyes twinkling. "You too, Zoe. I'll see you on the other side. Hopefully, it will be many, many years in the future."

"Good-bye, Hank. Be at peace."

He lifted a hand and turned to walk away from us. I couldn't hear the voices calling him or the light he spoke of, but the air around me buzzed with energy. I knew that the veil between the living and the dead had been lifted to allow him through. I could even sense its general location.

As I watched Hank disappear, something dark began pushing against the veil. I shivered as it tried to shove through.

"No," I whispered, but it was too late.

The presence slammed against the veil once more and I almost fell to my knees as it shot through, escaping the grasp of the portal.

Hank turned and gave us one last wave before he vanished completely, unaware of the darkness that had brushed by him.

I swayed on my feet from the burst of energy that accompanied the closing of the veil. Mal took my arm, keeping me on my feet.

"Are you okay?" he asked.

"Hank's gone," I replied. "But something else is here."

I felt the dark entity hovering nearby. Without addressing it, I knew that we were being watched. Before I could ask the specter any questions, it disappeared, zipping through the trees around us.

Unease settled over me. Whatever that was, it wasn't a regular ghost. Its presence was darker, heavier, almost like a physical touch. I hoped to God that it couldn't harm anyone, because it seemed almost...corporeal.

"It's gone," I told Mal.

"What's gone?"

"The dark spirit that came through the same portal Hank used to leave. I think it escaped from the other side."

"I don't understand," Mal stated.

"Me either. But whatever it is, I don't think it's here to spread cheer and joy."

"What should we do?"

I shook my head. "I don't think there's anything we can do, Mal. It left and I have no idea where it's going."

Somehow I knew that it wouldn't be last time I saw the spirit. I only hoped that I would know how to deal with it when I did come across the entity again.

CHAPTER

44

OVER THE NEXT week, I healed quickly. My doctor commented on how fast I recovered from my concussion. The bruising was still there, but it was no longer purple and black, but shifting from blue toward green. In another two weeks, it would be gone completely.

I managed to convince Mal that I would be fine in my house alone as soon as the doctor gave me the all clear to drive. It was a difficult task, but I needed to put some space between us. I was beginning to get used to having him around and looking forward to seeing him in the morning. He had rapidly become someone I considered a close friend. I felt I could share anything with him and loved talking to him about nearly everything.

The problem was that I was beginning to get attached, and not in a platonic way. Mal didn't hug me or hold my hand anymore and I realized I missed it. Which in turn scared the shit out of me. Not just because he was my boss but because now he was my friend. I didn't want to lose him in either capacity if a romantic entanglement didn't work out.

Once I convinced Mal that I would be fine alone, I read everything I could about evil spirits. I devoured book after book on spells, potions, exorcisms, and necromancy. Nothing I found seemed to describe what I'd felt and seen.

When I came across that evil presence again, I wanted to be able to deal with it. Instinct told me that I shouldn't face it unprepared.

I also invited everyone over for another episode watching party. We ate pizza and brownies and I found that I was getting used to seeing myself on camera.

Although Jonelle was still insisting that I wear more make-up. That was the only problem with having a hair stylist-slash-makeup artist as a best friend. They were very determined that you should look your best when you were on a YouTube show.

Teri even joined us, listening to our conversation and occasionally interjecting. I had to relay her statements to the others, but everyone seemed to take it in stride.

As the episode ended, Mal got to his feet.

"I have several announcements to make," he stated, raising his voice so that he had our attention. As we fell silent, he grinned. "And they're all good news. First of all, since Zoe Thorne has joined our ragtag group, our channel has increased to nearly one hundred and fifty thousand subscribers."

Stony and Blaine hooted and whistled, patting me on the back. "Good job, Zoe. You're awesome!"

I laughed and shook my head. "Whatever."

"I'm not done," Mal said, lifting his hands. "Because of all this extra attention, we have several networks interested in picking up our show."

Stony, Blaine, and Jonelle jumped to their feet, hugging each other and yanking me off the sofa as well.

"That's amazing!" Jonelle laughed.

Mal, Stony, and Blaine shared a man hug that included back-slapping and handshakes all around. Then they dragged me into the circle, hugging me as well.

Everyone was excited, but I couldn't help feeling concerned.

The idea of millions of people seeing me on television every week was daunting. Even more intimidating than hundreds of thousands of YouTube viewers. I wasn't exactly starlet material.

I smiled and laughed, congratulating Mal and the guys, but inside I was freaking out. I wasn't sure how I felt about this new development.

A couple of hours later, I was finally alone. I trudged upstairs and found Teri standing at my bedroom window, staring out into the backyard.

"I hear you're going to be a big television star," she murmured, never taking her eyes off the landscape behind my house.

"Yeah," I replied, my voice quiet.

Something in my tone must have garnered her full attention. She turned to face me. "You're not happy?"

I shrugged. "I'm not sure. Everything seems like it's changing so fast."

Teri smiled. "You're just used to your rut," she responded.

"Yeah, I guess I am," I answered with a sigh. "Do you think I'm making a mistake?"

"What do I know?" Teri asked with a shrug.

"Teri."

"Zoe, how long have I been telling you that you should get off your ass and start living your life?"

"Good point," I admitted.

"It's okay to freak out about it, sweetie. Your entire life has changed in just a few months. The important thing is that you're changing and growing. I'm stuck in this house forever. You have a chance to see the world and you should take it."

At her words, there was a pang in the vicinity of my heart.

"Do you want to leave, Teri?" I asked.

She smiled ruefully. "Your story about Hank Murphy got me thinking. I've been in this house for thirty years. I'm beginning to believe that's long enough. I'm curious about what's on the other side."

Though it hurt to think about Teri leaving, I couldn't blame her. "I understand."

She moved toward me. "Zoe, will you help me? Will you find out who killed me?"

I nodded. "Of course." I paused. "Do you think that's the only way you'll be able to move on?"

"I don't know," Teri answered with a shrug, "But I'd like to try."

"Then we'll try," I promised.

"Thank you, Zoe." She moved to the other window in the bedroom and looked toward Preston's house. "Though I do have to say that I'll miss watching Preston work out shirtless."

"Maybe there will be lots of shirtless firefighters on the other side," I suggested.

"I don't know," she demurred. "I wasn't on my best behavior all those years ago. I don't think I'll be allowed in Heaven."

I burst into laughter. "Well, you did save Mal's life just a week ago. That should count for something."

"That's true."

I could sense her sadness. "Teri, I will do everything I can to help you," I promised.

"I know you will, Zoe. It's just..." she trailed off. "You're not the only one who's scared of change."

Not for the first time, I wished I could touch her. However, it wasn't for the usual reason of wanting to throttle her. I could tell she needed comfort and I wasn't sure what to say. A hug would have conveyed that a lot more easily.

"Maybe a change will do you good," I offered.

She snorted. "I may have been dead for thirty years, but even I can recognize a line from a Sheryl Crow song."

"Sorry, I'm not very good at this."

Teri shook her head. "You're better than you think."

"You know what, I'm not so tired after all," I stated. "Wanna go watch something with hot guys in it?"

"Definitely," Teri replied.

"Great, I'll meet you downstairs in a few minutes. I'm going to put on my pajamas."

She laughed. "Some things will never change."

"Hey, I wear real pants when I have to. It's just that right now, I don't have to."

Still laughing, Teri disappeared.

Epilogue

H E WATCHED FROM the shadows as the two women moved away from the window, and he couldn't believe his luck.

She was still here.

Of the myriad of women he'd known all those years ago, she was his favorite. She'd fought the noose fiercely, even with the drugs he'd pumped into her system. Just thinking about it now made him hard.

It had been so long since he'd tasted death and the accompanying release. He was starving for the rush.

Now, he could watch her again, savoring the hunt. While he couldn't experience her death once more, there was always her friend.

The woman was younger and slimmer, but still gorgeous. As he watched her strip off her shirt, he palmed his cock. He'd never tried to fuck a human in this form. He wondered if it would be possible. He couldn't believe his luck. Where he was before, he couldn't touch anything. His fingers would pass right through. Now, he had a body; a big, strong body that could easily overpower a woman her size.

She shimmied out of her jeans and he groaned softly. He intended to find out exactly what his new body could do to her.

But not yet.

Though his blood leapt, he chose to wait and watch. While the hunt wasn't as enjoyable as the kill, he hadn't experienced this thrill in thirty years.

And he had nothing but time.

The End

Sign Up for C.C.'s Monthly Newsletter

www.ccwood.net/subscribe

Contact C.C.

C.C. loves to hear from her readers!

Facebook: www.facebook.com/authorccwood

Twitter: www.twitter.com/cc_wood

Instagram: www.instagram.com/authorccwood

Pinterest: www.pinterest.com/ccwood01

Email: author@ccwood.net

You can also sign up for blog updates and C.C.'s monthly newsletter on her website!

www.ccwood.net

About C.C.

A native Texan, C.C. grew up either reading or playing the piano. Years later, she's still not grown up and doing the same things. Since the voices in her head never shut up, C.C. decided to share their crazy stories and started writing books.

Now that she has a baby girl at home, C.C.'s non-writing time is usually spent cleaning up poopy diapers or feeding the poop machine. Sometimes she teaches piano, cooks, or spends time bugging her hubby and two beagles.

Titles by C.C. Wood

Novellas:

Girl Next Door Series:
Friends with Benefits
Frenemies
Drive Me Crazy
Girl Next Door-The Complete Series

Kiss Series:
A Kiss for Christmas
Kiss Me

Novels:
Seasons of Sorrow

NSFW Series:
In Love With Lucy
Earning Yancy

Westfall Brothers Series:
Texas with a Twist

Wicked Games Series:
All or Nothing

Paranormal Romance:

Bitten Series:
Bite Me
Once Bitten, Twice Shy
Bewitched, Bothered, and Bitten
One Little Bite
Love Bites
Bite the Bullet

The Wraith Files:
Don't Wake the Dead

Made in the USA
Columbia, SC
15 November 2017